D1260966

3

His heart replaced with a Q.R. Signum, Super Eva carries two swords, Kesara and Basara.

Gendo's Son!

■ Crimson A1 (Asuka and Eva-02's fused form) cruises over North Africa (going where she pleases).

NEON GENESIS EVANGELION ANIMA

VOLUME 3

BY
Ikuto Yamashita

CONCEPT
Khara
PLANNING & EDITING
Yasuo Kashihara

Seven Seas

Seven Seas Entertainment

EVANGELION ANIMA VOL. 3

©khara

First published in Japan in 2018 by
KADOKAWA CORPORATION, Tokyo.
English translation rights arranged with
KADOKAWA CORPORATION, Tokyo.

No portion of this book may be reproduced or transmitted
in any form without written permission from the copyright
holders. This is a work of fiction. Names, characters, places, and
incidents are the products of the author's imagination or are
used fictitiously. Any resemblance to actual events, locales, or
persons, living or dead, is entirely coincidental.

Seven Seas press and purchase enquiries can be sent to
Marketing Manager Lianne Sentar at press@gomanga.com.
Information regarding the distribution and purchase of
digital editions is available from Digital Manager CK Russell
at digital@gomanga.com.

Seven Seas and the Seven Seas logo are trademarks of
Seven Seas Entertainment. All rights reserved.

Follow Seven Seas Entertainment online at
sevenseasentertainment.com.

TRANSLATION: Nathan Collins
ADAPTATION: Peter Adrian Behravesh
COVER DESIGN: KC Fabellon
INTERIOR LAYOUT & DESIGN: Clay Gardner
PROOFREADER: Jade Gardner, Stephanie Cohen
LIGHT NOVEL EDITOR: Nibedita Sen
PREPRESS TECHNICIAN: Rhiannon Rasmussen-Silverstein
PRODUCTION MANAGER: Lissa Pattillo
MANAGING EDITOR: Julie Davis
ASSOCIATE PUBLISHER: Adam Arnold
PUBLISHER: Jason DeAngelis

ISBN: 978-1-64505-460-3
Printed in Canada
First Printing: June 2020
10 9 8 7 6 5 4 3 2 1

PART 1

NEON GENESIS

CHILDREN

EVANGELION: ANIMA

NEON GENESIS
EVANGELION ANIMA

CHAPTER 1

THE VALUE OF HUMANKIND
ALPHA

THE EARTH SHUDDERED and—at least for the moment—
went still again. Within the armored personnel carrier acting
as Nerv Japan's mobile command center, a cheerful tone chimed,
and an artificial voice announced, 《The preceding interplate
earthquake was centered twenty-five kilometers east of this location. The earthquake forecast has been updated. As of 1100 local
time, the probability of another interplate earthquake within the
next twenty-four hours has risen to forty percent.》

At the comms station, Commander Katsuragi Misato was
holding on to a metal rack to steady her balance when she heard
a man's voice—familiar but unexpected—over her headset.

《Commander Katsuragi.》

"Deputy Commander Fuyutsuki?" He no longer held that
rank—or *any* rank, for that matter—but old habits die hard.
"Why are you in the command center?"

《I'm here because you aren't.》

Misato didn't know what had happened in Hakone after her

11

sudden departure. She had a pretty good idea, however, of what was about to happen—a scolding.

In a valley within the Moroccan Atlas Mountains, crowded with bizarre and grotesque rock formations, Katsuragi Misato had met up with Nerv Japan's search and recovery team, which had come from Hakone under the leadership of Acting Deputy Commander Suzuhara Toji.

Misato handed over the broken rebel, Ayanami Rei Quatre— who offered no meaningful resistance—to the security intelligence team to keep her safe...and secret. Then, at the comms station, she reconnected with Hakone and Tokyo-3, half a world away, via the network of stratospheric airplanes that had replaced the satellites cast adrift by the Earth's shrinking.

She hoped to speak with Ibuki Maya, who was chief of both the science and engineering divisions, but instead, the person she reached was her former superior, an exacting officer who was not about to pass up the opportunity to put her through the wringer.

Rei Quatre had orchestrated Misato's disappearance. But Misato couldn't deny being at least partially at fault; when Chairman Kiel's booby-trapped visor overwrote Kaji Ryoji's mind in a hidden facility on the island of Cyprus, she'd gone into a state of shock and abandoned her duties. Now she felt like a truant student being scolded by her teacher.

Oh, come on, Misato silently griped. She attempted to run a hand through her hair, which she'd parted when she put on the headset, but the strands were too tangled by sand and dust for her fingers to pass through smoothly. Quatre had abducted her with the mutant Eva-0.0 and taken her on a strange trip, transporting her nearly instantaneously, like flipping channels on a TV, from Japan, to the eastern Mediterranean, and finally to North Africa. Each locale presented her with scenes that defied explanation. Only now was she able to focus on her own physical state.

Because Misato's disappearance had been kept under wraps, when the retrieval crew happened across the commander in far-off Morocco, they assumed that she was either here to perform an unannounced inspection or to embed herself within the European troops under a false identity, for anti-terror operations. But beneath her European army uniform—"procured" on-site—she still wore the same off-duty clothing she'd had on at the time of her abduction from Nerv HQ several days before. Her tight skirt and unkempt hair clearly marked her as out of place among the professionals bustling about in workwear and armored vests.

I don't even want to know what my face must look like right now.

Toji patted the top of her head and pointed to a door with a sign that read SHOWER ROOM. He placed a heavy-duty work uniform and an armored vest on the central table, where an analog map had been spread out. Without interrupting her call, he mouthed the words, *Wear these.* She waved him a thank you.

He could have at least warned me that Deputy Commander Fuyutsuki was back.

As if reading her mind, Toji stopped on his way out of the room and stuck his tongue out at her.

Over the connection to Tokyo-3, Maya asked, 《Is that thing really Asuka *and* Unit Two?》

"To be honest, I don't know. But that's what the kids are saying."

The red giant looked like an Evangelion, with feminine features breaking through the surface here and there like a colossal idol to a goddess. The resemblance to Soryu Asuka wasn't immediately apparent to Misato, but once it had been pointed out to her, she saw the similarities. Still, she'd need more proof before she accepted, as Ikari Shinji and Horaki Hikari claimed, that this creature was a fusion of Eva-02 and Asuka.

The other Nerv Japan agents on the scene seemed to be taking the same stance as Misato. Among them, only Toji thought that the red giant was Asuka.

"I guess it's something only kids understand," Misato remarked.

《They're seventeen years old,》 Maya reminded her. 《If you keep treating them like children, you'll only make them angry.》

Misato scratched at her stiff, dirt-caked hair. "Well, how else am I supposed to treat them? They make decisions based on intuition and take absolutely no responsibility for their actions."

《I suppose that's the mark of an adult—requiring proof so that we can obtain a shared understanding with others.》

"I don't think those kids are looking for proof."

Fuyutsuki cut in. 《Commander Katsuragi, I'm going to be blunt. It doesn't matter whether that red machine is Unit Two or Asuka or both—their combat capabilities are lost. But now we face a new problem...the loss of our greatest weapon, Super Eva.》

CHAPTER 2

EVA-01, THE CORRUPT

MISATO CHANGED into the uniform, put on the helmet, and walked outside to where Eva-01 was squatting on the ground for emergency repairs. As she circled the giant, she wrinkled her nose at the stench of scorched metal, resin, oil... and decomposing flesh. Shinji's Eva hadn't undergone as radical a mutation as Quatre's Eva-0.0, but the foreign presence of the Q.R. Signum had discolored portions of the giant's armor and musculature.

The changes are only this minor, Misato thought, *because Shinji is still resisting.*

The Eva's EXW-038 Neyarl—an experimental shoulder-mounted energy cannon—had been destroyed. The recovery team had anticipated that the weapon wouldn't survive its first use in the field, and the necessary replacement parts were ready and waiting on the cargo plane.

But would handing all that over be wise?

"About Super Eva's armament," Misato said. "Keep it to swords... or blunt weapons."

"That's all?" Toji was incredulous. "The repair crew says we can restore the FCS as soon as we swap out the electronics. Once that's finished, ranged weapons should be working again, no problem." Misato pursed her lips and shook her head. Toji's eyes widened as he realized she'd mentally reclassified Super Eva as untrustworthy.

Super Eva hadn't merely been rendered ineffective; the giant might now be a net *negative*. The situation could be even worse than Fuyutsuki had indicated.

To keep Super Eva—and Shinji—alive after the Lance of Longinus ripped out their heart, Hikari had made the split-second, unilateral decision to replace the device with a Q.R. Signum—an object carrying a direct link to the apparent commander of their enemies.

And what had happened the other time a Q.R. Signum had been implanted into a Nerv Japan Eva? The scale had caused Ayanami Quatre's Eva-0.0 to go haywire in orbit—disrupting Quatre's psyche, giving her self-awareness, and even mutating her Eva's physical form. Quatre had attacked her allies and gone fugitive. She and her Eva had, in effect, joined the enemy.

For now, Shinji and Super Eva remained of sound mind, but there was no guarantee they'd stay that way. As Misato and Toji walked back to the mobile command center, the commander couldn't help but feel uneasy about the future.

Shinji spoke over the comms channel. 《Super Eva to Mobile Command.》 Before his heart had been stolen, Shinji had begun to hear and speak through his shared perception of Super Eva's senses; but now he was relying on a newly replaced communications module. 《Please commence the communications and data link tests.》

"Command acknowledges," Toji replied. "We'll handle the transceiving of the test patterns and the diagnostics on our end—" He stopped and looked around in confusion. "Wait! What happened to the Soryu-looking one?"

The red giant had disappeared.

《Doesn't seem like she's willing to sit still for us,》 Shinji said. 《She went running after the Akashima—Oh, they're back again.》

"Yeah," Toji said, "she's always never been much for waiting around. The Akashima should be bringing you two shoulder units from the transport. I want you to put them on. Let's get you looking proper, even if it's just for show. Once we get back to Japan, we can do something about your eye, your broken bones, and, well, everything else."

"Shinji," Misato added, "have you felt any changes—physical *or* mental—since the Q.R. Signum was put into your body?"

In other words, *Are you still on our side?*

There was a small pause before he answered. 《My chest feels like it's on fire, but my arms and legs feel cold and numb. It's... confusing. And I really, *really* don't like it.》

"And how is Super Eva? Give it to me straight."

《The Eva isn't putting out as much power as before. This restraint armor feels heavy. And it's strange, but it's like the Eva is stirring up...negative emotions. It's disquieting. I feel as if I have to keep my guard up around it now.》

With the militaries of numerous nations present in the valley,

Misato couldn't do anything that might suggest that Nerv Japan was in danger of losing control of Super Eva. If word got out, the UN—which held authority over Nerv, at least on paper—would almost certainly seize Shinji and Super Eva. After all, they'd tried it once already with their failed raid on Hokkaido just days before.

It was imperative that Nerv Japan continued to act like they could effectively wield their Evangelions. For that reason, rather than sending Super Eva back to Japan damaged and unarmed, Nerv Japan needed to make a show of re-equipping it on location.

Toji gave the orders for the cosmetic repairs, despite resenting such ridiculous procedures amid a global crisis.

Arming Super Eva carried its own risks, as Quatre had shown, but Misato saw no other choice but to walk that tightrope.

But without any ranged weapons, even if Super Eva succumbed completely to Armaros' influence and turned against humanity, the colossus could only cause damage within the reach of its swing.

The replacement of Super Eva's shoulder modules began, but the Akashima had to assist in lifting one of the giant's arms.

《Misato-san,》 Shinji transmitted from inside the plug.

"What is it?"

《I'm sorry.》

Well, I'll be, Misato thought. "I'm at fault for all this, too. When we return, we can get chewed out together."

Loud, purposeful footsteps and a knock at the command center's door announced the arrival of a man with a soldier's physique and matching haircut.

"Lieutenant Colonel Kasuga?" Toji asked.

"Commanding Officer Suzuhara," the lieutenant colonel of the JSSDF Anti-Angel Rapid Response Unit replied. "All the heavy equipment is assembled and in place. My engineers there can handle the installation of the shoulder modules."

"Yes, I heard," Toji said. "I know this was a sudden request, so I appreciate the effort."

"With Super Eva soon able to walk again, we shouldn't need any more assistance from Akashima for the time being. The multinational forces have requested our assistance in disposing of the giant creatures' remains. I was thinking I'd send Endo in the Akashima to deal with it, if you don't mind."

"*I* don't mind. But do *you*? If you'd rather not to be tasked with that kind of grunt work, I'd be happy to come up with an excuse for you."

Kasuga smiled. "Are you kidding? I couldn't ask for a better demonstration. After all that chaos kicked up by your side and the Euro Eva, a lot of hope is being put into the Akashima—a machine operated by human touch."

The lieutenant colonel noticed Misato and raised an eyebrow. "I didn't expect you'd be joining us. I appreciate a commander who takes a hands-on approach. If you're traveling in secret, we can save formal introductions for another day."

He offered a casual salute and exited through the door, leaving his laughter behind as he went.

Misato stood frozen for a moment. "Who was that?"

Toji sighed. "I guess you could say he's Six's friend."

NEON GENESIS
EVANGELiONANIMA

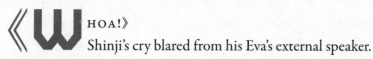

CHAPTER 3

《W HOA!》

Shinji's cry blared from his Eva's external speaker.

Startled by this exclamation, the crew looked skyward. Toji moved closer to the mobile command center's one-way mirror—which, from the outside, was indistinguishable from the other armored panels—for a better look.

The Asuka-like red giant pulled the entry plug out of its own back, opened the hatch, and gave it a good shake.

"What?" Toji sputtered. "Wait! Don't do that!"

To the watchers' relief, Asuka didn't suddenly come plummeting out of her cockpit. But it wasn't all good news.

As the giant swung the plug, the open hatch offered a brief glimpse of the empty seat within.

Shinji sighed. "I thought that might be the case."

Asuka had lost her physical form and had merged with her Eva. She now existed as part of the red giant.

Those who knew Asuka were devastated, but the giant just kept shaking the plug. Finally, she seemed to give up, and her shoulders slumped. She held the plug out to Super Eva and went still.

"What?" Shinji asked. She seemed to be waiting for his reaction.

Toji shouted up to him. 《Shinji!》

The young deputy commander had removed his communications headset and was waving it at Shinji. There was a camera attached.

Shinji stepped into Asuka-Eva's entry plug. Whatever transformation the Eva had undergone, the entry plug's layout remained unchanged from when it had been a part of Eva-02. Only the colors were new—every surface was red. The headcam Shinji had borrowed from Toji transmitted the video to Nerv Japan's HQ in Tokyo-3, where Maya was watching.

《Did you bring the sensor with you? Place it over there,》 the chief scientist instructed. 《You said that, at first, she looked like a lump of mud? I wonder if everything we're seeing here was recreated from Asuka's memory.》

"From...Asuka's memory?" Shinji repeated, confused.

《In some places, Eva's new form resembles Asuka, and in others, Eva-02. But not Eva-02 as it was when it last departed, equipped for space travel. What I've seen looks like Eva-02 as it was on land—as would have been most familiar to Asuka.》

The interior of the entry plug was damp, like it had just been drained of the LCL as part of the standard exit procedure. "Oh," Shinji said, noticing a book clinging to the wet surface of the side wall. The book's blue cover was conspicuous amid all the red.

When Asuka had embarked on her reconnaissance-in-force mission to the moon, her friends had given her as many gifts as the storage space permitted to help stave off boredom and homesickness on the long journey. Shinji had given her this book, a collection of marine life photographs. Its pages were coated in resin for bathtub reading.

It was Shinji's attempt at being thoughtful—he reasoned that a waterproof book would give her something to read in the LCL—but when Asuka saw his gift, she was underwhelmed. Annoyed, even.

"Is *this* all he gave me?"

Shinji flipped through the pages and landed on a two-page spread of Pacific white-sided dolphins jumping out of the water. *What must she have felt when she saw this,* he wondered, *after becoming stranded in space?* He thought of Ayanami Rei Cinq, who'd died before reaching the moon. Overwhelmed with grief and regret, he continued absently flipping the pages, but he wasn't actually looking at them anymore.

《Shinji-kun, stop right there!》 Maya said. 《Show me that.》

"Sorry," Shinji said. "I was just..."

《Do you see anything odd about those pictures? They've triggered Magi-2's text recognition.》

Shinji was confused. "No, they're just ordinary photographs," he said, but he angled the book into better light and squinted at the pages.

That's when he realized that the marine life images weren't ordinary at all. They were composed of miniscule symbols.

"What is this?" he asked.

《Whatever it is, it's not normal writing.》

Shinji resumed turning the pages, looking closely this time. It was the same with every picture—the beautiful waters and curiously shaped creatures were all formed from tiny symbols.

Had the red giant—the apparent fusion of Asuka and Eva—wanted to give this to him?

Shinji hopped onto his parked Eva's outstretched hand, and Asuka-Eva withdrew the plug. As the red giant's arm rose, her muscle fibers made a loud scraping noise. Her hand pushed through what Shinji supposed was her hair, and she reinserted the plug. Nothing in her actions indicated whether or not she was aware that she'd left the book for Shinji.

Her attention turned to the European Eva, Heurtebise, kneeling a fair distance away. She began to walk toward it.

"Huh? What?" Shinji stammered. "Asuka, stop! There are people on the ground that way! You're going to step on them!"

The red giant paused and looked over her shoulder at him. Then she resumed walking, following the path cleared by a large, camouflaged transport vehicle that had just passed by her feet. For the time being, at least, it seemed she'd decided to avoid trampling anyone. As she approached the other Eva, her body language so strongly evoked that of an excited child finding a turtle at the edge of the water, that Shinji blurted, "Asuka, don't poke that Eva! You'll surprise it!"

What am I saying? Shinji thought. *And why is she acting like a child?*

But he could only guess at what was going through her mind. She still hadn't spoken a single word.

NEON GENESIS
EVANGELION ANIMA

CHAPTER 4

▷ **A DISTANT REUNION**

A TECHNICIAN ARRIVED with a new headset to replace the one Toji had given to Shinji.

"Commanding Officer Suzuhara," she said, "I've reset the system to your communications credentials. You have a transmission from Lieutenant Colonel Clausewitz, the direct commission officer with the Euro Sixth Rapid Response Unit under Hartmann's command."

"I was waiting for this," Toji said cheerfully, but then he hung his head. "Wait, how are we supposed to understand each other?"

The technician was ready with a short cable, which she stretched out between her hands. "Your tablet can auto-translate. Don't worry, we'll also be monitoring your conversation from the command center to catch any translation errors in the software."

"You've thought of everything. Thanks."

Watching from a distance, Misato admired how the organization had adapted to Toji's leadership style.

Clausewitz... Misato thought. *The head of Nerv Germany.*

"Misato-san—I mean, Commander Katsuragi," Toji said, catching himself. "I can't return command to you until we get back to HQ."

"Because I'm not supposed to be here. I understand."

"And, er..." Toji cleared his throat awkwardly. "Could you do me a favor?"

Again, Misato understood. She knew why he'd been so determined to see this mission through himself.

"You have a chance to meet her?" she asked.

Toji stopped fidgeting and stood up straight. "Yes, but on one condition. I must speak with her alone."

"Then go. I'll hold down the fort."

"Thank you."

Toji hopped out of the mobile command center and scrambled down the red rocky slope.

"Go to her," Misato said cheerfully as she watched through the window.

At the bottom of the slope, the security team's SUV was ready and waiting, along with an escort.

In this valley, surrounded by red mountains and teeming with soldiers from any number of nations, Nerv Japan's recovery team went about their duties in a professional and orderly manner. Toji was an inexperienced leader, but rather than falling apart, the Nerv staff had come together, shoring up each other's weaknesses. Even when given minimal orders, everyone was working hard.

The JSSDF had even lent the use of their giant robot, crew included.

Is Deputy Commander Fuyutsuki calling the shots? No, I don't think so—if he were, he probably would have left Suzuhara-kun and come himself. Whatever the case, I need to get back in gear.

Nerv Japan's Acting Deputy Commander Suzuhara Toji had put in the request to Euro-II's control team for a face-to-face meeting with their Eva's pilot. He figured that if they refused, he'd be no worse off than he already was. But they'd said yes.

Euro-II's unit seemed to hold a special place within the European forces. They didn't mix with the other soldiers and instead had claimed a section of the red mountains for themselves. Though the European military was primarily composed of units recruited from member nations on a provisional basis, the Sixth Rapid Response Unit was a standing force reporting directly to the European Joint Forces Command. Though their numbers were small, they held nearly absolute authority over the army, navy, and air force—since their sole purpose was to deploy Heurtebise into battle at a moment's notice.

Toji's SUV was waved past the perimeter without being asked to stop, but he knew he was being subjected to any number of electronic scans. Because this was a personal meeting, no grand reception awaited him. The SUV proceeded straight to the feet of the kneeling white giant.

As Toji got out of the car, he immediately noticed the Eva's positron rifle, currently undergoing maintenance. This was a different model from the Japanese ones. The particle-generating cyclotron wasn't a torus. Instead, it began in a cone—much like Eva-00 Type-F's long rifle, the Angel's Backbone—before continuing into the accelerator's long barrel, which curved back on itself in a U-shape. This form, combined with the golden color of the weapon's electromagnetic-field-resistant coating, resulted in an appearance not unlike a brass instrument.

"I guess that *is* something an angel would carry," Toji remarked.

A reflection moved across the weapon's shiny exterior, and a familiar person stepped into view. Toji walked toward her, while his bodyguards remained behind. In his peripheral view, he saw the Euro guards forming a perimeter, but that was only to be expected. After all, they were protecting an Eva pilot.

"So," Toji said, "they still have you in the old plugsuits."

As if only just noticing what she was wearing, Hikari quickly moved her hands to cover herself.

"C-can we maybe skip the fashion advice?" she stammered. "And stop staring at me."

Her arms settled into a crossed position, and her posture drooped.

She's still herself, Toji thought with relief. After Heurtebise had confronted Super Eva in Hokkaido, Shinji reported that Hikari had been acting strangely—like she was under someone's control.

"What's next for you, Hikari? You could come back with me to Japan. I can get the request put through."

"I want you to take this."

She handed him an aluminum tube. He opened the lid and retrieved a glass ampoule. White crystals rattled around inside.

"That's Kodama," she said. "My sister."

"What?!" Toji's mind raced. Hikari's family had been taken to Europe—her older sister included. The Lance of Longinus had turned people across North Africa, Europe, and Russia into pillars of salt.

Was she caught in the lance's light?

Toji knew Kodama. She had a cheerful personality. He even called her "Sis."

"What...?! No..."

No words could express his shock.

Toji wanted to scream, but in front of him was the person hit hardest by the loss, and she was somehow remaining calm. He needed to keep himself in check. He closed his eyes and focused his thoughts on his artificial arm so that his racing heart wouldn't cause the limb to twitch. Then, slowly, carefully, he returned the ampoule to the aluminum tube and closed the lid tight.

"Take her back to Hakone," Hikari said.

What?

"No, no, no, hold on. This isn't the kind of thing you can just hand off to someone else. You should take it. Keep it safe. And..."

He trailed off, at a loss for words.

She gave him a kind smile. "If you take it for me, then I know I'll be able to come home one day."

Which means she won't come back now. Is that what she's saying?

She'd made up her mind. Now he understood why the Europeans had so easily agreed to this meeting.

Hikari slowly walked toward Heurtebise, and Toji followed after her.

"Nozomi is still in Germany," she said without stopping.

That was Hikari's younger sister.

Toji dropped his voice to a whisper. "Are they making you say this? Is that what's going on? I can find Nozomi, and—"

Hikari shook her head gently. "It's more complicated than that. I've come to understand many things."

She tapped Euro-II Heurtebise's foot with her hand. "For now, I'm the only person who can ride inside this Eva."

That sounded like Europe's problem. Toji couldn't understand how she could be so cavalier about the situation when she'd practically been kidnapped.

"You don't have to bear that responsibility," he said.

She turned. "Eva-II Heurtebise is Asuka's mother, too," she said, as if introducing someone very important.

"What? That's not..." *Possible? But who's to say what's possible anymore?* Toji searched his recollection of the reports from Eva-02's construction.

The German Nerv branch had originally built Unit Two, and both Maya and Hyuga had theorized that Euro-II had been built from a discarded production body.

"The Germans told me this morning—Unit Two's core failed to bind with this one's body. They say her soul is with Asuka in Unit Two, but traces might still linger in this Eva." Hikari sighed and flashed a sardonic grin. "I feel like I'm only just learning everything this morning."

Hikari pointed to the red giant. "Look at her."

"Crimson A1?" Toji asked. This was the provisional code name Nerv Japan had just assigned to the Asuka and Eva combination.

"Don't call her that." Hikari was still smiling warmly, but her voice was firm. "You have to keep calling her Asuka or her essence will fade. If you don't consciously pick her out from the mix, she won't be able to come back."

"Are you saying that's not Soryu?"

"Asuka isn't that big, silly," Hikari said with a giggle.

Toji didn't understand. She seemed to be suggesting that Asuka was still on board the Eva, but he'd already confirmed that that wasn't the case.

Seeing his confusion, Hikari explained. "She's not Asuka. When she returned, she was jumbled together with all kinds of different creatures. I don't know why or how. But amid that mishmash, her mother's soul tried to protect her by overwriting portions of the Eva with parts that were Asuka."

Every now and then, a huge boom echoed across the mountains as another giant, deteriorating corpse crumbled in the canyon below.

In the Valley of Human Bodies, the Asuka and Eva combination had shaken loose the ancient organisms' data, which had poured into the giant rock formations left behind after the final battle of the Evangelions and created an Eva-sized menagerie—a fleeting festival of life that had only lasted a single night. Now these life-forms were returning to dust.

Heavy machinery and CBRN monitoring vehicles were making the rounds through the canyon and collecting samples from the colossal creatures before they crumbled.

Maybe they thought these samples would help them learn more about the Ark. After all, the organisms' data had been stored in the moonside Ark before flooding into Asuka and Eva-02. But ultimately, these were just oversized corpses.

As the soldiers recovered the remains of their devoured comrades from the organisms' digestive tracts, they couldn't help but wonder why these creatures had appeared in such fervor the night before.

Other teams used ground-penetrating radar and seismic surveying equipment to search for the Ark itself. Humanity had turned to religious folklore in hopes of salvation. What they didn't know was that Armaros had carried the Ark off to a new location. Aida Kensuke—who'd managed to slip out of the valley undetected even after his arm had been turned to salt—hadn't divulged that information.

The European forces had arrived first, followed by a coalition of North African militaries, and each side kept the other in check. Their frenzied hunt the night before had given way to a more level-headed search, but after the earthquake, their movements had grown hurried again. They were now preparing for a full withdrawal.

Earthquake prediction centers in Europe, West Asia, and North Africa all agreed—another interplate earthquake would soon strike the region.

Heurtebise's control aircraft, a large VTOL, was parked on the rocky ground behind the white giant. A single, primary turbine had been running for some time—the plane's auxiliary power unit must not have been able to put out sufficient electricity for maintaining control of the Eva—but now the engine's noise raised in pitch. The crew was likely preparing to ignite the other turbines. Someone appeared from the control aircraft and called out to Hikari in German.

"He said it's time to leave," she explained to Toji.

At that exact moment, Toji's tablet vibrated in his pocket. He retrieved the device and saw an earthquake warning scrolling across the LCD.

"Are you going to be all right in Europe?" he asked.

"Nerv Germany promised they won't run Heurtebise using the dummy plug anymore. But they say I still have to be partially hooked in to keep the black scale from taking over my mind."

"Can you trust them?"

"It'll be fine. If they try to control me with those drugs again, Heurtebise won't move."

Toji nodded. "Because Asuka's mom will go on strike. It pays to have some leverage over the management, eh?" He still couldn't make himself accept her decision, but he forced himself to smile for her.

Hikari threw her arms around him.

The European guards tensed and raised their weapons, and Toji's retinue responded in kind. Toji raised both arms and slowly looked around, announcing with his body language that there wasn't—and wouldn't be—any trouble.

Hikari leaned her forehead against his chest and whispered. "My memories finally came back to me this morning, all at once." She'd removed all emotion from her voice, but Toji could feel her trembling. "Hundreds died in the darkness of last night. Some because of the Eva under my control."

"I won't tell you there's no point in thinking about it, but when an Eva's involved, that kind of thing just..." Toji suddenly remembered how he'd punched Shinji years ago. *What the hell has happened to me?*

He'd still never piloted an Eva into battle, but ever since he'd started commanding them, he'd learned to perform that dreadful calculation—victims versus results.

"And before that," Hikari said, "I tried to take down Shinji."

"But you were being controlled through the dummy plug, weren't you?" Toji asked.

"It was still me doing it. That's why I can't go back yet. I can't forgive myself, and I can't forgive the people who put me in this situation." She looked up at him, smiling through her worry. "Please, give me time."

She was asking for space to reconcile her new memories, but if she was going to blame herself for what she'd been through, she'd be better off at home.

"You know, I really think that—" Toji began.

But she cut him off. "I'm sorry I'm being selfish. I understand your perspective, and I hate to make you endure this."

You're the one who's bearing this burden alone! Toji thought.

But she'd spoken with finality. There was no point in arguing—and Toji wasn't so selfish that he'd try to use force. But his mind buzzed with frustration.

Hikari pressed her lips against his, then released her arms and backed away, her parting smile still betraying worry.

Then she had turned, her yellow plugsuit growing smaller as she walked away.

A suspended scaffold brought an engineer down from Heurtebise's entry plug. Hikari traded places with him, and the scaffold lifted her back up to the pilot's seat.

"Stubborn girl," Toji grumbled.

He was walking back to the SUV when suddenly he cried out in surprise.

There was Crimson A1—the Asuka and Eva-02 combination—evidently having grown bored watching the Moroccan army's heavy machinery. She'd approached without him noticing and was crouching with her chin on her hands as she stared at him.

She was staring as he walked all the way to the SUV.

She was still staring as he and his retinue climbed into the vehicle.

Just before he closed the door, Toji leaned out and waved his arms at her. "Well?!" he shouted angrily. "What is it? If you have somethin' to say, then say it!"

Asuka-Eva tilted her head—which, even while crouching, was still quite high up. For some reason, the sight melted Toji's frustration.

"Yeah, yeah. Nothing's going right. And we're just getting started."

Behind him, the white Euro Eva spread its wings, the graviton floaters roared, and the angel lifted into the sky.

CHAPTER 5

▶ # A WORLD FORGOTTEN

A S VARIOUS ARMIES' ALARMS sounded their evacuation, Nerv Japan personnel's smart devices displayed an alert. An AI read the message aloud from speakers within their encampment.

《The following is a revision of plate deformation forecast number twenty-two. The probability of a magnitude eight earthquake occurring between 1500 and 1600 Greenwich Mean Time is now seventy-five percent.》

Toji rushed into the mobile command center just as Misato was asking, "What was that warning?"

"An earthquake!" Toji replied, breathless. "And from the sound of it, the probability is high."

"Of being hit by another of the same magnitude, you mean?"

He shook his head. "According to the scientists, that was just the opening act."

Toji switched his headset to transmit to all Nerv devices.

"Er... All stations, please continue preparations to evacuate. We depart in one hour. Leave behind the heavy machinery along with any disassembled pieces of Super Eva's armor. And make sure everyone is accounted for." Toji looked to Misato, who still seemed to be processing the news. "A truly massive earthquake is coming."

"We're sure of that?" she asked.

"Plate deformations created these mountains. But this one's going to be severe. Simulations show that it will topple the mountains surrounding the valley. This place is going to be buried beyond recognition."

Misato looked out the window. "The Valley of Human Bodies will be no more."

After Seele had hijacked Kaji's mind, he'd said that a great flood would reset the world.

In certain circumstances, the thoughts and deeds of humankind left afterimages on the next iteration. The rock formations in the valley had been left by the final battle between more than a hundred Evangelions and were imbued with their desperation for survival. Then came a new input—Crimson A1's zoological data. The rocks metamorphosized...and died in one last gasp of freedom.

Misato thought of the next world described by Armaros and Seele, and said, "I think this valley will find peace."

On a flat expanse of land some ten kilometers southwest of the Valley of Human Bodies, the aircraft Nerv Japan had borrowed from the UN waited for the recovery teams to arrive, while the aircraft of the European mixed fleet flew overhead. The recovery teams were nearly an hour late now. They'd been delayed by the throng of African and European armies making their own hasty retreat.

Taking up the rear, behind the off-road tractor towing the mobile command center and the other military vehicles, Super Eva pulled Crimson A1 along by the hand.

"Asuka," Shinji said, "what's so wrong with going this way?"

For whatever reason, Asuka-Eva wanted to go east-northeast, away from the rally point.

In her agitated state, loading Crimson A1 onto the cargo plane seemed a daunting task, but the recovery team had come to North Africa with a signal-stop plug in case Super Eva had proven impossible to control. As a backup plan, they only needed to find the right opportunity to put Asuka to sleep.

When it came time to decide whether the second giant-sized cargo plane would transport Super Eva or the Akashima, Shinji insisted he could fly home himself—and that was when he ran into a problem.

He couldn't form an A.T. Field around Super Eva's Vertex wings.

He didn't realize anything was wrong until it was too late. Before, the giant had seared across the sky as if propelled by a tremendous force. This time, Super Eva leaped into the sky...and toppled over in full view of everyone. Shinji yelped in surprise.

"I'm not flying!" he said, stating the obvious. Then, with delayed realization, "I *can't* fly?"

Crimson A1 stepped around the collapsed Eva and leaped from the rocks. Her two long bundles of hair—or were they wings?—spread out ever so slightly, and Asuka-Eva began rising into the sky.

"What?" Shinji said, startled, as she grabbed Super Eva's arm and pulled him with her.

Completely off-balance, Super Eva flailed about, but Asuka-Eva deftly moved beneath him and began pushing him from below. She took hold of his other arm—the one broken and dangling—and moved back above him again, still pulling.

Shinji was too flabbergasted to feel any pain.

He snapped out of his confusion and tried to create an A.T. Field so he could find some kind of purchase.

Asuka-Eva soared even higher, keeping an eye on him. There was an accompanying roar—or rather, a chorus of vibrations.

On the ground, the science team stood awestruck, and Misato—who'd been about to attempt to load Crimson A1 onto the transport—remarked, "I don't understand how her graviton floaters are still active in her new form."

Familiar traces of the Allegorica's wings remained in Asuka-Eva's hair, but Misato had assumed the resemblance was merely vestigial.

"So then," Misato said, "those two disc-shaped parts are the N_2 reactors... And she's using them to lift something even heavier than herself?!"

Shinji searched for an explanation as to why he couldn't fly. *Is it because I've lost too much power?*

The Center Trigonus had been Super Eva's heart, the vessel that directed the wild torrent of energy flowing into the Eva from higher dimensions. His A.T. Field-powered wings had relied on that energy to fly, and now the heart had been stolen. On top of that, the Eva was in rough shape after getting battered by Armaros. Shinji didn't know if that was exacerbating the problem, but it certainly didn't help.

As Asuka tugged him upward and forward, Shinji generated thrust with his A.T. Field, albeit minimal and intermittent. But this effort taught him something about the Q.R. Signum in his chest.

Armaros' scale sent him power even as its darkness assaulted his psyche, but the farther he got from the ground, the weaker the power became.

Meanwhile, the intrusive thoughts seem to be getting stronger!

With Super Eva's eye crushed, the virtual display in front of Shinji showed only a limited field of view. And without this to distract his mind, he couldn't help but think about the uncertain future. He visualized the Q.R. Signum's darkness pursuing him, threatening to swallow him whole.

But then the bright splash of Asuka-Eva's red body danced across his limited vision, as if to chase his fears away. It almost seemed like she was trying to be playful, perhaps even smiling.

A memory returned to Shinji. The pulling on his arms felt familiar. Nostalgic.

Summer. The first swim day of the year. I take a deep breath. I flutter my legs in the water.

Then he was back in the present with a new realization. *Asuka is trying to teach me how to fly.*

And then another realization. *We're heading toward Tokyo-3. That's why she's been pulling me in this direction.* Shinji chuckled. *She's going straight back to where she belongs.*

The Akashima was loaded into one of the two giant-transport cargo planes, while the other, which would have transported Crimson A1, had no cargo. Both ignited their rocket boosters and lifted off, leaving tremendous smoke plumes in their wake as they departed the continent that had been the birthplace of humankind.

As Crimson A1 pulled Super Eva up and over the Valley of Human Bodies, the anomalous aurora painted eerie, rainbow-colored trails across the northern sky. Just then, a massive earth-quake struck the mountain range below. The ground turned pale and hazy, as if the Earth had coughed, but Shinji was too focused on his perilous flight to notice what happened next.

Everything they'd seen and touched down there crumbled into dust.

NEON GENESIS EVANGELION ANIMA

PART 2

A JOURNEY WITHOUT MAPS

CHAPTER 6

THE VALUE OF HUMANKIND
BETA

To recover super eva, Nerv Japan had sent two UN cargo planes—large enough to transport one Evangelion each—and six additional aircraft. But the red Asuka-Eva was pulling Super Eva across the sky, leaving one Eva transport empty. It followed the pair of giants, its searchlights illuminating them. Their only other escort was a single N$_2$ Flanker, which had peeled off from the retinue.

The Flanker was supposed to be Toji's transport, but right now, the exhausted leader was sleeping in the empty cargo plane, on the floor of the passageway outside the CIC, while the unmanned, heavily modified Flanker accompanied the slower, larger craft.

Even with Super Eva's meager assistance, Asuka-Eva was too heavily burdened to reach the cruising speed of the jet-powered transport planes. The other aircraft, fully loaded with equipment and staff, had no choice but to fly ahead. Otherwise, they risked running out of fuel. Shinji and the other stragglers were still flying eastward over the Indian subcontinent as night fell.

The Lance of Longinus continued to lengthen as it circled the Earth 20,000 kilometers above the surface. Its extremely thin, radiant line appeared over the southwest horizon and then traced a massive arc overhead on its journey northeast.

The scientific community predicted that the mysterious force constricting the Earth would reach its peak when the lance's head and tail met, forming a complete ring. But even though that day hadn't yet arrived, the Earth's crust was in continuous turmoil.

Even the skies had changed dramatically. The Longinus Curtain, a barrier the lance had created between the Earth and the moon, had shattered just days earlier, revealing a terrifying sight—the moon had swollen to nearly double its size.

In the night sky, the disturbance in the Earth's electric field made the curved horizon glow. To the south, lightning flashed, and to the north, the aurora cast its eerie lights. It was a beautiful view.

Inside the CIC, Misato was on the radio with Maya in Tokyo-3. She kept one eye on the monitor showing Crimson A1 and Super Eva. The image was washed out, its subjects lit by the plane's searchlights.

"The Q.R. Signum," Misato was saying, "belongs to Armaros— our *enemy*. Those black scales have been powering the corpses of the mass-production Evas. So why are they continuing to supply energy to Heurtebise and Super Eva?"

《Maybe Armaros doesn't actually regard us as an enemy,》 Maya said.

The reality was that they were fighting something that operated on an entirely different level from humanity.

《I'd wager its thought processes aren't as complicated as we assume.》

"You know, I think you might be right about that."

What does a god care for the tribulations of humanity?

It was early morning in Japan, and Maya had clearly been up all night. The chief scientist had no intention of dragging out this conversation, so she went straight to the heart of Misato's apprehensions.

《Commander Katsuragi, you fear that, in exchange for its survival, Super Eva has been contaminated and will become Armaros' vanguard, correct?》

"That's right."

《As for whether Super Eva will end up like Unit Quatre...I'm not so sure. The scale is inside the quantum wave mirror. What I keep thinking about is the stolen heart and how it's a window to higher dimen—oh... Hold on. Another quake. This one might be a bit bi—》

The transmission cut off.

"Maya?" Misato asked.

But not only was the encoded voice channel gone, the entire communication signal had been interrupted, including the navigation and weather data from Tokyo-3. The monitor in the comms booth stated that the contact couldn't be found and asked if Misato wanted to retry the transmission.

NEON GENESIS
EVANGELION**ANIMA**

CHAPTER 7

FALSEHOOD

NOT ALL OF THE RECOVERY TEAM'S aircraft were headed to Japan. One plane, bearing the security intelligence division, peeled off from the formation after takeoff, without announcing their destination. They returned to where they'd left—North Africa, post-earthquake—to search for Ayanami Rei Trois, who'd gone missing there.

Only Misato, Toji, and a select few other personnel knew that she'd walked away alone soon after Misato had come back. Later, Misato happened to come across Rei Quatre, who was in a near-catatonic state. For now, the commander was pretending she was Trois and had placed her in the cargo plane's medical bay.

Why had Misato done this? In order to bring Super Eva home.

Misato reckoned that if Shinji knew Trois had gone missing, he would have demanded to search for her until the bitter end and would have refused to evacuate.

But unlike Shinji, Toji was responsible for *everyone* under his command. He was, of course, concerned for Rei Trois, but the people on the rescue team had entrusted their lives to him, and it was clear now that he'd made the right call. Had he continued the search operations and not ordered the evacuation, everyone on the ground would have been buried under the collapsing mountains.

Shortly after takeoff, the departing personnel had looked down to see the great earthquake level the mountains and kick up giant dust clouds. While most of them had let out sighs of profound relief, Toji had shuddered with dread as he imagined what would have happened had he acted differently.

Managing to stay in flight, mostly thanks to Crimson A1, Shinji caught a glimpse of a figure through a window of the giant cargo plane overhead.

"Ayanami?"

He zoomed in his view without conscious effort. The interior of the plane was dark, but Super Eva's vision automatically compensated and increased its photosensitivity. The girl's features became more distinct. Shinji had been right. It was Ayanami.

Unaware that she wasn't Trois, Shinji said softly, "Ayanami... Trois, you offered to come with me, and I put you through hell."

Then he gasped.

A door near the window blew out in a cloud of smoke. The plane's safety systems forced open the hatch, and the difference in pressure threw Ayanami's body out into the sky where she blew about like a scrap of cloth.

"Wh-why the hell...?!"

Moving quickly, Shinji initiated the entry plug release sequence.

He partially ejected Unit One's entry plug and opened the hatch. The LCL hadn't had time to fully drain, and it sprayed out in a fine mist. The low temperature instantly crystallized the liquid, creating a white cloud that trailed after the Eva.

"CIC!" Shinji shouted into his headset. "This is an emergency! Ayanami is—"

But the nearly five-hundred-kilometer-per-hour wind swallowed his voice.

As Ayanami fell toward him, Shinji reshaped his unsteady A.T. Field in an attempt to catch her and pull her into the plug. He forgot to focus on his flight, and Super Eva's hands slipped out of Asuka-Eva's grasp. Now he and Super Eva, like Ayanami, were in free fall.

The low-temperature, low-pressure atmosphere squeezed the air from Shinji's lungs, and he began to feel faint. But even as his consciousness faded, he managed to catch Ayanami by the arm and pull her into the plug. The pair collapsed into the pilot's seat.

"Seal...seal the hatch," Shinji commanded his Eva's systems. "Commence entry sequence."

Ever since Super Eva had been given a heart, Shinji hadn't needed to go through the entry sequence. He and the Eva were one entity. But the legacy commands remained in the system, and the plug's environment rapidly stabilized from the emergency ejection. The plug filled with LCL—warmer than usual—and Shinji filled his lungs, letting out a deep breath.

His lungs thawed—expanding, contracting, and hurting like hell.

That was close, Shinji thought.

He realized he still had his arms around Ayanami. She was dressed in orange coveralls and work clothes. Flustered, he sat her upright on his knees.

"What the hell were you thinking, Trois?!" Shinji yelled. "What if you'd hit something when you were getting sucked out of the plane? What if you'd blacked out from the pressure change? Do you have any idea how many different ways you could've gotten killed with that stunt?"

But something wasn't right with Ayanami—specifically, her movements.

She gave the impression of a broken puppet, her red eyes fixed on a point somewhere off in the distance.

Oh, no. She must have hit her head.

"Ayanami! Breathe in the LCL. Breathe it in deep!"

Her eyes focused on him. Super Eva was still falling toward the Earth's surface. Ayanami floated, weightless inside the plug. Behind her, an array of alert windows popped up in rapid succession. Their red glow accentuated the outline of her face.

One of the windows reported a system error: PILOT THOUGHT-PATTERN REFERENCE INDISTINCT. The entry plug was picking up Ayanami's thoughts.

Damn!

In his haste, Shinji had brought someone else inside Super Eva without any thought-shielding equipment. In the old Eva-01, the additional presence would have resulted in a decreased field-generating capability and impaired command recognition, but with Super Eva...well, no one had ever tried it before..

Ayanami, her eyes still locked on Shinji, spoke softly.

"Take Ikari-kun—and take me—someplace far away. The farthest place."

Shinji felt a sharp knot in his chest. He grunted in pain and clutched the front of his plugsuit.

Intuitively, he knew why. The Q.R. Signum implanted in his other chest—Super Eva's chest—had responded to Ayanami's call. The girl's words were an incantation directed at Armaros' black scale, the source of Super Eva's power.

"If Ikari-kun won't set this world free, and if I can't escape... then at least take us to the edge of the Earth!"

Shinji was clutching his chest so tightly his fingers had nearly dug between his ribs. "You're...Quatre?!" he realized. "But how?"

Super Eva continued to fall toward the Earth—one arm extended, the other trailing limply behind.

If the heavily armored, four-thousand-ton Eva continued falling unchecked, the giant's impact would crater the Earth. But the Indian subcontinent was already sliding north, violently pushing the mighty Himalayas up and slipping under the Eurasian plate. Any mark Super Eva left would pale in comparison.

The giant-transport plane was in an uproar.

A shrill alarm announced the release of the outer door and

awoke the off-duty personnel in their sleeping bags, which they now scrambled out of. The primary compartments maintained normal operating pressure, but the UN pilots followed protocol and immediately shed altitude. The massive plane's wings pushed through the clouds, and everything inside began to rattle and shake.

"Stop the low-pressure alarm!" Misato shouted up to the cockpit. "Is Super Eva all right?"

The expelled door and any other objects that had been sucked out might have hit it.

She looked to the external camera feed where Super Eva plummeted toward the Deccan Plateau—and then, like magic, was swallowed into the ground.

"He's gone," Misato said. "No emissions detected."

One explanation came readily to mind.

Again and again, they'd fought enemies with the Q.R. Signum's ability to teleport into and out of battle. Had Super Eva been contaminated, like Unit Quatre, and joined the enemy?

Misato pressed the button on the intercom by her seat. "Medical bay, is Quatre there?"

But she already knew the answer.

CHAPTER 8

▷ **THE ILLUSORY PASSAGE, PART ONE**

T HE Q.R. SIGNUM TELEPORTATION wasn't instantaneous. The traveler experienced a passage of time, however brief, as they journeyed through the domain of the Victors.

When Misato had first experienced that otherworldly realm, she'd likened the place to the roots of a forest that ran through the Earth—or a roller coaster twisting and turning underground.

But the subspace didn't have a classically physical structure. The traveler felt no acceleration, and any branches save for the one being traveled were invisible.

Super Eva passed through the tunnel and was spat out into the air.

Shinji was fully expecting to crash into the ground, back first. He'd lowered his head and tensed his back muscles to brace himself, but no impact came. Instead, his back was skyward now, and he'd been expelled on an upward trajectory.

Apparently, a traveler left the tunnel with the same velocity they'd entered.

He looked down and saw an expansive white forest of dead trees, perhaps done in by pests or pestilence.

Super Eva's mighty bulk reached nearly five hundred meters before descending again, and the receding landscape came rushing toward them.

Super Eva covered his face with both arms, and Shinji felt the snapping of dried-out tree limbs. In the last moment before the crash, he was once again swallowed into the ground and found himself briefly back in the tunnel before appearing near a glacier-covered mountain. He fell into a valley and leaped across space again.

Super Eva appeared near plateaus and plains, leaping from one place to the next without rhyme or reason.

"Where is this taking us?" Shinji cried out.

Super Eva was tossed out onto a peninsula buried under sea waters surging from a recent earthquake, or maybe a tsunami. A caldera rose, island-like, from the water. The ring of mountains didn't stand as tall as they once had, but they were still tall enough to shield the city and lake nestled within from the giant waves pressing in on every side.

Inside the next tunnel, Shinji realized what he'd just seen. "That was Tokyo-3!"

He felt himself being carried farther away.

"Quatre! Take me back to where we just were!"

Quatre said nothing.

"Quatre!"

Shinji had had enough.

Wasn't this the person who'd killed him? His hair stood on end as he relived the memory of his body boiling away under Unit Quatre's gamma-ray laser cannon.

"Move!" he shouted.

He grabbed Quatre by the back of her collar and pushed her aside as hard as he could. She didn't offer any resistance, floating up in the flow of the LCL, which was moving faster than normal in order to deliver enough oxygen for two.

Shinji was still gripping her collar, and the zipper of her coveralls tore open. The girl flew sideways, where, hidden behind the plug's holographic display, she crashed into the sidewall and rebounded. But Shinji wasn't paying any attention to her. He was staring straight ahead.

I have to go back there!

"Take me back to where we were!"

His right hand clutching the torn-off section of her uniform, its free end floating in the LCL, Shinji grabbed the control stick with his left hand and jostled it back and forth.

"Go back! Go back!"

But Shinji's pleading went unanswered, and Super Eva raced onward through the mysterious passage.

CHAPTER 9

RECOVERY TEAM,
ABOVE THE DECCAN PLATEAU

THE CARGO PLANE entered a holding pattern over the site where Super Eva had disappeared.

The pilots switched the N_2 reactors to standby and directed the planes' complex sensors below, but Misato knew they would find nothing.

Q.R. Signum dislocation left no traces detectable by current methods.

As the retinue debated what to do next, the red giant, Crimson A1—who'd been pacing the ground where Super Eva had vanished—suddenly leaped into the sky and resumed her previous route.

"It looks like Asuka has realized that Shinji and Unit One are gone," Misato said, "and that they're not coming back."

She didn't have concrete proof, but no one offered a counterargument.

"Let's go, too."

There was nothing left to be done here.

Word had spread among the crew that communications with Tokyo-3 had been lost, and everyone was anxious to get back. Now that Asuka-Eva was no longer saddled with a flight partner, she took off at incredible speed. Likewise, the cargo plane had no further reason to fly slowly. Its massive array of half-lowered flaps rose back in line with the wings, and it picked up altitude and speed.

CHAPTER 10

THE ILLUSORY PASSAGE, PART TWO

EVERYTHING WAS RECEDING into the distance.

This displacement jump was longer than the others—long enough for Shinji's impatience and rage to drain away, leaving him empty.

When he came back to his senses, he noticed that Quatre's upper body was exposed, having spilled out from her torn uniform. Her right cheek was red and swollen in the flow of the LCL.

Shinji looked down in horror at the hand he'd used to toss her aside.

Hastily, he guided her back to him, then got out of the pilot's seat and sat her down in his place.

"Ayanami," Shinji said. "Quatre..."

She stared forward in silence.

Guilt weighing heavily upon him, Shinji arranged Quatre's clothes back into place, but no matter how many times he tried, he couldn't get the broken zipper to close back up. From the display screen, flashes of light silhouetted the graceful curves of Ayanami Quatre's chest. But the sight of her only sharpened his remorse.

"Damn it," he muttered. His face burned with embarrassment. "If...if you hadn't done that, none of this would have happened."

Shinji regretted what he'd done, but he couldn't bring himself to apologize. He gave up on the zipper and crudely closed her collar with an attached fastener.

Her red cheeks moved pitifully as she faintly said, "This...is the future you chose."

"Could you please not make *everything* my fault?"

Just then, Shinji realized they weren't alone in the passage.

Ahead of Super Eva, a two-hundred-kilometer-wide molten ball of rock was flying through the tunnel at the same rapid speed.

The large, dark-red mass followed the path through the low-gravity, near-vacuum subspace.

The sky, if it could be called sky, was an empty darkness. But everything in the passage was brightly lit—washed out, even—as if under intense sunlight. In the next moment, Shinji lost sight of the rock.

Did we pass an exit? Where did it lead?

The tunnel continued. Apparently, their exit was still ahead.

For a moment, Shinji wondered if the space inside the tunnel was expanding, like when he'd fought Victors Two and Three, and that maybe he wasn't moving at all. But the increasingly sparse background was still passing at great speed. It seemed like their destination truly was that far away.

The next thing Shinji knew, the overbearing, tangled arterial network of root-like tunnels was behind them. He sensed that they were now in a single, one-way tunnel.

And that tunnel was narrowing.

NEON GENESIS
EVANGELION ANIMA

CHAPTER 11

RECOVERY TEAM,
ABOVE MAINLAND SOUTHEAST ASIA

"**A**SUKA!" Misato shouted. An analog-modulated laser beam hurled her voice toward the red giant. "Don't go that way! Go right—the side you hold your chopsticks!"

With visible reluctance, Crimson A1 altered her course.

The giant was attempting to take the shortest possible route home without any regard for national boundaries. Each time she was about to cross into some country's sovereign airspace without clearance, Misato had to grab the microphone and redirect her.

Tokyo-3 remained radio silent. As the giant cargo plane was crossing over Southeast Asia, they received a transmission, marked urgent, from the group that had flown ahead.

It was an aerial photograph of what at first seemed to be an island off the coast of a large landmass.

"Where was this taken?" Misato asked.

A murmur arose as multiple people simultaneously came to the same realization.

"Wait a minute," Toji said. "Where's Odawara and Numazu?"

The two cities had been on the boundary between mainland Japan and the mountainous Izu Peninsula directly to the south of Hakone. But now the lower-lying cities were underwater, and the peninsula had become an island stranded at sea.

A sudden uproar filled the CIC.

"Quiet!" Misato hissed as she listened to the rest of the transmission on her headset. "They're saying the entire boundary between the tectonic plates has sunk."

From the crowd, one crewman shouted, "But that's..."

Impossible, Misato finished in her head.

Earthquakes were common in the region. The Izu Peninsula rode atop the Philippine Sea Plate, and the eastern half of Japan's main island, Honshu, rode atop the North American Plate. The two plates would scrape against each other, with the most stress located just north of Tokyo-3.

But a mere earthquake didn't cause this kind of damage. The tectonic plates shifted atop a far thicker mantle. For both plates to sink, as if the ground had been pulled out from underneath them, wasn't normally conceivable.

"In other words," Toji said, stunned, "the foundation got pulled out. Is that what this means? Is the ground under our home being taken from us?"

Deep inside the planet, the Earth's mass had been disappearing. This was the direct cause of its constriction, and Toji had witnessed the cataclysmic effects as he flew over Central Eurasia for this mission.

Scientists had first confirmed the loss of material by beaming

particles from an accelerator underground. Various scientific facilities had since been reequipped with seismographs to continuously monitor the situation on a global scale.

But of all the losses to date, this was the closest to home.

"What about Tokyo-3?" Toji asked.

Another closer image arrived. An island poked out from the
newly formed waterway between Honshu and the former Izu
Peninsula.

Toji gasped. "Is that...Mount Hakone?!"

On the northern part of the depression inside the island stood
a cluster of white buildings laid out in an orderly, geometric pattern.

It was Tokyo-3 and Nerv Japan HQ.

The staff inside the CIC looked at the aerial photograph with
frozen expressions. They didn't know whether to be elated that
the city survived or horrified at the destruction around it.

The inside of the caldera looked just as Toji, Misato, and the
others remembered it, but their surroundings had sunk hundreds
of meters. Fortunately, the caldera's previously high elevation had
kept it safe.

As best could be seen from the high-altitude photograph, the
city hadn't suffered major damage. But there was no question that
the area had been shaken badly.

As much as the crew wished they could run straight back to
their home, they were still far away. And even when they arrived,
what help could they possibly offer?

Nervous murmurs arose from the typically stoic crew.

"The earthquake shrank Lake Ashi," Misato commented.

"Ah, not exactly," Toji replied with a hint of embarrassment. "Six did that when she drained the water."

Piloting Eva-00 Type-F, little Rei Six had confronted Sandalphon's larva when the Angel infiltrated the old Geofront. She'd fired the Field Piercer—a.k.a. the Angel's Backbone—up through the lake's bed and flooded the underground domain.

Misato hadn't yet heard. This had occurred while she was with Rei Quatre.

"Just...what the hell were you all doing while I was gone?"

Her exasperated tone brought a sense of normalcy back to the CIC, and the crew looked a little less panicked and pale.

"Even at its lowest point, the crater still stands seven hundred meters above sea level," Toji reassured, to himself as much as everyone around him. "It's gonna take more than a little drop to finish us."

Our families are there, Toji thought, *and they're going to be all right.*

More than eighty percent of the structures inside the caldera had been built to be earthquake-resistant, including Tokyo-3's residential districts—although the original intent was to withstand attacks from the city's many uninvited guests. Tokyo-3 and Nerv HQ also possessed an independent power grid—a lesson learned from the siege they'd faced three years ago.

Additional reports brought word that the airports in Suruga Bay and Sagami Bay had been destroyed, either by land collapse or tsunami, and were completely unusable. The advance group was in the process of choosing a new landing site.

This group included the other oversized cargo plane, which held the JSSDF's giant mecha, the Akashima.

The Akashima's commander, Lieutenant Colonel Kasuga, made contact with the base at Hamamatsu and was informed that at the tsunami's peak, the surge waters had submerged the grounds. But a shelter in a rise near the runway was still functioning. The landing strip could be recovered.

After flying halfway across the world, the metal birds turned their wings toward their new destination.

NEON GENESIS EVANGELION ANIMA

CHAPTER 12

THE ILLUSORY PASSAGE, TERMINUS

T HE DISPLACEMENT JUMP went on a long time, and silence stretched between Shinji and Rei Quatre.

Her pleas had sent them on this journey to an unknown destination where no one would be and no one would come.

Within the root-like corridor, Shinji had difficulty perceiving what was around him, but he could sense that the passage was narrowing.

On and on it narrowed, extending farther and farther. Shinji could do nothing but wait to be expelled into some desolate place.

Just when he was thinking the road must be nearing its end, Kaworu's voice came to him unbidden.

I'm glad you didn't spill out of your human vessel... Though perhaps your current situation doesn't call for celebration.

Where are you? Shinji asked.

Kaworu wasn't actually in the tunnel, but Shinji thought he felt him point to the Q.R. Signum in his chest.

You're the lead actor, Kaworu said, *you're supposed to be in the spotlight. And yet you're here, under the stage, where the stagehands scurry about.*

"What's that supposed to mean?" Shinji demanded. In response, his ears began to ring.

He realized Kaworu was laughing.

This was only supposed to be an interlude. You've outperformed my expectations.

Kaworu's voice began to distort. The ringing in Shinji's ears rose in pitch and intensity.

"It's...too much."

Shinji felt himself begin to black out.

In the next instant, he was nearly himself again.

He'd emerged from the tunnel.

Much to Shinji's surprise, there was air where he came out. He'd assumed he was being transported to somewhere even farther than the moon—maybe some remote planet, like Venus or Mars. But no, he was seemingly still on Earth.

The surrounding area was dry and desolate—not unlike the Atlas Mountains.

"Kaworu-kun?" Shinji asked, but he no longer sensed his presence. His remote-transmission friend always conversed on his own terms.

Once the ringing in his ears and the pain in his chest had eased a little, Shinji drained the LCL from the plug.

Quatre's hair and work uniform had been swaying like aquatic plants in a fish tank, but as the fluid gradually lowered, they pressed flat against her skin. No longer buoyant, her body sank deep into the plug seat.

As Shinji stood beside her, the weight came back to his legs. He lifted his heels and broke their adhesion to the wet floor.

Shinji ejected the plug. Just as he was about to open the hatch, an alarm sounded. It was the environmental sensor.

"A decompression sickness warning? Why would that be an issue?"

The display indicated low air pressure outside—on par with the atmosphere atop a tall mountain.

A sudden change in pressure could be dangerous, particularly after time spent in the LCL. Then the AI announced another hazard—high radiation—and a recommendation to avoid prolonged exposure. At first, Shinji thought he might have been transported to a former nuclear test site, a nuclear waste repository, or something along those lines, but according to the computer, the radiation didn't match a human-made source. Apparently, these were cosmic rays from above.

Without exiting, Shinji opened the hatch, and bright sunlight illuminated the chamber—but the air was cold. The atmospheric pressure was low, the sky a bluish black. *Are we on a high-altitude plateau, maybe?*

Shinji didn't see the swollen moon anywhere, but he didn't have a full view of the sky, nor did he know what direction he faced.

But something else was odd.

"The Longinus Ring is gone."

"Super Eva to Mobile Command."

Shinji tried to establish a connection through the wireless transmitter, but no reply came. He couldn't pick up any guide beacons belonging to the stratospheric airplane network. In fact, all the signals had gone quiet.

Shinji looked away from the blindingly bright exterior and back to the relative darkness inside the plug.

"Quatre," he asked, "where are we?"

Her terse reply came from the shadows. "A distant place."

"Distant how?" Shinji asked, annoyed. "Tell me where we are."

"In a distant place... Aren't we? Where is this?"

"I'm asking you."

This conversation was going nowhere. He sighed, his breath turning white.

It's like hopping onto a train without knowing where it's going... and deciding to stay on until the last stop.

Where have I heard that before?

He was thinking back to when he'd first arrived at Nerv.

I ran away, but Tokyo-3 was mostly on lockdown, and I couldn't get anywhere. I bounced around between the city and the foothills. And that was when I met Kensuke.

Back then, Shinji hadn't known how to cope with his Eva and the people around him. And now, Rei Quatre seemed to be struggling in much the same way, except she was also dealing with a deluge of unfamiliar emotions, and the trauma of being shackled by Armaros.

At the side terminal, Shinji entered the command to transmit a distress signal and muttered, "So, does that mean I'm Kensuke today? What a fine turn of events."

Quatre gave him a puzzled look.

Not sure what to do, are you? Shinji thought. *Well, what did you bring us here for?*

Shinji groaned. "Why did this happen?" To Quatre, he said, "So, we're here. Somewhere far away, just like you wanted. Are you satisfied?"

"Satisfied?" Quatre asked. "I don't know what that feels like. When the one of me was split into four, I was afraid. I knew fear. Commander Ikari was gone. You didn't choose me. Though I didn't realize that until I learned how to be afraid."

She'd been sitting in the pilot's chair—not by choice but simply because that's where Shinji had put her—but the cold air had begun to freeze her wet clothes, and she curled forward, shivering.

"I *want* instrumentality," Quatre said. "You're the one who chose this world for us, Ikari-kun—and without you, maybe our world won't have to end. Maybe we could try the Human Instrumentality Project again."

"I get it now," Shinji said. He placed a hand on his chest, where his heart had been before she'd melted him with her Eva's laser.

"But I was wrong," she said. "The black giant won't change his decision. The world *will* be reconstructed. But if I could just get you far enough away—outside the world, even—then maybe..."

She let the thought trail off, and he filled in the rest. "Maybe we could let the apocalypse go on without us. Is that it? And who knows, with me out of the picture, he might change his mind after all, right?"

She buried her head in her knees and nodded.

"Ikari-kun...I'm cold."

Shinji closed the hatch and slid his finger across the temperature control to turn up the heat.

Super Eva walked across dry land. There was nothing green. The earth rose and fell in monotonous brown waves across the seemingly endless plateau. He had no GPS—the satellites had long since scattered, due to the Earth's weakening gravitational pull. The topography didn't match anything in his geological database, and nobody replied to his transmissions. Shinji began to take measurements of the sun's angle to try and get even a rough approximation of his location. He realized something was off.

Even after several hours, the shining sun hadn't moved from its zenith.

The planet wasn't rotating.

CHAPTER 13

THE DORMANT LAND

O NCE SHINJI BEGAN to suspect something was wrong with this place, the two-tone world of desert hills and empty sky began to resemble a surrealist painting created by an unbalanced mind.

Nothing moved. That, in and of itself, felt wrong. At the very least, the sun should have been shifting overhead.

Shinji didn't know what kind of danger to expect, and Super Eva proceeded with caution.

After some time, Super Eva's survey module broke the silence with an alarm—a series of short beeps that Shinji hadn't heard before.

Or maybe he had.

"Wait...I think I heard this alarm during the connection tests for the swords I got in North Africa."

The two blades were a new design, with experimental sensors dangling from each end—one on the pommel and another at the end of the sheath, making four in total. He'd only received a brief overview of the devices, but each sensor contained an array of quantum wave mirrors repurposed for detection.

When the alarm sounded, Super Eva's automap opened to show a twenty-kilometer range around his current location. Because he didn't have any matching topographical data, the map had only been filled with his direct visual observations. Everything beyond the range of sight remained blank, and it was in that blank space that an icon blinked.

"Predicted arrival?" Shinji wondered aloud. "What's that?"

Who had heard Super Eva's distress signal, and how were they arriving?

Apprehensive, Shinji switched off the signal. At first, the arrival icon bounced around within a three-kilometer-wide area, but it soon began to focus on a single point.

The alarm gave one last, long tone, and the icon stopped flashing. It turned solid red, indicating an enemy.

Beside the marker, a label appeared: MUTANT EVA-0.0 (CONFIDENCE 62%).

"What?!" Shinji sputtered, speaking to the display. "H-how do you know?"

Until now, the enemy had always been able to get the drop on him. Shinji wanted to know what had changed, but—

I can think about that later!

Shinji readied himself. The designation referred to Quatre's Eva-0.0, which had been corrupted by Armaros' Q.R. Signum. Shinji had been told that Kaji—now a vessel for Seele—had hijacked Unit Quatre.

He looked over at the Eva's former pilot, but she remained silent and expressionless. He realized he knew nothing of what she'd been through.

Strangely, Shinji felt a sort of relief upon seeing a familiar enemy marked on the display. He'd begun to feel stir-crazy, trapped in this place where time itself was caged, where the terrain never varied and the sun never moved.

Armaros' attendants—the Angel Carriers, the mutant Eva-0.0, and the Victors—had always arrived without warning. For the first time, Shinji knew one was coming and could choose his response. He elected to advance toward the enemy's entry point in hopes that he might find some answers about the place where he found himself.

Without hesitating, Shinji refilled the plug with LCL, and then, on the map display, he overlaid the shortest route to his target that still provided cover and started walking.

I wonder if I can—he focused his thoughts on the Vertex wings—*jump!*

He tried to fly low along the ground.

"Whoa," he said. as Super Eva listed forward. The giant's toes scraped along the ground and kicked up puffs of sand. It could hardly be called flying, but he was moving much faster than he could have by running.

His chest tingled with heat. The closer the unstable Q.R. Signum was to the ground, the more stable it was—relatively speaking, at least.

"I must have had a good teacher," he said, thinking of Asuka-Eva pulling him along.

The red giant had flown freely, innocently.

At first, Shinji had assumed she'd regressed into some kind of early childhood mental state. But as he'd watched her, he'd realized that wasn't the case. She was simply free to be who she was on the inside.

Asuka was easily fascinated and easily surprised, but she hated showing it. And so she kept her true self hidden, feigning disinterest and reacting instead with weariness and derision.

"Of course, I'd never say that to her face," Shinji said, "or she'd be pissed."

He wondered if Misato and Toji had been able to convince her to keep flying to Japan.

CHAPTER 14

▶ **A CHANCE MEETING AT THE END**

WITH HIS APPROXIMATION of flight, Shinji neared the mutant Eva-0.0's predicted arrival point quickly. He stayed four kilometers away, with a mountain for cover, and extended an external camera just above the ridgeline.

The camera panned from side to side and then stopped.

And there it was, malformed and monstrous, the chimera-like mutant.

The giant's gamma-ray laser cannon had merged with its right arm. A mass-production Eva's external S^2 Engine had been hacked off from its owner and jammed into the mutant's misshapen body. It even had black wings stolen from an Angel Carrier Type-3.

This is what the Q.R. Signum's influence had made of Unit Quatre.

Chief Engineer and Scientist Ibuki's sensors had worked. Though she wasn't around to hear, he couldn't help but compliment her. "Maya-san, you're a genius."

The monstrous giant hadn't noticed Shinji's presence. It seemed to be searching for something. Moving from vantage point to vantage point, the mutant Eva-0.0 surveyed its surroundings.

"Damn it, Toji, why couldn't you have given me a gun?"

Shinji held the control stick from his position beside the plug seat, and his attention was fully on the outside view. He didn't notice when Quatre's vacant expression changed to one of distress.

When she began to howl, "You...you!" Shinji finally looked over at her.

"Quatre?"

"Why are you here?!" she screamed.

Super Eva's transmitter, which was only supposed to respond to Shinji's voice commands, reacted to Quatre and blasted out her yell with the transmission code assigned to her before she'd been designated an enemy.

The mutant Eva-0.0 turned.

Shinji gasped. As he shifted Super Eva into a defensive stance, he glared at Quatre. "You gave us away! We had the drop on it!"

But she ignored him. Her eyes were locked on the mutant Eva-0.0 on the screen.

And then she shouted as loud as she could.

"Trois! The me who unifies!"

"What?!" Shinji blurted.

Super Eva picked up on his thoughts and zoomed in with his uninjured eye.

A figure stood in front of the Q.R. Signum jutting out from

the Eva-0.0's chest armor. Kaji's black coat hung from his shoulders, flapping in the wind.

When he spoke, his voice came over the hydrospeaker.

《Gendo's puppet... I thought you were broken. And who is that with you? Gendo's son? How did you know we were here?》

Seele had hijacked Kaji's mind, but the man still spoke with Kaji's dry, teasing tone. It might have been endearing once, but now it served as a painful reminder to anyone who'd known him.

Hearing what had happened to Kaji still hadn't prepared Shinji for the reality. Shaken, he said, "Kaji?!"

Staying behind the mountain, Super Eva circled around to the Kaji-vessel's front, and Shinji saw another person standing inside Kaji's open coat. She wore the same black mini-dress that Quatre had previously taken from Trois.

"Ayanami?" Shinji asked. "Trois, is that really you?"

She stirred faintly but kept on staring straight ahead.

Holding her from behind, Kaji smirked. 《Is this where I say, "Haven't you heard, Shinji-kun?"》

"Now that you're our enemy, the way you talk is really starting to piss me off," Shinji retorted.

But inside, he was distraught. Why was Trois here...and with the enemy?

Seele had manipulated Quatre and taken control of her mutant Eva-0.0, but once she went into a near-catatonic state in the Valley of Human Bodies, the Eva had malfunctioned and crashed.

Meanwhile, Ayanami Rei Trois had separated from Misato and the others to strike out on her own, bereft of any kind of home. The Kaji-vessel had found and captured her. She remained a fully functional Evangelion control device, and that was all he needed, so he'd discarded her broken counterpart, Quatre. Misato had gone searching for Trois, but instead found Quatre, and took the girl into her protective care.

"Trois, can you hear me?" Shinji asked. "That Eva is dangerous. Its contamination will spread to you, too!"

When Trois replied, her expression remained placid, even though her voice faltered.

《I couldn't stop you, Ikari-kun. And I couldn't be turned into salt, either. I'm a puppet. I'm not capable of expressing myself. But if I'm here, I don't have to think about anything anymore. So...leave me be.》

Shinji searched his memories for anything that could help him make sense of her incomprehensible answer.

"Oh....!"

He remembered. When he'd confronted Armaros, Trois had become distressed and tried to stop him, but he'd refused.

He tried to explain. "I was just—"

"Don't be ridiculous!" Quatre cut in. "You're the version of me who has everything! Why are *you* acting like you're the puppet?!"

Ayanami Rei Quatre, who'd been like a marionette with its strings snipped, leaned forward, her red eyes brimming with fury, and glared at the girl who looked almost exactly like her.

Her outburst sent Shinji's fingers digging into his chest even harder than before, and he grunted in pain.

Is she activating the Q.R. Signum inside me?

One after another, error windows appeared on his holographic display. But this time, the black force pushed back against his attempts to resist. The Q.R. Signum's contamination was spreading.

But Quatre wasn't finished.

"When the black giant went through me to get into your clones, you—the me who unifies—pushed your burdens onto us."

The mental feedback caused the control stick to jump and twitch, and Shinji scrambled to hold it in place.

"You gave each of us one disparate, incomplete piece! Six became the me who is childish and selfish. Cinq was me the problem solver, but she passed that back to you when she died. And—"

"Quatre!" Shinji shouted. "Please, stop!"

He could feel Super Eva's body—*his* body—approaching some kind of transformation.

But Quatre didn't ease up.

"And you put into *my* body the me who cowers in fear!"

Her fury drove Shinji's fingernails into his chest, and blood began to seep out, dissipating into the LCL.

"You have everything!" Quatre yelled.

As if on cue, the Q.R. Signum began pouring the black force into Super Eva with even greater intensity. Shinji had thought he could keep the raw power contained within the darkness, but now it threatened to run rampant within the giant who'd lost his heart.

PART 3

NEON GENESIS
THE APPLE'S CORE
EVANGELION: ANIMA

NEON GENESIS
EVANGELION ANIMA

CHAPTER 15

EARTH SIMULATION

A BRILLIANT BEAM of golden light struck the barren mountain, vaporizing the sand and rock. The ground detonated, as if it were made of explosives.

Shinji counted the seconds. "Two, three, four, five..."

But how long, he wondered, letting the count trail off, *until the mutant Eva-0.0 recharges its cannon?*

"Fifty-seven seconds," Ayanami Rei Quatre said. It had been her Eva, after all.

"Fifty-seven seconds," Shinji repeated. Then he winced. "I lost track."

"Fourteen, fifteen, sixteen..." Quatre filled in.

The mutant Eva-0.0's gamma-ray laser cannon was the most powerful human-made long-range weapon, and it could pierce the ridge of a mountain as if it were air. But for all its unnatural modifications, the mutant Eva still couldn't see through solid rock. The targeting systems relied on predictions based on Super Eva's last known movements. As long as he could find cover, Shinji had a chance of evading the blast.

"Fifty-five, fifty-six... Now!" Shinji shouted as he slid across another mountain ridge. He dove down the slope on the other side, kicking up sand clouds. In the next instant, the mountain split open just to his right, and a tremendous wave of heat grazed Super Eva's head. The beam struck and exploded another sandy rise ahead to his left.

"Jump!" Quatre shouted. "We don't know the terrain."

The cannon's recharge time could allow them to survey their surroundings.

"I was just gonna!" Shinji said with the indignant tone of a child being nagged to clean his room.

Preparing for the jump, Shinji planted Super Eva's feet firmly on the ground, while Quatre began drawing power from the Q.R. Signum—at a far greater rate than Shinji had yet been able to access.

"Is the Q.R. Signum connected to Armaros through the ground surface?"

"Yes," Quatre said. "At least, I think so. The gateways to the tunnel network seem to work on the ground, too. Every time my feet left the ground, I could feel the power source fading. You feel that, too, don't you?"

With more experience using the Q.R. Signum, Quatre had already drawn the necessary power by the time Shinji was ready to jump. Super Eva hurtled skyward into the cloud of sand and smoke that had risen from the last laser strike.

Shinji gasped. The power felt different from what he'd tapped into through Super Eva's heart. It was like a drug.

With tremendous energy, Super Eva shot through the mushroom cloud, through the gathering bands of electrified lightning clouds, and into the open sky above. For the first time in too long, Shinji experienced the thrill of flight.

Then he looked down, with full view of his surroundings. "The valley is sloped!" he said. "It runs down that way, and then..."

But Shinji's sentence ended there. The valley's edge led to... nothing.

The land abruptly terminated at a dark blue sky that faded into darkness below.

What is this place? Shinji thought. *Can't anything make sense?*

In exasperation, Shinji called out to the man who was trying to kill him. "The sun is stopped. The ground is missing. Kaji-san, can you tell me what the hell is going on here?! The Lance of Longinus isn't in orbit, and the bloated moon is gone!"

《There's no moon here at all,》 Kaji replied. Electromagnetic interference from the ionized air caused the signal to crackle and made his overly casual tone somehow even more grating than before. 《The moon that *was* here was carried off long, long ago on a collision course with Earth, to provide the material and energy to form *your* moon.》

Shinji couldn't process what he was hearing. His mind seized up as he tried to work it out.

"Huh?" he blurted in confusion. "Where are we? Where on Earth is this place—"

The Kaji-vessel continued, not waiting for Shinji to catch up.

《As I understand it, the natural satellite didn't have enough mass on its own. But since this place wasn't needed once the test was over, the material to make up the difference was torn off from this land. That's why it looks like it does. And without any moon, this place eventually stopped rotating. The side we're on now permanently faces the sun. Does that answer your questions? Are we good now?》

Shinji glanced to Quatre, next to him in the flowing LCL. She frowned and shook her head. At least Shinji wasn't alone in his confusion.

"My question is," Shinji replied, "where on Earth is this place, and why is it like this?"

《Come on, Shinji. This isn't the Earth.》

"What?" Shinji gasped, though less from surprise than denial. This wasn't the answer he wanted to hear.

But he'd known it was a possibility the moment he'd looked up and seen the sky without the now-familiar presence of the Lance of Longinus.

And yet, he still fought acceptance.

"But there's air here. There's gravity!"

《Of course there is. This was the testing ground for the Instrumentality Project, after all. It wouldn't make for a very good simulation of Earth without air and gravity.》 The Kaji-vessel paused, sensing Shinji's confusion. 《Oh, I see. You didn't know. But then, why are you here at the Apple's Core?

"The Apple's Core?"

Super Eva began to descend, and Shinji quickly appraised

the updated topographical map. He was seeking cover behind another ridge, when—

Boom!

The mutant Eva-0.0's gamma-ray laser cannon blasted the brittle rocks of the mountain and sent a shower of sand onto Super Eva. In order to maintain a high enough transmission rate, the reciprocal comms link used a rather high frequency, which had the unfortunate side effect of making the transmission source easily detectable.

"Wait! Simulator? Core?" Shinji shook his head to refocus his thoughts. He could figure the rest out later. Right now, he had one question. "If this isn't Earth, then where *is* Earth?!"

While Super Eva moved around behind cover, the mutant Eva-0.0 slowly turned to keep facing him. Standing atop the giant's chest armor, the Kaji-vessel brought his right hand out from the shadows of his coat—keeping his other hand wrapped around Trois—and pointed skyward to the motionless sun.

《Forever hidden on the other side of the sun. You now stand upon a mirror Earth on the exact opposite side of the sun from the Earth you call home. So, if you come across an electrical outlet, be careful which way you insert any plugs.》

Neither Shinji nor Quatre caught the reference to an old science fiction movie.

The Kaji-vessel chuckled to himself. 《Welcome to the Apple's Core. Maybe you've heard of its other name—the garden of paradise, Eden—where humankind was created and tested.》

"What, like the myth?" Shinji blurted.

《You know, I'd appreciate it if you stopped interrupting and just listened. Anyway, this planet and its moon were packed together and hurtled into the Earth. In other words, ultimately, the Earth *itself* is what bit the apple. Isn't that funny?》

All trace of humor vanished from the Kaji-vessel's face, and he whispered into Trois' ear, "Fly, Ikari's puppet."

Ayanami Rei Trois jolted but then immediately opened a gateway to the tunnel network. Shinji was still trying to figure out what was going on when the mutant Eva-0.0 abandoned the fight and began sinking into the ground.

《On your way here,》 the Kaji-vessel said, 《you probably noticed that the connection to this place is thin and faint. I'll give it one last nudge and then separate it for good. You'll die here with no way to return home.》

Shinji moved quickly, but it was too late.

By the time Super Eva jumped over the ridgeline, the mutant Eva-0.0 was already gone.

"Quatre, follow them!"

"I can't! I don't know where they went. If we were closer, I could have tuned in to the same flow, but we're too far."

Super Eva landed with a thud sending up a cloud of sand and dust.

Shinji raised his fist, but he had nowhere to direct his anger. Instead, he screamed. "Let's just go home. Hurry, while we still can!"

With Rei Trois out of sight, Rei Quatre's temper quickly subsided. But Quatre and Shinji had been at a frustrating impasse from the moment they'd stumbled onto this world, and Shinji could already sense that impasse returning.

He gave his head a vigorous shake to snap out of it. *Patience,* he told himself. *Calm down.*

Now that the target of Quatre's rage had gone, the Q.R. Signum was easing up on its assault against Shinji's psyche. But if he let himself succumb to fear and anger, he might still be swallowed by the darkness of the black scale.

Much like Super Eva's heart had been stolen from his chest, the moon had been stolen from this unfamiliar planet.

According to prevailing scientific consensus, the Earth's moon had been formed from the debris of a collision with a Mars-sized body. Though the moon had been Earth's companion through the ages, humanity was only recently beginning to understand the satellite's vital role in regulating Earth's celestial movement and ecology. In that sense, the moon was like a metronome...or even a heart.

Was the former satellite of this strange planet the object that had slammed into Earth and created the moon?

Regardless, this planet had lost its beating heart and grown still. Then Shinji had arrived, his heart stolen as well.

Now everyone else had left, and the place was quiet once more.

Shinji brought Super Eva over to the edge of the land he'd seen from above. The deep blue sky darkened into a rich navy-black hue at the horizon and continued down, below the edge of the world, into a pure black void dotted with stars.

If the Earth had been flat, as was once believed, the edge of the world would have looked just like this. It was an overhang, and Shinji couldn't see the underside. But far below, a sphere of clouds had gathered as if surrounding something. Super Eva's feet knocked a few rocks over the side, and they tumbled down toward the clouds.

When Shinji's thoughts calmed, he realized something didn't add up.

"Wait a minute," he said. *If Seele wanted to leave us here to die on this forsaken planet...* "Why did he bother telling us?"

CHAPTER 16

— THE COMMANDER'S RETURN

T HE BASE OF THE IZU PENINSULA had sunk some four hundred meters and was now swallowed by the sea.

The Hakone Caldera, with Nerv Japan cradled inside, became an island stranded in the middle of this newly formed strait. When the great sinking happened, the ground turned fifteen degrees counter-clockwise, and anything aligned to the cardinal directions became skewed. Miraculously, the ground within the caldera sank straight down rather than tilting to one side or the other.

After two agonizing days in Hamamatsu trying to secure a VTOL, Misato and the others had finally arrived home. Elated to see that Maya was all right, Misato remarked, "At least the ground didn't tip over. That was some good luck."

"Good luck?" Maya shook her head. "You must be joking. The ground within the caldera titled *point four* degrees to the east. That's a huge deal! I've been working this whole time to re-level the particle accelerator's framework. Do you want to ask me how many doors won't open because they're misaligned?"

"Take care of what you can," Misato said with a placating smile. "I'll straighten out the supply situation."

After the initial jolt, the sinking had been smooth. There had still been many injuries, and the dead numbered in the double digits, but the greatest difficulty Nerv Japan faced was the loss of the roadways and railways.

Hakone had no airports, and of course no seaport. The most pressing concern was securing new supply routes for the immense volume of materials needed to rebuild.

Hyuga came rushing into the command center, wearing a hard hat and a cheerful smile. "Welcome back!"

Fuyutsuki was the next to arrive on the middle deck. "You're back."

Misato bowed her head. "Deputy Commander Fuyutsuki. Thank you for stepping in." She turned to Hyuga. "I'm glad you're all right, too. So, can you tell me what that thing in the lake is?"

"Ah. I take it you've seen it, then."

A massive, egg-like object peeked out from the lowered waters of Lake Ashi. The object was semi-transparent, like colored glass, with one solitary hole in its surface. The hole had been plugged up by a rush of debris and silt when the lake had partially drained. Hastily erected scaffolding around it indicated that a survey had at least been attempted.

"We don't have a clue," Hyuga said. "Except... The outer diameter is exactly the same size as the Chronostatic Sphere in the old Geofront." He looked to Maya.

"This is just conjecture," she continued where Hyuga had left off, "but if Armaros was telling the truth, and this world is repeating itself for the purposes of the Instrumentality Project, then that object might be the remnants of the vessel that carried Lilith from the past world into our own. In other words, it might be Lilith's *previous* Chronostatic Sphere."

"So the sphere," Misato said, "has a shell? Like an egg?"

"We don't know. We don't even know if that thing is a physical object or a stabilized distortion in space."

"Before we began Tokyo-3's construction," Fuyutsuki added, "we performed underground—and underwater—imaging of the surrounding area, including down to the bottom of the lake. But whatever that thing is, it didn't show up on any of our scans back then."

"The object is tough," Maya said. "We can't even tell if anything we do to it makes an impact."

"The Japanese government sent a team to relocate the object," Fuyutsuki continued, "but when the ground sank, they weren't sure what to do, and they withdrew to Matsushiro. They left just before you returned. Another team was looking into repurposing it as a makeshift shelter, but their work is on hold. They found a large, bow-shaped object among the silt inside, which they handed over to us as 'repayment,' but..."

Maya shrugged. "But we can't make anything of it. It's junk."

NEON GENESIS
EVANGELION ANIMA

CHAPTER 17

— # UNDERSTANDING THE PLANET

SUPER EVA FLEW LOW along the clifftop's edge, keeping the drop-off to his right, until he came upon his own footprints at the place he'd started. The loop took two and a half days. Apparently, this was the full extent of this world.

Shinji thought back to a pre-medieval world map he'd seen in a history textbook. "I think the people living before the Age of Discovery had more reasonable ideas about the workings of the universe than this."

Shinji seemed to be standing atop a flat expanse of arid land the size of a continent, about five thousand kilometers across at its widest.

"I wonder if there's any way down," he muttered.

He couldn't help but wonder what was under the continent's overhang, several thousand kilometers below.

"I feel like I can smell water. Can you?"

Apparently, Quatre thought the remark too illogical to be worth a reply.

But at least she seemed to be cooperating for the time being.

Without her help, Shinji wouldn't have been able to fully utilize the Q.R. Signum, and he wouldn't have been able to get the lay of the land without her powering Super Eva's flight.

They only had two days' worth of emergency food and water left, give or take. But Shinji was hoping Rei Quatre might be more amenable to making the leap back home once her survival was at stake.

Super Eva once again looked over the impossible cliffside. Far, far below was the unidentifiable mass obscured by clouds.

The parasitic Q.R. Signum had increased Super Eva's functions, and the Eva had begun to automatically repair its injuries. Shinji realized he could once again see with the giant's left eye. With fully restored vision, he squinted down. Beyond the clouds and the dark mass, he saw the faint, jagged, rose-colored outline of something else.

He realized that their floating continent, the dark mass below it, and the distant red outline were all lined up on the same axis. He suddenly remembered that Kaji had called this place the "Apple's Core."

"An apple core..."

Shinji imagined a dumbbell-shaped planet. Except...that didn't seem physically possible. Asteroids could possess unusual shapes, but this was a *planet*, with enough mass to experience 1 g of surface gravity. On that scale, even the strongest rocks behaved like liquid. The planet would deform under its own weight and become a sphere.

But, supposing this planet somehow has the shape of an eaten apple, then what am I looking at?

If the dark, cloud-covered area beneath the cliff was the left-over, uneaten and seeded core, then what was Shinji seeing even farther beyond?

"The opposite side of the core," Shinji said. "Could there be another continent over there?"

Another continent, with rough edges like flower petals.

If this side was always illuminated by the sun, was the other side a world of eternal night?

"Quatre, do you think we could fly to the other side?"

"What would be the point?" Rei Quatre replied, as if she couldn't care less.

"Er..."

Shinji recognized that he was going to have to get along with Quatre for the time being. Bossing her around wasn't going to get him anywhere. He gathered his thoughts and chose his words carefully.

"You wanted to take me to the farthest place, right? Well, the *farthest* place might be over on that side, don't you think?"

Come on, Shinji. That was the best you could come up with?

The suggestion was so transparent that Shinji regretted saying it almost immediately.

But Quatre replied, "That place in the middle, covered with clouds... There's a spike in gravity there. Not a gravitational pull naturally arising from mass gathered together but from mass held in place by some other gravitational force."

"What does that mean for us?"

"If we approach it, that gravity will pull at us stronger than the surface of the planet's far side. And if we get pulled in, we might not be able to leave. If we're going to fly across, we need to make sure we avoid the center."

At least she thinks we can avoid it, Shinji thought.

"So let's fly," he said.

"Are you serious?"

"Yeah. Lend me your help?"

For a moment—too brief for Shinji to notice—she didn't know what to do.

But in the end, she said, "Okay."

From the moment Ayanami Rei Quatre gained self-awareness, she'd either been on the giving or receiving end of demand after demand. This was the first time—including when she'd been consolidated with the others in Trois—that she'd ever been *asked* for help.

Quatre measured the distances with Super Eva's optical sensors, though, even at full functionality, they left a little to be desired. The quantum flux inclination sensors—the same sensors that had predicted the mutant Eva-0.0's arrival—measured the distribution of the eccentric gravity near the core.

The cloud-covered center was a little more than 6,300 kilometers away, and the red continent on the opposite side was roughly the same distance again, for a total of about 12,700 kilometers—almost exactly the same as Earth's diameter.

As far as Super Eva's sensors could determine, the planet's shape matched Kaji's description—an apple eaten to the core.

Curiously, despite so much of the apple having been bitten off, the planet's gravity and heliocentric orbit matched Earth's.

As Quatre calculated a trajectory that would take them to the red land on the far side, without falling into the middle, she muttered, "This continent is like a five-thousand-kilometer-tall umbrella. I don't understand how it doesn't collapse."

Then, she added, "We'll fly. And we'll fly true. But there's no doubt about it. Some strange force is acting upon this entire planet."

CHAPTER 18

TRANSCONTINENTAL FLIGHT

THE FLIGHT TO THE OPPOSITE CONTINENT ended up taking several hours of intense concentration.

Along the way, just as Super Eva passed over the core, a gap between the clouds offered a glimpse of the shadowy surface.

"It's an ocean," Quatre said. "A spherical ocean."

Assuming that Super Eva wouldn't have continuous access to the Q.R. Signum's power so far from the ground, Shinji and Quatre had elected a ballistic trajectory, including something of a flyby around the planet's core to aid in their descent.

"That can't be—" Shinji said. "Wait, something moved! What could stir up waves large enough for us to see up here?"

"Normally, extreme gravity influences organisms to be smaller, but who knows what's normal on this planet. Accelerate on my mark, Ikari-kun. We're about to hit the lowest point of our trajectory. Mark!"

As hard as he could, Shinji pushed against the upper atmosphere of the apple's core with the Vertex wings' A.T. Field.

He gritted his teeth. "The Eva...is so...heavy!" But he provided the boost they needed.

Once they'd passed the core, they saw why the opposite landmass appeared red.

It was the same reason Earth's moon appeared red during a lunar eclipse. The ground and the atmosphere on the planet's sunside, along with the clouds around the core, scattered the bluer wavelengths, letting only red light—like that of a sunset—pass through to the nightside.

As they sailed around the edge of the continent, Shinji said, "Look, Quatre."

A vast forest ringed the nightside, with tree limbs stretching out over the shelf to catch the gloaming light.

Super Eva reoriented himself on the other side. They'd made it across. Relief flooded Shinji, and he suddenly felt like he couldn't maintain flight a single moment longer.

The Eva crashed through the trees, toppling them and scattering branches and leaves. When Super Eva came to a stop at last, and Shinji no longer had to concentrate on the flight, he gasped for air as if he'd been holding his breath for a full day. He slumped forward, then drained the LCL from the entry plug and opened the hatch.

The plug slid out from Super Eva's back, and thick, humid air rushed into the chamber.

Without waiting to perform the customary atmospheric analysis, Shinji took in a deep lungful of air. How all the air here didn't fall down into the apple core was yet another mystery. As he took in the relaxing smell of the forest, he felt his exhaustion melt away.

"Quatre, let's put our feet on the ground."

The view outside was peculiar. The land and sky of the sunside was now upside down beneath them, and diffuse sunlight came up from the cliffside, bathing the nightside in red and silhouetting the trees.

There's something familiar about this evening light... Shinji thought.

Hopping down from Super Eva's palm, Shinji noticed a geometric pattern of bumps on the ground—too regular to be natural. He followed the pattern with his eyes. In the shade of a tree, the undergrowth thinned, revealing a long, narrow piece of rusted metal.

"Metal," Shinji said. "Train tracks?"

He seemed to have found an abandoned railway line. He could think of only one explanation.

"The remains of civilization." Though upon saying it, he grew less certain.

If he accepted Kaji's story as the truth, then whatever used to be on this planet would be ancient on an astrological timeline. No way could a piece of exposed steel remain in anything approaching identifiable form.

He walked up to the rusty red rail and touched his hand to the metal.

Shinji gasped as the ground began rhythmically jolting beneath his feet with a *ka-clack, ka-clack*. Reflexively, he reached for a hanging strap to steady himself.

He looked around in confusion.

He was standing on a moving train.

Ka-clack, ka-clack.

A man was seated on the bench seat in front of Shinji. The man kept his head down, but his shoulders seemed familiar.

"Shinji," the man said, "will you keep on going?"

Shinji's answer came naturally. "I will. It's not over yet."

"Sometimes, moving in a new direction means you aren't able to stop."

"That's fine. The only thing troubling me is that I don't feel like I'm advancing."

"I see."

Warm, early evening light flowed in through the train windows as Shinji shared an unusually tranquil conversation with his father.

He was starting to forget where he'd been before this train. He let go of the hanging strap to move to the seat beside his father, when—

A hand gripped his arm from behind, and Ayanami's voice said, "Ikari-kun!"

He turned with a start.

"Quatre?" His eyes went wide, and his mouth gaped. "Wha?!"

He hadn't expected to see Ayanami wearing a high school uniform. Even more surprising, she wasn't the Ayanami he'd been with only moments before. She was Cinq, and Cinq was dead.

He recognized her immediately. She was a little taller than

the others, and her mannerisms came off as just slightly more mature. When she looked at someone, her expression carried a feeling of urgency. Of the four Ayanamis, she was the only one capable of that expression.

"Cinq?" Shinji said.

But she'd tragically died in the lonely space between the Earth and the moon. *Wait, is this Trois under Kaji-san's control?*

When Cinq was killed, her memories had crossed the vast distance and flooded into the primary Ayanami—Trois.

But when Trois was with Kaji, she'd been wearing a black dress, not a school uniform. Moreover, she hadn't acted on her own like this. She seemed like she'd gotten tired and given up.

So, is this really Cinq?

She didn't give him time to work through his confusion. Before he could ask another question, she squeezed his arm tight.

"You can't stay here! Maybe if your body were still in the other world, it would be different, but you're here. If you let these thoughts take hold of you, you won't be able to leave!"

The train carriage was filled with the warm glow of the setting sun, and the wheels made a rhythmic sound as they passed over the crossties. The scene felt comforting and familiar, without even a hint of danger. Shinji's mind brimmed with memories of better days...

Cinq put more force into her grip, and the pain brought Shinji out of his reverie.

"See!" she said. "That's exactly what I mean. Try to remember where you were before here. It was a different place, wasn't it?"

He lowered his head in thought. "That's right," he said. "I was with Quatre, on the edge of a continent on a strange planet. I found a rusted train track..."

When he looked up again, Cinq was giving him a kind, motherly smile, the corners of her eyes crinkling.

"Let's meet again, Ikari-kun."

"Cinq," he said, "You're..."

Doubt briefly clouded her expression. But then she let go of his arm.

She turned her head away. "I don't know what form that will take, but...let's meet again."

She looked up at him, seeming to have decided something.

Directing her voice somewhere beyond Shinji, she said, "Quatre! The me at the mercy of fear! You're near, aren't you? Quickly, pull him back to you!"

Then the train was gone. With one foot forward, Shinji was poised to run down the rusted tracks, while Ayanami Quatre, in orange coveralls, pulled on his hand from behind, holding him in place. They were in the forest of eternal dusk.

O N THE TWILIGHT RING of the nightside continent, the flora resembled normal photosynthetic plants, with trees recognizable in shape and appearance, at least to the point where Shinji could still comfortably call them trees. But deeper into the continent, the story changed.

There, Shinji and Quatre found a silent forest thick with white flora and undergrowth—or more likely, some kind of fungus. Whatever they were, they didn't require much light to thrive. Although, the forest wasn't *completely* dark. Some vegetation emitted light, either redirecting it from the shelf's edge or somehow creating it. Around them grew clusters of photosynthetic organisms muscling in to soak up the light, which came in all different colors and reflected off the plants in a soft glow.

After four excruciating assaults on his taste buds, Shinji found a fruit that was edible. He and Quatre ate it as they flew Super Eva over the nightside continent, colorful clusters of flora passing below.

The view reminded Shinji of a night market.

"It's like someone cast a magic spell and erased all the people from a festival," he said softly.

He realized Quatre was staring right at him and immediately grew awkward.

"Magic?" she asked.

"I-I just meant that the forest looks festive," Shinji stammered, "but at the same time, still. That's all."

"Oh." Ayanami took a crunchy bite of the red fruit.

But to Shinji, the stillness of the forest felt more like absence than order. He sensed an unknown presence all around them, and he suspected there might be more than train tracks buried underneath these forests.

They came upon a giant tree towering far above the surrounding forest. It stood nearly five times the size of their Eva.

The tree had thousands upon thousands of branches—at least, that's how Shinji thought of the appendages—which glowed as if from countless hanging lanterns. Shinji narrowed his eyes, attuned his senses to wavelengths outside the visual spectrum, and observed that the light wasn't being produced by the tree itself but by flowers on a crawling vine that had colonized the barren tree.

"In my foster home, I saw a glowing tree like this in a picture book with paper-cut art. But this tree is dead. I wonder what it was like when it was still alive."

"The picture book... Did you..." Quatre trailed off.

"Did I...?"

"Did you like that book?"

Shinji searched his memories and then shook his head. "I don't remember it very well. Except that it was scary but beautiful."

"Scary but beautiful," Quatre repeated. "Scary" was the only part she understood. Her self-awareness had been driven by fear. She'd turned traitor and even killed Shinji once.

But, unexpectedly, the pairing of the word "beautiful" with "scary" seemed to resonate with her. "So then, this must be scary but beautiful, too."

As Super Eva circled the majestic tree—large enough to make even sequoias seem like saplings in comparison—Quatre's gaze remained transfixed upon the spectacular, three-dimensional constellation of its lights.

Then an alarm announced a hostile presence.

Shinji and Quatre jolted upright. Super Eva dropped altitude and quietly approached the target.

This time, they didn't find the mutant Eva-0.0 with Kaji and Trois, but instead an Angel Carrier, standing still as if hiding, deep within the white fungal forest.

NEON GENESIS
EVANGELION ANIMA

CHAPTER 20

WHITE GUARDIAN

T HE WHITE GIANT stood perfectly still among the fungal trees.

The Angel Carrier had wings and two Q.R. Signum scales—a Type-3. But in place of the typical cocoon, a black sphere floated within its open rib cage. Occasionally, a white interference pattern flashed across the sphere's surface.

"Leliel!" Shinji shouted.

This was a smaller, larval form of an Angel that Shinji had encountered before. The black sphere was only a shadow. The Angel's true body existed in imaginary space and could swallow anything that fell inside it.

Standing among the giant trees, their trunks like ancient ruins, the Angel Carrier remained completely motionless. Even when Shinji came closer, the carrier didn't move.

Is it dead? Shinji wondered.

The carrier's Q.R. Signum scales were intact, but they were completely black and lacked their typical dark-red glowing pattern.

The Angel inside—Leliel—had swallowed Shinji and Eva-01 when he was in junior high.

But this was Shinji's first encounter with a larval Leliel. The Angel Carrier bearing Leliel's cocoon had attacked Hakone while Shinji was dead—after he was evaporated by Quatre's gamma-ray laser and before he was reborn as Super Eva.

After his revival, he'd learned that Asuka, piloting Eva-02, had managed to impale the cocoon with the Lance of Longinus—not knowing that the larva within was Leliel. The larval Angel had swallowed the lance into its imaginary space and promptly disappeared.

Shinji knew of two Lances of Longinus.

The one that currently encircled the Earth had previously been on the moon. The lance had landed there after Rei, in Eva-00, had hurled the weapon at the Angel Arael.

The other had been hidden among the weapons wielded by the mass-production Evangelions in the Battle at Nerv HQ. During the final stages of the Instrumentality Project, they'd impaled Eva-02 with the weapon to carry out the sacrificial ritual. After the Instrumentality Project had failed, Nerv Japan took possession of the lance. That was the one stolen by Leliel.

The latter was a reproduction—a copy of the original made by Seele.

Back when Nerv still possessed the Lance of Longinus, Commander Ikari Gendo had wanted to put the lance somewhere out of Seele's reach in order to prevent them from initiating the

Instrumentality Project according to their own plan. He'd managed to strand the lance on the moon, but Seele had prepared a duplicate instead.

"What does this mean?" Shinji said, thinking aloud.

In all likelihood, the black giant, Armaros, had purposefully stolen the Lance of Longinus from Eva-02—from humanity. Wouldn't the Apple's Core be an ideal place to store the weapon out of humanity's reach?

Seele/Kaji had come to this planet in search of something. Then he'd threatened to strand Shinji and Quatre here, hoping this threat would compel them to try to escape.

"Kaji-san was looking for this Angel Carrier," Shinji said. "He was looking for Leliel. And Leliel holds the lance—the same copy that Seele created."

CRIMSON A1, the Asuka/Eva synthesis, left the city, where recovery operations were underway, to visit Shinji's watermelon patch, as had become her habit. She bounded across the countryside, landing beside the field.

She sat on the northern side, so as not to block the sunlight, and noticed three small, round dots weaving through the watermelons. Rei Six had come to water the plants, and the three Type-N robots had accompanied her, along with the two golden retrievers, Azuchi and Momo. But Asuka/Eva must have thought the robots were harmful pests. She plucked one from the ground and flicked it away with a loud *pwing* that reverberated through the caldera. And just like that, with a little help from Earth's decreased escape velocity, the Type-N robot began its journey through space.

"Noooo!" Six shouted as she ran up to Asuka/Eva's feet. She waved her arms furiously while the dogs barked in objection. And so, the other two robots, currently running in fear, were spared the same fate.

The straightest section of the Hakone Caldera's outer ridge lay along its southern rim, from Mount Daikan to Mount Shirogane. Before the caldera had been leased to the UN, the area was known for its picturesque driving routes.

But now, Six was ruthlessly blasting apart those peaks with Eva-00 Type-F's rifle, Angel's Backbone.

After her A.T. Field-accelerated baryon cannon flattened the land, Nerv engineers compacted the ground with a monomolecular vibrating ribbon, and where that wasn't sufficient, they used soil-hardening agents to reshape the sediment. This feat of rapid construction remade the ridgeline into a four-thousand-meter-long runway for what was provisionally being called the Daikan Airport.

But the new airport wasn't finished in time for Commander Katsuragi Misato's return from the United Nations conference. Instead, her heavy VTOL craft landed at the Nerv HQ heliport, which was crowded with containers and pallets of supplies.

Deputy Commander Suzuhara Toji met her as she deplaned.

"Welcome back, Commander," he said. "The *Yamato* will be coming from Hiroshima to be refitted with our N_2 reactor at the end of the month. We're going to provide them the one we were planning on using for Power Plant Number 2. Is that all right?"

"It's a generous gift, but with everyone stretched thin from all these disasters, wielding our power like a stick will only take us so far."

"So," Toji said, broaching the main topic, "how did the Security Council respond to the Euro's op?"

"They approved the plan. The council said they were still narrowing down locations for launching the offensive. And they've given us some work to do to prepare."

"That must mean they've seen enough evidence that the imitation heartbeat will lead the carriers where we want."

Toji opened the depot door, and Misato walked through, keeping a hand on her officer's cap so that the wind wouldn't blow it away.

On the other side, she removed the cap and said, "We can lure Armaros' underlings to any place of our choosing, and we'll have total freedom to set up the ambush how we want it. If we set the bait, we're sure they'll come. At least, we're mostly sure."

"I FOUND YOU," the Kaji-vessel said.

Using Ayanami Trois to pilot the mutant Eva-0.0, Seele had searched the nightside continent for over half a month before finally finding Leliel's Angel Carrier. Perched atop the Eva's shoulder, he held Trois in front of him with one arm and commanded her to approach the white giant. But then Kaji's innate caution—Kaji's, not Seele's—sent up a warning.

He'd keenly spotted a place where Super Eva had trampled the vegetation, despite Shinji's attempts to conceal any tracks.

The misshapen Eva flapped its wings and generated a gravity field to bring itself to a quick stop.

"Gendo's son," the Kaji-vessel said. "You were here. Did you figure it out?"

Scratching at his beard, the Kaji-vessel looked around.

But there was no sign that Shinji had retrieved the lance. The Angel Leliel only swallowed objects. It never let anything back out. Any attempt to forcibly remove an object from the imaginary space would surely kill the Angel...and spray blood everywhere.

Neither did the Kaji-vessel sense Super Eva anywhere in the vicinity.

"Puppet," he asked, "do you know what Gendo's son is thinking?"

Trois' cheeks were flushed from exhaustion. She'd been piloting the Eva nearly without rest, and she was starting to get mildly feverish.

"I don't," she answered expressionlessly.

The Kaji-vessel clicked his tongue. "I don't know why I bother talking to you."

Kaji found another of Super Eva's footsteps and attempted to trace his movements. He was done listening to Trois, but she kept on muttering—perhaps due to the fever.

"I don't know what he's thinking. He'd distancing himself from me, and I..."

I've become more like his mother, she thought. *I don't know if that repulses him, or if he's expecting something more of me. Either way, he doesn't see me as my own person. But what does it matter? It's not like I can tell him any of this from here.*

"He left the area," the Kaji-vessel said. "Maybe four or five days ago." He shrugged. "All right."

With Kaji's concerns quelled, Eva-0.0 approached the Angel Carrier. The Eva charged the gamma-ray laser cannon on its right arm.

"Do it!"

Trois responded immediately. Eva-0.0 thrust its non-cannon arm into Leliel, and the Angel Carrier moved.

All at once, color returned to the carrier's seemingly dead Q.R. Signum scales, and it awoke. That must have been the trap.

The carrier reached out its right arm to grab the mutant Eva-0.0. The Eva raised its cannon arm and fired.

KRA-KOOM!

For an instant, the dark fungal forest was as bright as mid-day, and the gamma-ray laser obliterated one of the carrier's Q.R. Signum scales.

The Angel Carrier reeled backward, taking Leliel with it, and the mutant Eva-0.0's left arm slid out from inside it. Clutched in the Eva's bloody hand was the lance's shaft.

The Lance of Longinus could pierce anything and had been the master key to unlocking the Human Instrumentality Project.

"That's the way," the Kaji-vessel said. "Keep pulling!"

The lance's long shaft kept sliding out of the imaginary dimensional space.

"Do you hear me, black giant? You're just an oversized cog with no sense of time, mindless of any element missing from the original plan, no matter how useful. Do you have any idea how much work we put into making this duplicate?"

A shrill sound shook the air. It was Leliel's death cry.

"We're done here."

Ayanami Rei Trois let out a small gasp, her face registering surprise.

As Leliel shrieked, from inside the Angel appeared a hand, clenched around the lance, then a strong-looking arm, and a shoulder.

"Puppet!" Kaji shouted. "Stop!"

He'd been taken completely by surprise. He quickly realized what was happening and moved to stop it, but he was too late.

"Gendo's son!"

Blood exploded from Leliel, and out came a curved horn, then a visor that opened to reveal two gleaming eyes.

《Trois!》 Shinji shouted. 《Cut the mental feedback link!》

Super Eva sprang from the Angel with his bloodied left hand clutching the lance. In one moment, his right arm was pressed close to his side, and in the next, it flashed out a sword. The force of the swiftly moving blade sent Leliel's blood flying in an arc.

Eva-0.0 didn't even have time to lift its shield.

In another instant, the blade would shatter the Q.R. Signum in the mutant Eva's chest.

Trois yelped as the Kaji-vessel roughly seized her right arm and moved it in front of her chest. The mutant Eva-0.0 mimicked the motion, blocking Super Eva's blade with the gamma-ray laser cannon.

The sword cleaved the cannon cleanly in two, and the long convergence barrel flew off into the distance.

But the cannon had turned Super Eva's sword—Basara— aside, and the blade narrowly missed the Q.R. Signum, tearing deep into the mutant Eva's chest armor. A piece of flying shrapnel gouged Kaji's cheek and severed his ear.

This all happened in moments. The next instant, Super Eva had completely freed himself from the prison of Leliel's imaginary dimension space. His feet slammed into the ground.

Using his forward momentum, Super Eva rammed the mutant Eva and sent it staggering backward. The mutant's grip loosened on the lance, and Super Eva seized the weapon and swapped it with the sword in his dominant hand.

He kept moving—not into the mutant Eva, but past it, like a javelin thrower making a run-up.

"Time for Plan B!" Shinji said to Quatre. "I hope you got the calculations right!"

"Don't mess up the throw, Ikari-kun," Quatre replied.

Super Eva ran forward and raised the lance aloft. He planted one foot, leaned his upper body back, and—

《What are you doing?!》 the Kaji-vessel shouted.

But Shinji wasn't listening. "Go!"

Super Eva hurled the lance with tremendous speed, and the weapon whistled through the air, easily breaking free from the gravity of the Apple's Core. In the blink of an eye, the Lance of Longinus disappeared into the starry sky.

《Gendo's son! What do you think you're doing?》

"What am *I* doing? *You're* the one with a hostage."

Shinji had decided that if he failed to disable the mutant Eva-0.0, he would throw the Lance of Longinus away before Seele/Kaji could try to use Trois as leverage to take the weapon back.

It was the wrong decision.

The original Lance of Longinus was constricting the Earth to cataclysmic effect. If humanity could be armed with its duplicate, then why worry over the sacrifice of one person?

"You were the same way when you stopped the Instrumentality Project," Quatre muttered. "You only see the world that's directly around you."

She was wearing Shinji's plugsuit. The current-issue suits could suppress synchronization rates as high as 400%. Wearing it prevented Quatre from becoming disembodied inside Leliel due to over-synchronization. Having become one with his Eva, Shinji assumed he could no longer be dissolved himself, and he'd exchanged his plugsuit for Quatre's engineer's uniform.

If he'd been truly committed to saving humanity, he would have reclaimed the lance the moment he'd found Leliel and then compelled Quatre—by any means necessary—to make the jump back to Earth.

But Shinji hadn't done that. As long as he knew Trois would eventually come, he wanted to rescue her.

And this was the result.

Quatre sighed. "See? Now you've got nothing."

"I don't want to hear it," Shinji replied as he returned Basara to his right hand and retrieved his other sword, Kesara, from his right shoulder pylon.

"Kesara on standby, and...mark."

"You know, Ikari-kun," Quatre said. "All this time, I'd thought you made a mistake."

The pylon's cylindrical chamber tilted forward and opened with a loud thud, and Shinji unsheathed the second sword.

"Wait," he said. "You *had* thought?"

"Three years ago, you made this flawed world because it was the world you wanted. It wasn't by mistake."

PART 4

NEON GENESIS

SYMMETRICAL COMPONENTS

EVANGELION: ANIMA

NEON GENESIS
EVANGELION ANIMA

CHAPTER 23

AT THE FOOT OF THE GREAT TREE

"**B**UT I WON'T SAY it was the *smart* choice," Quatre said, seeming to understand, if not accept, Shinji's decision.

"I know," Shinji replied. "I mean, I think I know."

Deep in the fungal forest on the nightside of the Apple's Core, Super Eva stood before two hostile giants with his twin swords drawn.

One was the mutant Eva-0.0, formerly Quatre's, now controlled by the Kaji-vessel and his hostage, Trois. The other was an Angel Carrier Type-3. The carrier's shoulder was injured, and its larva, Leliel, was dead.

But the white giant was still moving.

"The carrier is down one Q.R. Signum," Shinji said. "Did Kaji-san do that? The carrier was undamaged when Leliel swallowed us up."

"Well," Quatre responded, "whatever happened between them while we were inside, that carrier is obeying Seele now."

"You can tell?"

"Seele can control Q.R. Signum scales by touch, and through the scale, he can influence the pilot. That was how he hijacked my Eva in Cyprus."

The Kaji-vessel called out. 《Do you really think you managed to fool me? You sent the lance into an orbit that will bring it back down to Earth in a matter of months.》

Behind Shinji in the entry plug, Quatre whispered. "He saw right through us... But at least he can't do anything about it."

Shinji remained silent, watching through a zoomed-in view on the holographic display. The Kaji-vessel still held Trois in one arm. He raised his other hand and placed his thumb and middle finger against her carotid artery.

《You know what happens next,》 he said. 《I'll kill this puppet.》

Shinji shot upright, but Quatre placed a hand on his shoulder. "Don't panic."

She opened the comms channel so that her next words would be transmitted.

"He can't do that, Shinji. Seele can access the Q.R. Signum and nothing more. He can't control that Eva without a compatible pilot, let alone make the jump through the tunnels. If he could, he would've come alone."

Seele chuckled. 《But Shinji-kun, Gendo's son, do you really think the Earth can afford to wait around for the lance to finish its long journey?》

That was, in fact, Shinji's greatest worry.

Shinji and Quatre had been on this misshapen planet for

more than half a month. The Kaji-vessel called this planet the Apple's Core, but he'd also mentioned a second name—one that it had gone by as a testing ground for the Instrumentality Project. Eden. Though this was a strange land, it must have been a paradise compared to the destruction on Earth.

And how much worse had the situation become since Shinji was last on Earth?

《What will happen to your planet is simple,》the Kaji-vessel said. 《Once the moon is large enough, it will approach the Earth and drink up the land and seas.》

What?! Shinji looked to Quatre in surprise.

"Wait," Shinji said. "Is that the..."

Shinji remembered a phrase Armaros had spoken through the Ayanamis' mental link.

《That's right. The Great Flood.》

"The carrier is moving!" Quatre hissed.

The Angel Carrier leaped over the mutant Eva-0.0 and came rushing at Super Eva, thrusting its staff forward.

If what he's saying is true, thought Shinji, *then what could we possibly do to stop it?*

All three giants, including Super Eva, were drawing power from identical sources—Armaros' Q.R. Signum scales. It was a fact Shinji found ironic—and chilling.

Those given a scale could draw upon a terrible power. In return, they faced a gradual corruption, and every now and then, were made to speak on Armaros' behalf. Beyond that, they were free to act as allies or enemies. Their actions were beneath the concern of a being who could create worlds.

The tip of the Angel Carrier's staff formed two prongs with sharp, jagged edges, and the carrier's rushing attack, strengthened by the giant's A.T. Field-like shield, only barely missed Super Eva.

But Super Eva had purposefully dodged at the last minute to set up a counterattack with his swords.

"Show me what you can do!" Shinji shouted.

He parried his enemy's charge with his left-hand sword and slashed with his right.

The blade moved faster than the speed of sound, yet it still failed to penetrate the Angel Carrier's shield. The moment the sword made contact, a strong force repelled it.

Shinji grunted in surprise as the carrier sailed past him and landed on the ground, scattering dirt and toppling a cluster of the white, softly glowing fungal trees. Shinji leaped backward to get some space.

"That wasn't supposed to happen!"

His twin swords, Kesara and Basara, were code named "Field Penetrators."

But even when swung with all of Super Eva's might, the blades hadn't lived up to their name.

Shinji looked at his swords through the holographic display. "Are they too dull?"

A sub-window opened, and Maya's voice spoke through the seat's speakers.

《You've drawn both swords, Shinji-kun.》

"Maya-san?!"

《This is a recording,》 Maya said from the sub-window. 《I don't have time to prepare a field manual for you, but I can tell you the basics. If the swords are working, that's great. But if they don't work, put them back in their sheaths right away, and the system will deal with it.》

That was *too* brief.

With nothing else to do but to trust Maya's instructions, Shinji returned both swords to his shoulder pylons.

"What now?" Quatre asked.

Shinji's eyes went wide as he realized Super Eva was now weaponless.

《Oh, but do be careful,》 Maya's voice added. 《The swords will need 201 seconds to retune.》

"Whaaaat?!"

This was no time to go unarmed for well over three minutes.

Super Eva grasped the swords' hilts, but the sheaths had locked the weapons firmly inside; they wouldn't budge. Another new window opened on the display, this time showing a three-dimensional cube along with a too-technical message saying that something was happening to his equipment, but that was hardly helpful now.

Super Eva had left Africa equipped with nothing but the swords and a single knife. Misato hadn't allowed him to carry any ranged weapons, out of fear that the Q.R. Signum might cause him to lose control while flying over some sovereign state.

With the swords locked away, all he had left was the knife on his right leg. He was reaching to draw it, when—

"Ikari-kun, on your left!" Quatre shouted.

He noticed the Angel Carrier's attack too late. The white giant was flying toward him, low—and this time it was coming at full force.

Shinji couldn't get out of the way in time. He barely managed to bring up his A.T. Field as a shield.

But he grunted in pain as Super Eva took the tackle head-on and was tossed backward, carving a path of destruction through the fungal forest.

At first, Shinji thought Super Eva's back had slammed into a rough patch of ground—but the object beneath him shattered into dry, fibrous splinters that scattered all around.

A root of the dead tree?

The giant tree, which stood many times taller than an Evangelion, swayed faintly from the impact, and luminescent spores of the parasitic fungus fell like snow from its branches.

The mutant Eva-0.0 transmitted Kaji's voice.

《Would you like to die at the foot of the old Tree of Life? It was one of the two great trees that represented this place, you know. It would make a fine grave marker, don't you think?》

Unlike the Angel Carrier, the mutant Eva showed no sign of pressing the attack.

The Kaji-vessel had come to this planet to find the duplicate Lance of Longinus, but Shinji had hurled it into space.

SRM-61A FIELD PENETRATOR, A.K.A. KESARA

One of a pair of Field Penetrator swords. Generates a special A.T. Field that can be tuned to penetrate a target's field. Like the Vertex wings, the sword utilizes experimental field-induction elements. The arrangement of those elements affects the sword's field pattern. The sword is stored in a pylon capable of "baking in" specific arrangements.

The shape of the sword slightly differs from that of its twin, the SRM-62b (Basara).

The weapon was traveling too fast to pursue directly, and the tunnel network only connected points on land. The Kaji-vessel had no way to recover the lance now.

But he could still try to force Shinji to give up the trajectory data.

So why isn't he moving?

"Be careful," Quatre said. "Eva-0.0 is repairing the end of the laser cannon where you cut the barrel off...so that it can be fired at that length."

The gamma-ray laser cannon—when working at full power—was the strongest weapon available to any Eva.

So that's why he's leaving the fight to the Angel Carrier.

Shinji pretended not to have noticed. "Two great trees, you say? Where's the other one?"

《Didn't you see it in the center of the sunside continent? That one has mostly weathered away. It may once have been the Tree of Knowledge, but it died and toppled a long, long time ago. All that's left is a flat patch of ground where the stump used to be.》

The Tree of Knowledge, the fruit of knowledge...the forbidden fruit?

I'd eat just about anything that got me expelled from this paradise.

Both sides were trying to buy time.

"Let's see if I can even the score before you jump back in the fight," Shinji said to himself.

The Angel Carrier was the first back on its feet. But the white giant's stance wasn't normal.

The carrier's left shoulder was already damaged. Did it break when it tackled me?

Super Eva stood, knife in hand. But the carrier kept its distance. Instead of charging in for another tackle, the giant aimed its power shield at Super Eva and fired it like an invisible fist.

Shinji wouldn't have seen the attack coming if it weren't for the glowing ripple spreading through the fungal spores.

Super Eva leaped to the side, and in the next moment, the ripple reached the spot where he'd been standing. The ground exploded.

Shinji glanced back at Quatre's face. She looked feverish, like she was under even more strain than he was.

"Quatre, are you all right?"

"I've run the calculations on what will happen once Eva-0.0 has repaired its cannon. With the convergence and laser pumping capabilities at that barrel length, we should be safe from a distance of thirty kilometers. He won't be able to attack us from the horizon. But at close range, the laser will still be putting out a quarter of its maximum power. That's more than enough to be a serious threat."

She paused. Her chest rose as she took in a deep breath of LCL and slowly let it back out again.

"This Eva can draw in unlimited power," she said, "but every time we maneuver in battle, the Q.R. Signum takes a little more control."

"I wish I could say, 'don't push yourself,'" Shinji said. "But it's not that simple, is it? We need that power."

By observing the lights of the forest, Super Eva had dodged several of the Angel Carrier's invisible fists, but eventually, it read Shinji's movements and aimed an attack directly at the spot where he was about to land.

Below him, the ground exploded, and a giant sheet of rock flew toward Super Eva. Even with the prog knife running on high power, the rock looked too large to smash. He hadn't yet been able to control the Q.R. Signum's power shield as well as his A.T. Field, but at the last moment, he focused the shield's power into the knife, and—

KA-CRACK!

The rock shattered into tiny fragments. Shinji had discovered how to use the shield as a weapon, like the Angel Carrier was doing.

"Are you up for this?" Shinji asked.

Quatre nodded. "I'll back you up."

Super Eva's shoulders tingled with unfamiliar heat.

The next time the Angel Carrier fired a shield projectile, Super Eva countered with one of his own—using the same technique Shinji had previously employed to generate his A.T. Field at a remote point.

"Go!" he shouted.

The two projectiles shot through the forest and collided head-on, but the Angel Carrier's was stronger, and it batted Shinji's shield aside.

"Quatre?!"

"I'm losing power!" she said. "It's slipping through my fingers."

Super Eva's shoulders were growing hotter.

"The swords!" Shinji realized. "The heat is coming from Super Eva's shoulder units, from within Kesara's and Basara's sheaths. What's the status?"

Quatre's eyes scanned the armament display window. "It says, 'Tempering process underway. Rearranging blade crystalline structure.'"

Whatever that meant, at least it wasn't an error message.

"I think those swords are made out of the same A.T. Field-induction elements as the Type-F's cannon," Quatre said, "or your Eva's wings."

"What does that mean?"

"The system can read the data from when the swords failed to penetrate the enemy's shield and then reconfigure their field pattern on the spot."

Super Eva shuddered. Shinji felt like his blood flow had changed. Gasping, he clutched at his chest. The Q.R. Signum was now causing him physical pain.

"See?" Quatre said. "The field type is changing."

VWWMMM.

"Wait, this is strange," she said. "The swords drain a lot of power, but I'm not having to direct the power *to* them. The Q.R. Signum is spreading its energy into the sword system on its own. It's as if..."

The sound was like the earth rumbling, the vibrations like a low-amplitude earthquake. The black scale's power flooded into the swords in raging waves.

"It's too hot!" Shinji cried. "Something's wrong!"

"It's as if the scale is trying to possess the swords," Quatre said.

A loud, metallic *wham* sounded from Super Eva's shoulders, and they both jumped. A happy chime followed, and a new message appeared on the display: REFORGING COMPLETE.

The cylindrical tumblers swiveled open, offering the two swords.

Bubbling with impatience, Super Eva crossed his arms in front of his face and seized the twin hilts.

"What?!" Shinji shouted.

"What's wrong?" Quatre asked.

"Super Eva didn't move the way I told him to."

He wasn't completely sure, but it seemed like the Eva had moved *ahead* of his conscious thoughts.

Maya's voice spoke again. 《Cool the blades to bind the new crystalline structure. If you're near a river or a large body of water—》

Shinji didn't hear the rest. Super Eva took another direct hit from the carrier's projected shield, but he continued drawing Kesara and Basara as he tumbled backward.

Super Eva tore a swath of destruction through the fungal forest, rolling from the impact. Shinji shifted his grip on the swords, turning their pommels upright, and thrust their red-hot blades into the ground.

The earth swelled as the swords' tremendous heat dumped into it, and the forest's underground moisture instantly vaporized. Steam exploded upward, filling the air with white mist.

Despite losing sight of Super Eva, the Angel Carrier held its staff aloft and jumped into the dense cloud in search of its quarry.

"Gendo's son...what did you do?" Kaji muttered.

A wrenching sound echoed from the steam, then the carrier's staff flew out of the cloud and impaled itself in the ground in front of the mutant Eva-0.0.

The carrier's arm was still holding on to the shaft.

"Did he cut through the shield?" Kaji wondered aloud.

The Angel Carrier was ejected from the steam cloud and crashed into the trees. As it rolled, the giant raised its blood-soaked stump and threw one invisible fist after another into the mist.

Super Eva came leaping out from the cloud, breaking through the outer wall and leaving a black trail in its wake. The Eva held both swords crossed and focused the strongest part of his shield at the point where the blades overlapped. He didn't try to evade the carrier's attacks but simply shrugged them aside. He closed the distance and broke through the Angel Carrier's shield.

With a scream like metal slicing through metal, Super Eva's crossed swords sank into the carrier's shield, reaching either side of its neck. Super Eva threw his arms wide.

Kesara and Basara passed each other inside the carrier's neck, and, almost as an afterthought, smashed through the remaining Q.R. Signum scale in the carrier's right shoulder.

Super Eva's hands were gripping the swords, but to Shinji, his own Q.R. Signum's uncanny power seemed to be reaching black arms out to wield the swords directly.

"The swords," Shinji gasped, breathless. "They've attuned *too* well. The power... I can't..."

He couldn't control it. Super Eva—or rather, the two swords—wanted to slice through anything that moved, friend or foe.

Without a moment's pause, Super Eva leaped to attack the mutant Eva-0.0, as if there were nothing else it would rather do.

The mutant Eva-0.0 grabbed the Angel Carrier's staff from the ground and held the weapon in front of its body. But Super Eva's sword, Basara, smashed into the staff with a shower of sparks, scraping all the way down its length and into the mutant's A.T. Field.

The Field Penetrator was attuned to the Angel Carrier's power shield, not the mutant Eva's field, and couldn't slice through easily. But the field still crackled and splintered as the weapon forced its way through with murderous fury. The blade's tip inched inexorably toward the Q.R. Signum in the mutant Eva's chest.

The Kaji-vessel stood on a platform in front of the Q.R. Signum, holding Trois.

Shinji cried out through gritted teeth as he forced the blade to stop at the last possible moment.

Shinji breathed heavily, and the sword's tip trembled—centimeters from Rei Trois' face.

Trois remained motionless. With a resigned expression, she spoke.

《Yes, Ikari-kun. This is what you should've done in the first place. If you had, then you and Quatre—the me who loses hope to fear—would've been able to go home, lance in hand.》

What is she talking about? As Shinji strained to hold the sword back, Quatre responded from behind.

"She's right. Instead of throwing away the Lance of Longinus, you should've driven it through Trois, the me who unifies."

《Yes. Kill me now and correct your path. I can accept that. I'm nothing. I'm less than nothing. I'm a hindrance. I want you to do it.》

"She's right," Quatre said. "If something stands in your way, you eliminate it. My other selves would reach the same conclusion."

Shinji's shoulders heaved as he fought against the sword. If he lost focus, the weapon would kill Trois and Kaji in an instant.

"Shut up," he grunted. "Both of you!"

The A.T. Field at the tip of the blade rumbled. *How can they so easily tell me to kill, when I'm fighting so hard not to? How can Trois look at me like that's a sensible thing to say? And what about Kaji-san?*

The Kaji-vessel held Trois in front of him as he listened to the exchange with his same damn smirk.

"Kaji-san," Shinji said, "release Trois and the Eva. Or keep the Eva, if you want. Just let Trois go. Please."

《That's not what the puppets are saying.》 The Kaji-vessel said and laughed. 《Don't you think you should all get on the same page? I suppose we could decide by majority vote, but I don't think that would go the way you want.》

The Kaji-vessel glanced at the mutant Eva-0.0's right arm. The tip of the sawed-off gamma-ray laser was nearly repaired.

Trois spoke. 《It's only a matter of time, Ikari-kun, before I... I'll become your mother.》

Not this again. Shinji's eyebrows furrowed. Rei Quatre had already ambushed him with that subject once.

Trois continued. 《When that happens, I can't imagine being able to claim I'm a different person from her. Not when I can't see who I am.》

What is she talking about?

《I don't want to be like that. When the time comes, I don't think I'll exist anymore.》

Her words offended Shinji. "Look, I'll say this as clear as I can. I don't see any of you as my mother. All right? When Quatre first said something to that effect, I admit, I felt something. But that was just because—"

Trois cut him off. 《The dress you gave me... It was *her* favorite color.》

"I'm...I'm sorry. I didn't give enough thought to how that would look from your point of view."

《You were telling me to become Ikari Yui.》

"That's not true!" Shinji yelled.

Trois fell silent.

Shinji lowered his head and shook it back and forth in the LCL. "Just listen to me. Asuka and everyone else... They *enjoy* picking out presents. I never know what to pick. Even thinking about it makes my head hurt! All I wanted was to give you something...to give *us* a chance to connect. Do you have to be so critical?!"

Whenever he thought too hard about something, other people always ended up meddling. The Shinji of three years ago—the fourteen-year-old Shinji—had considered that sort of social interaction an unwanted intrusion.

He'd made too much progress discarding those feelings to have them revived now. Revisiting them made him feel nauseous... and angry.

"You think you lack something that would define you," Shinji snapped. "Well, I don't know what that thing is. Maybe you really *don't* have it. But stop assuming that I—or anyone else for that matter—know what defines me. I don't!"

He'd only been venting, but his words sank in. Her expression shifted. "You're right, I don't know what it is... And you don't, either?"

Too clouded with rage to notice her shift, Shinji barked, "That's right! I don't know! I don't know what other people are feeling! I don't know what I'm missing!"

"Is...Is that true? That thing I don't understand. The missing part I can't see. Not everyone can see it in themselves?"

"No! How could they?!"

Simultaneously, both Ayanamis said, "Oh..."

"Fire!" the Kaji-vessel ordered from behind Trois' back. The girl shuddered, and the mutant Eva's arm muscles groaned. The shortened gamma-ray laser cannon swung toward Super Eva and fired.

At the exact same moment, Super Eva slammed his right shoulder into the mutant Eva-0.0, swinging Kesara upward. The severed cannon-arm sailed through the sky, spraying blood behind it, and the laser roared past Super Eva, slamming into the Tree of Life.

Trois gasped. For the second time, she felt the Eva's arm being sliced off, as if it were her own. She was going into shock, unable to even scream.

"Ayanami!" Shinji cried out to Trois. "The next time I give you something, I'll find a color that suits *you*. I swear!"

Racked with pain, Trois lost focus. Her A.T. Field had been allowing her and Kaji to stand in place on their moving Eva, but now that field weakened, and Super Eva's collision had tilted the small platform under their feet. They fell precariously close to the edge.

The LCL inside Super Eva's plug had stopped flowing. After a moment of confusion, Shinji realized that the entry plug was sliding out from Super Eva's back. He turned to see Quatre opening the hatch.

Before he could ask what she was doing, she pressed her lips to his. The roar of the ejecting LCL faded into momentary silence.

"You can see me as part of Ayanami, too," Quatre said.

"What are you doing, Quatre?!" Shinji sputtered.

She slipped out from the seat and stood. She was holding her arm, her face contorted in pain.

"I'm synchronized with Trois right now," she explained. "I told me—I mean her—the way back home. And the duplicate lance's trajectory."

"What are you saying?"

The mutant Eva-0.0 had gone still, leaning against Super Eva. Even though the two Evas were touching, they were still dizzyingly high off the ground. Yet Quatre nimbly jumped across to the titled platform.

She approached Trois and said, "The me who unifies, the one in control—close off my access to memories of the duplicate lance. Lock away my knowledge of the lance's trajectory."

"What do you think you're doing, broken puppet?" the Kaji-vessel said, clinging to the edge of the platform.

Quatre was still wearing Shinji's plugsuit. Using the built-in controls, she instructed the medical telemetry unit to inject a sedative into her arm so that she could take on the full amount of the feedback pain.

Then, to Kaji, she casually said, "Seele, I'm going with you. We could kill you right now, but I have some acquaintances who don't want your vessel to die."

Trois was struggling to stand. She looked up weakly. "Why are you doing this?"

"This Eva-0.0 was mine in the first place, and I want it back. Go home to Tokyo-3 with Ikari-kun. We can't put an end to this with you two stranded here."

"An...end..." Trois repeated. "If the worst happens, the me who is fulfilled... I want to say...thank you."

"No more running, the me who doesn't realize she's fulfilled."

The two girls had arrived at a settlement.

Super Eva had finally shaken free of the curse on his swords. He reached out to carefully scoop up both Ayanamis, but when his hand got near, Quatre shoved the now-standing Trois over the edge. Shinji quickly caught her.

He fumbled his grip on Kesara, and the blade landed tip-first into the ground.

Before the sword even had time to topple, the mutant Eva was already sinking into the tunnel network. Shinji rushed to the entry plug's hatch, leaned out, and shouted, "Quatre!"

She turned to look up at him, but before he could say anything else, the misshapen giant, carrying Quatre and Kaji, was swallowed by the ground.

"Trois!" Shinji called out from the hatch. "Are you all right?"

She didn't respond. She was curled up on Eva's hand with her arms around her own shoulders, staring at the patch of ground where the mutant Eva-0.0 had disappeared.

Worried, Shinji climbed down to her.

"Let's go home, Ayanami." He knelt and added, "Trois?"

That's when he saw something he'd never expected to see.

Her blank expression had shattered. She was bawling.

CHAPTER 24

► THE PEOPLE LEFT BEHIND

OBJECTS EVERYWHERE on the Earth were no longer moving as they should have been.

People first noticed when the number of traffic accidents began to skyrocket. Everyday things, from cars to tap water, began turning, or stopping and starting, in new and unpredictable ways.

Unable to disperse their kinetic energy, ocean waves began reaching higher and farther inland than had previously been thought possible. The cause was simple physics. Between the Earth's loss of mass and its shrinking circumference, gravity had observably weakened.

As a consequence, despite whatever urgency they felt in their hearts, humans were now forced to slow down.

In the Hakone Caldera, now geographically stranded in the strait where the Izu Peninsula used to be, supplies were beginning to arrive through the hastily constructed Daikan Airport, and the reconstruction efforts were finally taking shape.

Super Eva and Shinji were still missing, but they were known to be alive. One day, about half a month earlier, little Ayanami Rei Six had suddenly let out a squeak, as if someone had put a pickled plum in her mouth, and she made a surprise announcement.

"Ikari-kun's eating a tart red fruit with Quatre."

The Ayanamis' mental link had only been sporadically present, either due to a malfunction or their new self-awareness. This momentary reconnection gave Six the knowledge that Shinji and Quatre were together—but not where.

Still, even knowing that they were out there somewhere, alive, was good news.

Maybe next time Six could locate the pair, and a search party could be sent out.

But when anyone asked Six about Ayanami Trois, whom the Security Intelligence Department had failed to find after her disappearance in North Africa, the girl always said she hadn't heard anything.

And she always added, "I think she's closed herself away."

A location in Russia had been chosen to launch the counter-offensive against Earth's enemies, and the Euro military would be leading the assault. But the exact composition of the multi-national force was still up in the air, and consequently, a date had yet to be chosen.

Crimson A1—the Asuka/Eva synthesis—still showed no concern for the affairs of society. She circled the skies above Nerv HQ slowly, as if going for a lazy swim.

"How is she making such a good sound?" Ibuki Maya asked.

The chief scientist was talking about the hum of the cascading graviton floaters that gave Asuka/Eva flight.

Asuka had flown to the moon courtesy of the angular, mechanical Allegorica wings. Now those wings had fused with the Eva's N_2 reactors into a far more compact form as part of the giant's long, flowing hair. The harsh, dissonant drone of the Allegorica wings had been replaced by a beautiful refrain that harmonized with the wind.

The wings should have lost efficiency in the transformation, but they were more effective than ever before. If this had been the product of some power beyond human comprehension, Maya might not have been bothered, but the wings had been created through human innovation, technological expertise, and rigorous calculations. For some cheap trick to come along, miniaturize the wings, *and* make them more efficient was, from an engineer's perspective—

"Unacceptable." Maya rolled her shoulders with a frustrated sigh.

That's just how it is, she told herself.

In the Eva-related fields, knowing when to let go was vitally important. Countless distinguished figures had burned out trying to decipher an indecipherable puzzle.

Maya entered the cage where the engineering team was giving Eva-00 Type-F's Allegorica system its final adjustments. The work was part of Nerv Japan's preparation for their role in the counter-offensive, but developing the system was in their best interests either way. Nerv HQ currently had no other Eva at their disposal.

The Type-F configuration turned part of the Eva's body structure into a specialized weapons platform. Notably, the Eva was missing one leg, which restricted its movement. The Allegoric Wings would compensate for this.

Nerv Japan could have remotely recalled Six's Eva-0.0 from orbit, or sent a pilot up to it, but the Eva would have to be respec'ed for use on land all the same. Plus, Six was assigned to Eva-00 Type-F anyway. Even with another Evangelion on hand, they'd be a pilot short.

As Crimson A1 drifted lazily overhead, the Asuka/Eva hybrid's wings offered inspiration for Eva-00's design.

Asuka/Eva had come home with nothing but a single blue book.

Shinji had given Asuka the book, a collection of marine life photographs, to help her pass the time on her reconnaissance-in-force mission to the moon. During the synthesis between Asuka and her Eva, the book alone had retained its original shape, although a great volume of data had been written into its pages.

In the command center, Maya presented a report on her team's analysis of the book, with the main screen providing visual aid.

"Of course," the chief scientist was saying, "Asuka didn't write this data by hand. The book had dissolved in the chaotic stream of information and was reconstructed, incorporating the data into its pages. Now, the contents of that data were written in what can only be called a new language, created by Asuka's subconscious.

The language itself changes as it goes along, which makes the translation quite difficult."

Of everything Misato, Fuyutsuki, and Toji had learned from Asuka's journey—including that the moon's expansion was due to Armaros taking matter from deep within the Earth and depositing it on the moon—the book was the part they had the most trouble understanding.

"The data includes, in a compressed form, the things Asuka witnessed at her final destination at the far side of the moon," Maya explained.

The picture on the main screen switched to a 3D reconstruction of Asuka's memories and Eva-02's sensor data. A massive, blue structure made of many cubes was half-buried in the lunar surface.

Misato had seen the same thing in Africa.

"The Ark?" she asked.

"What?!" Toji gasped. "*That's* the Ark?"

Beads of light collected on the structure's surface, then slid down to the lunar soil and took the shape of a small Angel. A mass of Angel Carriers' arms sprouted from the ground, grasping for it.

"What, is that the enemy's main base?" Misato asked.

Maya shook her head. "That's what Asuka thought. If only it were. The structure doesn't just contain the Angels' information. Stored within those cubes is the data for everything needed to start our world. When Asuka flew her Eva inside, she was absorbed into it."

"The data for everything?" Misato repeated.

"What did you see that night in Africa?" Maya asked.

Misato thought back to that one-night orgy of evolution.

At the beginning, a giant jumble, unidentifiable as either Asuka or her Eva, had run past Misato, and then the colossal rock formations began transforming.

"Life-forms of every kind rose from the surface," Misato said.

"While Asuka's consciousness was swallowed within that swarm of information," Maya said, "she wrote one last note explaining the true nature of the Ark. Whether it's a fact or her conjecture, I can't say. But this is what she left for us: 'The Ark contains the saved data of all life, so that each attempt of the as-yet-unsuccessful Instrumentality Project can be made in tens of thousands of years, rather than hundreds of millions.'"

The black giant Armaros had made his pronouncement though the Ayanamis' voices, while across Europe, many people—not a great many, but enough—heard Armaros' voice inside their heads and repeated his message. Namely that a great flood would clear the stage so that the next curtain could rise.

One interpretation of this message was that Earth was perpetually proceeding toward fulfillment of the Instrumentality Project, like a stack of rocks toppling over only to be rebuilt anew, stone by stone. But Asuka's note suggested something else.

"Good God," Fuyutsuki said. "The path of evolution isn't natural to our present world but a shortened reconstruction of some distant past. Why do I suddenly feel like everything around us is a matte painting on a movie set?"

"Why is there another on the moon?" Hyuga demanded.

"And what?" Aoba followed. "Next time around, the moon will be the Earth?"

Toji remembered something else as he looked at the book's contents. In his brief reunion with Hikari, she'd told him, "But amid that mishmash, her mother's soul tried to protect her by overwriting portions of the Eva with parts that were Asuka."

So, he thought, *Not only did Soryu make it past the Longinus Curtain, she tried to leave a record of every single thing she saw on the moon.*

"Damn show-off."

Oh crap, I said that out loud.

The adults all turned to him with confused expressions, but he forged ahead. "Let's say we can't do anything about that world-creating jack-in-the-box for now. What about splitting Soryu and the Eva apart?"

The question was on everyone's minds, but they all were too afraid to ask.

Maya drew in a sharp breath and shook her head. "It doesn't look good. As far as we can tell, she's still carrying the information for a significant number of organisms. Even just from a raw data standpoint, Magi-2 still hasn't been able to disentangle them all."

"I was under the impression that everything had left during that stampede," Misato said.

"The majority stayed dormant and never came to the surface, but they've influenced her genetic structure. Her DNA is a complete mess."

"Is there anything we can do?" Misato asked.

Maya thought for a moment. "Let's reach out to Nerv U.S. They've been working on genetically modifying pilot candidates in order to *create* pilots the Evangelions will deem worthy."

"What kind of modifications are we talking?"

"I don't know the details, but it has something to do with simplifying the thought patterns shared between the Eva and its pilot. They've been splicing animal DNA into both."

"Commander Ikari knew about that project," Fuyutsuki cut in. "In theory, the genetic modification could drastically lower the pilot requirements. But it also comes with a high risk of producing something no longer human. Characteristics of the contributing animals can rise to the surface. Potentially, those manifestations could lead to better combat performance, but Seele forbid us from exploring the possibilities. They claimed that such a pilot couldn't be counted upon to unlock the Instrumentality Project." He frowned. "I'd heard the U.S. branch dispersed after the failure of Unit Four."

"That was the cover story," Aoba explained. "Off the books, they've been continuing several projects, using funds and resources from the federal government. I wouldn't be surprised if the reasons they gave for Unit Four's failure were a cover story, too. If the American public learned Nerv was splicing animal DNA into humans, the religious groups wouldn't stay silent. My guess is that Nerv turned the accident to their advantage and took the opportunity to go underground."

"But we're not talking about putting animal genes in," Misato said, "we're talking about taking Asuka out."

"Reverse the process, you mean." Maya nodded. "An attractive notion, isn't it? Well, whatever the process ends up being, we'd be starting the research from scratch, so we might as well see how far they've gotten. While we're at it, we should get the Europeans to share their imitation heartbeat tech. It wouldn't be too difficult to replicate on our own, but why go to the trouble if we don't have to?"

"You make it sound like we're popping out to pick up pizza and ramen. I'm not sure it'll be that easy."

"Near the Ark on the moon, Asuka found a German quantum wave mirror truck that went missing from the battle in Hokkaido. Use that as a bargaining chip."

"You're kidding."

PART 5

NEON GENESIS

AN INVITATION NORTH

EVANGELION: ANIMA

CHAPTER 25

RETUNING HUMANITY

THE UN GIANT-TRANSPORT PLANE landed at Hakone's Daikan Airport. A crane arm removed a tarp with U.S. military markings from the cargo plane's payload. The makeshift airport's personnel expected to see a humanoid giant strapped down in the supine position for transport. But they saw something different.

"What the hell is that?" someone in the crowd asked.

The giant looked humanoid, but it was on its hands and knees. When the entry plug was inserted—at a different angle than was typical—and the giant began to move, the figure suddenly didn't seem so human.

Walking on all four limbs, the giant carried itself with the distinctive, smooth motions of a quadruped. Its movements flowed from front legs to torso to rear legs without any clear demarcation. The tips of its fingers and toes were narrowed into sharp points.

A Q.R. Signum provided its forbidden power to the giant.

"Is *that* the American Eva?" a member of the ground crew asked.

Apparently, the Americans had taken after the Euro's Heurtebise and obtained a Q.R. Signum of their own. The source of the Eva's body wasn't immediately evident, except that it didn't appear to be one of the dead mass-production Evangelions that had gone missing after the Battle at Nerv HQ three years prior.

"What are its weapons?" asked another. "How's that thing supposed to hold a weapon with its hands on the ground?"

From his station in the command center, Aoba was observing the U.S. Eva's arrival at Daikan Airport.

He called Fuyutsuki over. "That Eva looks specialized for close combat. Do you think the idea is to rely on the military for suppressing fire?"

"Statistically speaking, the majority of our conflicts are hand to hand. Besides, there'll be plenty of ranged support available."

"They can call that thing an Eva all they want, but I'm not sure I can think of it as one."

Fuyutsuki clicked his tongue. "I'd remind you not to judge based on first impressions. Commander Ikari shared Seele's opinion that an Eva without its human form loses its reason to exist."

"To play out a role dictated by some myth, you mean? That's ridiculous." Aoba shook his head and sighed. "I guess I can't say that anymore, seeing how we're living through mythical events. Hell, three years ago, we watched a giant diagram of the Tree of Life appear out of thin air."

When Maya asked Nerv U.S. to share their data on genetic modifications to create compatible Eva pilots on demand, no one

had expected the Americans to offer proof of the project's success in the form of a direct visit.

The date for the final battle had been set. One week before the operation, Nerv U.S. had abruptly come out from its long hiding and announced that they would act as reserve forces. On the way to Russia, the detachment stopped in Nerv Japan to refuel and pay their respects.

The Eva pilot meowed.

Six's interest was piqued. She stared at the pilot, a chestnut-haired girl near her own height.

A man in an engineering officer's uniform introduced the pilot. "This is Mari."

Despite seeming to be the same age as Six, the young girl was the Evangelion pilot the Americans had genetically altered in secret.

"She looks like a normal girl to me," Hyuga said. "A human girl."

But as soon as he finished speaking, his mouth dropped. On top of her head were two cat-ear-looking bumps that he'd assumed were some kind of cosmetic cover for her interface headset. But the cat ears had twitched.

"Er...maybe not entirely normal," Hyuga said.

What had at first appeared cute suddenly seemed freakish.

Not that Nerv Japan had any right to criticize anyone for tinkering with the human body. But humans were self-centered creatures capable of great hypocrisy.

Perhaps reading Hyuga's reaction, the officer offered an explanation.

"She has human ears on the sides of her head. We didn't put the other ones there on purpose. In order to eliminate issues with the mental connection between Eva and pilot, we've strengthened the Evangelion's animalistic impulses. Over the course of repeated synchronization tests, the animal's physical characteristics have begun to manifest on the pilot."

Commander Katsuragi crouched down to Mari's eye level. "Nice to meet you, Mari. How do you do?"

"I'm fine," the girl said. "So are the rest of my pack."

Her...pack? Misato thought. *Does she mean her team?*

The engineering officer sighed and shook his head. "She thinks that the other animals are living inside her as individuals."

"Not inside me," she corrected. "They're *with* me."

The officer looked exasperated. "Of course that's nonsense."

But one person and one dog took her seriously.

"Lucky!" Six said, eyes twinkling.

"Woof!" Azuchi barked.

The giant-transport plane's too-long wings rocked as it circled the runway, back to where it had touched down. Its engines roared, powering up for takeoff. With the aircraft refueled, the U.S. Eva's retinue concluded their hurried introductions and reboarded. Without further delay, the plane took off, aiming its nose toward the staging area in Russia.

"Fuyutsuki, why do you think they stopped by here?" Misato asked. "They could've flown over the Arctic Ocean without re-fueling. They had to go out of their way to come this far west."

"They might have been signaling a positive stance toward our request for their technology, but I can't say for sure. Either way, they're bringing their Eva out into the light, so I'm sure they want to make a good impression. What did you charge them for the precious jet fuel they hauled off in that cargo plane?"

"Let's just say it's a seller's market."

CHAPTER 26

———— OFF THE SHORE OF TOKYO

U NFORTUNATELY FOR HER, Ibuki Maya hadn't been there to witness the U.S. Eva. The chief scientist was on the deck of the battleship *Yamato* with Asuka/Eva flying overhead. After returning home at the end of World War II, the last-century super-large battleship had undergone many improvements, including having its coal-fired boilers switched over to heavy fuel oil, but it was later moored and converted into a museum memorializing Japan's defeat. Now the battleship had been further modernized, gaining an N_2 reactor in the process, and was back at sea. The ship had just completed its sea trial in Kanto Bay, where there weren't freak swells like there were in the open ocean.

Rumors were circulating that the *Yamato* was intended as a shelter vessel for select citizens.

Nerv Japan had been uncharacteristically generous in providing the N_2 reactor to the Japanese government. The global cataclysm was breaking down supply chains of every kind, and the reactor was one way Nerv Japan could drag the government to the bargaining table.

Talking to herself, the chief scientist remarked, "Even with the reactor, this ship is still…" She tried to remember what Fuyutsuki had called it. "Fudara-something-or-other."

Fuyutsuki had called the government's plans for the ship a "twenty-first-century version of the Fudaraku tokai," which was an extreme religious practice where pilgrims committed suicide by boarding themselves up within a boat bound for a paradise. But Maya didn't know the reference.

The *Yamato* had passed its sea trial, but Maya still had work to do.

"Asuka, please come down," Ritsuko said.

Asuka/Eva was making a game of disappearing into and appearing out of clouds in the pre-storm sky. She'd been carrying a giant, unstrung bow—or at least, something that looked like one—and was still holding it as she landed on the stern end of the flight deck, which was currently being used for takeoff and landing of helicopters and VTOL aircraft.

"Sorry to interrupt your game," Maya said.

Unfortunately, the research into separating Asuka back into human form was only just beginning. But the Asuka/Eva synthesis was responding to her own name, and through the repetition of some simple exercises, she was even learning to communicate. She had a lively curiosity and was surprisingly agreeable, which seemed unlike her previous self. But maybe that was closer to her true nature than anyone had known.

Maya thrust her fist forward as if she were holding a bow. "Hold that with your left hand, like this."

Asuka/Eva thought for a moment and then mimicked the action. The bow's bottom tip slammed down onto the flight deck, and the red giant turned her torso, pulling her rear leg back into an archer's stance.

The bow had been discovered along with the giant, semi-transparent eggshell that had appeared from the bottom of Lake Ashi. Maya was treating the mysterious object as an Evangelion-sized weapon. The bow possessed no string. Instead, each half contained a particle accelerator that met at a shared focal point. When the particles collided at an angle in the middle, the resulting energy shot forward like an arrow—or, as Maya thought of it, an energy slingshot.

The bow's construction remained a complete unknown, but Maya figured that if it was an Eva-sized weapon, having an Eva wield it might lead to new discoveries.

"So, the bow is a little larger than an Eva," Maya remarked. "Almost like it's sized for Armaros."

Ibuki Maya had given herself two assignments—to recreate the guided cannon, Neyarl, which had performed beyond expectations and destroyed a Victor with particles drawn from Super Eva's heart, and to identify the guided particle that had done it.

The resulting magnetic field had either destroyed Super Eva's full data records or, at best, left them temporarily inaccessible. But in North Africa, Maya had been able to retrieve one valuable piece of information—when Super Eva fired the weapon, time stretched out so much that he perceived the behavior of elementary particles. "Without ever touching the enemy, or undergoing any change itself," Shinji had said, "the beam tore through the Victor and made its protons decay."

That was enough to give Maya at least part of an answer—magnetic monopoles. They were particles that had existed only in the first moments of the birth of the universe, and even then, only in vanishingly small numbers.

Whether humanity liked it or not, Armaros had displayed acts of godlike power. But if such particles could defeat him and his retainers, then those fearsome giants were fundamentally no different from any other entities born after the beginning of the universe. There was no reason for humanity to simply hang their heads and accept defeat.

Ask others what that knowledge changed about the present situation, and they would likely struggle to answer, but to a scholar like Maya, it changed everything. Here was an enemy who defied all measuring, and maybe, finally, she'd been given a set of laws that could place him on a scale.

"Don't worry, Asuka," Maya said, looking up high. "I don't think that bow will do anything without a lot of energy being dumped into it."

Horaki Hikari had been the first to call Asuka by her name, so that she might reclaim her identity, but now everyone followed suit.

"Today," Maya continued, looking down at her tablet, "before we completely hand over the N_2 reactor, I want to take one last opportunity to make use of it, along with those two miniaturized ones you've got, and see if we can test-fire that bow. So if you could hang on to it until it shoots, that would be great."

A storm looked like it was brewing, but for now, the waves were calm, as was everything else.

Asuka looked over her shoulder.

The red giant froze, as if she'd heard a voice she recognized.

"Asuka?" Maya said. She looked back up from the screen and noticed that Asuka/Eva was staring at a point somewhere in the distance. "What's the matter?"

Maya tapped on the tablet and pulled up Asuka's status display. According to the data, the giant wasn't particularly alarmed. She was just focusing her attention in that direction.

BANG!

Maya yelped. Asuka/Eva must have let go of the bow, and the weapon had dropped to the deck.

The graceful red giant stood completely erect, as if someone had called to her.

Her Allegorica wings billowed upward, like long hair caught in the wind. She took one smooth step and then began gliding toward the coastline in the direction she'd been looking.

"Asuka!" Maya spoke into her tablet. "Where are you going? Is something there?"

On the shoreline of Kanto Bay stood the ruins of the old metropolis abandoned after the Second Impact. Suddenly, black, root-like tendrils burst out from the rubble and coiled around Asuka.

"Asuka!" Maya shouted.

Asuka didn't resist as the tendrils pulled her into the ground. Just like that, she was gone.

Alarms sounded throughout the battleship, and the close-range autocannons swiveled their daruma-doll heads, but by then, it was all over. Still surrounded by the upgrade crew's scaffolding, the main battery cannons swept their barrels across the sky at nothing.

Where the Asuka/Eva synthesis had disappeared, the rubble had been scattered away, leaving the barren ground exposed. But other than that, there was no trace that anything had passed through.

CHAPTER 27

▶ ——— # AN ISLAND AWAKENING

UPON LANDING AT ROGACHEVO, a Russian military air base on the southern side of Novaya Zemlya, an archipelago that divided the Barents and Kara Seas, a Euro soldier exhaled white breaths and grumbled, "What the hell kind of place are they choosing for the last battle?"

The Europeans, after discussing with Russia, had selected this location for the final confrontation and were rapidly preparing the ambush site.

The black giant Armaros, who'd brought calamity to every part of the globe, along with his underlings, the Victors and the Angel Carriers, were drawn to the heartbeat produced by Super Eva's window to higher dimensions. An imitation heartbeat produced the same effect. Even now, after the Lance of Longinus had stolen Super Eva's heart, the rumble of that imitation would still bring humanity's enemies calling.

With the Evangelion—Heurtebise—and their combined combat forces, Europe and Russia intended on forcing a final showdown on this remote island.

Both seas, to the east and west, adjoined the Arctic Ocean. And at this high latitude, the pull of the gargantuan moon had a lesser effect on the tides, so damage from the water's ebb and flow had been kept comparatively low.

Countless gray warships, constituting the bulk of Russia's navy, were spread out across the water as far as the eye could see. Their cannons had been raised, and waterproof coverings removed, for thorough testing of their safeguards and controls.

The ground troops were outfitted with CBRN gear (airtight suits and gas masks) to protect against being turned into pillars of salt—if that phenomenon could indeed be protected against.

At least the protective gear wouldn't be uncomfortably hot this far north.

But even if the soldiers grew too warm for comfort, no one would remove the gear by choice. In the previous century, Novaya Zemlya had been a nuclear test site, and even now, Russia maintained a stockpile of N_2 weapons. They tested these weapons so heavily that the northern edge of the island wasn't just cratered, it looked like the bottom of a giant pot.

The N_2 reaction didn't produce radiation—at least, not officially—but the testing had unearthed soil contaminated by the previous century's nuclear tests. Everyone present had heard rumors of radioactive soil turning to dust and drifting away on the wind.

The angry bark of a drill sergeant echoed from inside the passenger plane that had brought the latest batch of soldiers here, and they rushed off the plane as if it were on fire. They were holding up the endless stream of aircraft queuing to land, refuel, and take off again, empty.

From the airport, soldiers and supplies were shuttled by truck, helicopter, and VOTL aircraft to the battleground—the bombed-out test site—which the locals had taken to calling Misha's Frying Pan.

A strange aircraft circled the center of the basin like a wayward leaf as it attempted to land. It was Nerv Japan's Platypus-2, a.k.a. the N_2 Flanker.

The N_2 Flanker was the progenitor of the graviton floater technology—the combination of N_2 reactor and diamond-slit array. The experimental plane was a joint effort between Nerv Japan and the JSSDF, with a Russian-made aircraft serving as the testbed. In a certain sense, the aircraft was coming home, though its birthplace was hard to pin down. According to one story, the JSSDF had piled a bunch of graviton floaters onto a used Russian aircraft that had been purchased for tactical appraisal and subsequently mothballed. Another suggested that the graviton floater test unit had been built first, and later retrofitted with a nose and wings, so that the fore and aft could be differentiated.

Either way, the Allegorica wings on Eva-02 and Heurtebise were expanded versions of this plane's systems and had been created from its accumulated data. The Flanker was later equipped with a railgun that drew power from the N_2 reactor. Nerv Japan had hoped that, with its ability to fly freely at any speed up to Mach 2, the plane would serve as air support for the Evangelions. But once Hakone was leased to the UN, Nerv Japan lost the cooperation of the JSSDF.

Due to the Flanker's overall reliability, and its resilience against electromagnetic interference, the plane had been recently serving as a transport for Acting Deputy Commander Toji's frequent travels.

"Let's get to work," Toji said. He'd come to observe the planned battle site. The UN had requested Nerv Japan's participation in the main event.

But Super Eva had gone missing, and Eva-02 had fused with its pilot and might not follow orders. Meanwhile, the pilot of the last orbital Eva-0.0 was in the final testing phase of Eva-00 Type-F's Allegorica system—but the engineers would do whatever it took to be ready in time for the battle.

Toji's visit primarily served as a clear signal that Nerv Japan didn't intend to ignore their allies' call. Still, he dutifully observed the battle formations as he descended. He spotted Heurtebise's control plane, of the Euro Sixth Rapid Response Unit, touching down on the dry, barren ground. He was changing course so that he could set the N_2 Flanker down beside them when a warning came over the radio from the garrison.

《Japanese plane, maintain your distance from the Eva.》

"Aw, man. I was hoping I could use the bathroom."

Toji hadn't intended on staying for more than a quick look. Nerv Japan still had a lot of preparations ahead. For now, he just hoped they wouldn't push the German Eva-02 Heurtebise too far. Down below, Hikari's pure-white Eva was kneeling.

《Ritter?》 the command plane's bridge called to Hikari in her entry plug.

It took a moment before she remembered that Ritter—knight—meant her.

"Oh, er, yes!" she hastily replied. "Kommandobrücke?"

《Did we interrupt you? Were you on the phone with your boyfriend?》

"I would never do that on duty!"

That had been a joke. All her communications were kept under strict control. But she was a stickler for rules anyway.

《Hikari, the additional quantum wave mirror trucks are here. Do you think you could start the calibrations?》

"Affirmative."

Leaning out from the cockpit of his parked Flanker, Toji removed his helmet and waved it to get Hikari's attention. The helmet tumbled from his fingers and rolled away. He yelped in surprise and then scurried down out of the plane to chase after it.

"What is he doing?" Hikari laughed as she watched through the Eva's partially zoomed-in side view.

Just as Nerv Germany and the Euro Sixth Army had promised, Hikari was no longer being hypnotically controlled.

At this point, she—and her human rights—were being treated with deference. With no other Eva-compatible pilots within their command, they'd adapted a new strategy—to use her natural amiability against her. They'd learned that as long as they apologized for their earlier discourtesy, and took a completely honest and cooperative stance with her, she didn't have it in her to refuse. And yes, she knew what they were doing.

Her older sister had been caught in the Lance of Longinus's light and turned into a pillar of salt, but she still had a younger sister in Germany. And while the mysterious presence inside the abandoned prototype body of Asuka's Eva-02 might have been nothing more than vestige of a long-gone consciousness, Hikari believed it was Asuka's mother. She didn't have any evidence aside from her own belief, but she couldn't just leave Heurtebise.

"This is Eva-02 Heurtebise requesting authorization to initialize my graviton floater array and take flight."

《This is Rogachevo Air Base ATC. Keep clear of the aircraft staging area.》

《Kommandobrücke to Hikari, you are authorized for your calibration flight. Be careful of the VTOL aircraft to your south.》

Heurtebise's graviton floaters began to hum and then roar, and the three-thousand-ton giant lifted off the ground.

The Eva rose about twenty meters, held altitude there, and then glided sideways to the right. The quantum wave mirrors, mounted on large armored trailers, swiveled to follow Heurtebise's movements.

"Measuring for tracking misalignment," Hikari said.

In far-off Hokkaido, the quantum wave mirrors had reflected and focused the spatial distortions created by Heurtebise's graviton floaters into a single point in midair. Heurtebise had used the effect to knock Super Eva off-balance and send the giant to the ground. Since then, the Euro military had upgraded the trucks and increased their number. Now there were sixteen. With this many, the quantum wave mirrors could further amplify the imitation heartbeat. But that wasn't all. The trucks could also create weaponized spatial distortions of drastically higher magnitude. Even as humanity continued to suffer under the weight of Armaros' boot, they weren't just lashing out like a cornered rat. They'd prepared a serious counterattack.

As Heurtebise glided through the air, the quantum wave mirrors swiveled atop the sixteen armored trucks. Every now and then, Heurtebise's spatial distortions reflected between the mirrors and burst at the focal point, sending an explosive roar reverberating across the basin.

"Ah, I hate that sound," Toji said with a wince. He thought back to how Super Eva had fallen to the ground again and again. Shinji had nearly lost his mind.

But back then, humanity was fighting among themselves. This time, they'd be fighting together against a common enemy.

He switched on the comms channel. "Hello? This is Suzuhara. Are you guys seeing this video?"

From his helmet speakers came a reply.

《Woof! Woof woof!》

《A cat! Cat ears!》

That was Azuchi—the golden retriever—and little Ayanami Rei Six.

"Huh?" Toji replied.

"What?" Aoba spoke next.

《This is Nerv Japan. The sound quality is great. We're getting some hitching on the video—it's being routed through the stratospheric airplane network, and we're running into some digital noise—but it'll do.》

"Where's the American Eva?"

《They're on their way to you. Misato should be back in the command center any moment now, and Chief Ibuki should be watching your stream from the deck of the *Yamato*.》 There was a brief pause. 《Hm? Why are you outside your plane? Your suit and helmet should keep out the dust, but I'm not sure I'd advise it.》

"Oh, er," Toji said, rubbing the back of his helmet where it had gotten dinged in the fall. "It's nothing."

He switched the head-mounted display from a direct view to a zoomed-in view, aided by extra side-mounted cameras. Toji liked to think of it as his "bird of prey" view. The new picture was transmitted from the helmet, to the Flanker, to the stratospheric airplane network, and then to Nerv Japan HQ.

A giant trench had been dug around the outside of the basin's rim. The tip of a massive railgun peeked out from the trench. The gun seemed to be a kind of mobile artillery.

"Hm?" Toji said.

Even farther behind the mobile railgun, he saw a convergence reflector that he recognized from the Japanese maser howitzer.

A voice came not from Toji's headset but from directly beside him. "Hey, Acting Deputy Commander Suzuhara."

Toji placed the voice immediately. "Lieutenant Colonel Kasuga?"

Toji returned the display to normal view and saw the large man standing beside him, wearing a winter-camouflage CBRN combat suit.

Everything Toji saw through his head-mounted display was being automatically processed by computer algorithms, which analyzed the man's silhouette and estimated bone structure and, within moments, added the name "Kasuga" to the screen. But Toji didn't need to read the digital name tag to know. This man could be none other than the commanding officer of the JSSDF Large-Scale Threat Unit. Kasuga was burly to begin with. And with his bulk stuffed inside, he made the protective gear look like a suit of power armor.

The soldier's affable eyes smiled from behind his goggles. Kasuga touched his gloved hand to the side of his helmet's covering in salute, and then turned in the direction Toji had been looking. "First Africa, then Russia. And here I thought all kaiju headed for Japan."

"That's never been a rule," Toji said.

"But we've always been the ones on the front line. Don't you feel like we've had something taken from us?"

"Er...maybe," Toji said, noncommittally.

"Let's go out for yakiniku sometime, while there's still meat left to eat."

Toji didn't mind that Nerv Japan wasn't commanding the operation, but he did care—greatly—that Hikari was being put on the front lines. Still, he was relieved to see that the Europeans had brought more forces than he'd anticipated. With sixteen whole trucks' worth of quantum wave mirrors, maybe they could even make that black colossus eat dirt.

Don't be so sure, he warned himself. *Dangerous is dangerous.*

A voice in his helmet brought him back from his thoughts.

《This is Ibuki from the *Yamato* in Kanto Bay. It's an emergency!》

Hikari made her way through the quantum mirror truck calibration checklist.

After she finished testing the gravitational field control of several dozen different attack patterns, she made a soft beat with her graviton floaters. The sound matched Super Eva's heartbeat perfectly, only much more subdued.

On the day of the battle, she would drive the beat with full power to summon the enemy.

In Heurtebise's control plane, the crew were pleased with the results and were feeling reassured. Among them were Lieutenant Colonel Clausewitz and the officer serving as his chief assistant.

"I think we'll be ready just in time for next week," the assistant said.

"I think so, too," said Clausewitz. "Hikari, stop the test heartbeat. Each truck, move to a new position and prepare for a second try."

《Heurtebise acknowledges. The heartbeat is stopped.》

At once, everyone in the command center relaxed. Some stood from their chairs, while others reached for their coffee cups.

"I'd like to get more data on the wave interference," the assistant said, "in case things get a little confused out there. We've got more trucks to coordinate than before."

"I'm concerned about the opposite problem, too," Clausewitz replied. "What will happen to the amplitude if more mirror trucks are destroyed than our estimates—"

A panicked voice came over the comms channel. 《Kommandobrücke, we have a problem! The echo is bouncing between Trucks Five through Sixteen. We can't stop it!》

The soldiers inside the command center tensed.

"The new trucks," Clausewitz remarked. "Heurtebise?"

《I'm not generating the waves.》Hikari replied.

"Is the echo bouncing between the trucks unaided?"

"Heurtebise's A.I. might have mistaken the command to stop for a change in output level," the assistant replied. "The system could be automatically stabilizing the echo. The new model trucks don't have enough output to generate the heartbeat on their own, but each does have an N_2 igniter capable of producing a small number of gravitons to make small corrections to the wave."

"Trucks Five through Sixteen," Clausewitz ordered, "lock the mirrors in place and unfocus the reflections. That will disperse the wave."

Thrum.

The test wave had amplified. The heartbeat was now loud enough to hear.

《This is Truck Six! I can't enter any commands. We've been locked out from the controls!》

THRUM.

The heartbeat grew louder still.

《This is Truck Eight! It's not just the mirrors. I can't even control the vehicle! The damn thing is driving on its own!》

The drivers of the newer trucks were all screaming now as they reported malfunctions. Their vehicles were moving of their own accord. Something else was controlling them.

THRUM.

The soldiers began to stir.

The twelve out-of-control quantum wave mirror trucks began to tighten their formation.

"Why is this happening?" shouted Clausewitz.

The assistant slapped a palm to his head. "This morning, we used new data code to us by Nerv Japan to update the trucks' computers with improved autonomy so that they can continue supporting Heurtebise in any eventuality."

"What do you mean, 'any eventuality?'"

"If the drivers are all dead."

THRUM!

Now the A.I. was issuing an alert over the speakers. 《Warning: The imitation heartbeat has reached call signal decibel level.》

"Damn it! We're going to invite company!" Clausewitz jumped to the microphone and shouted to Hikari. "Heurtebise! Destroy the quantum wave mirrors on the malfunctioning trucks!"

《Do what?!》

THRUM!

Alarms began ringing all across Novaya Zemlya.

THRUM!

The false heartbeat was the signal to commence combat operations. The combat A.I.s for all forces present—the Euro army, the Russian navy, and the local garrison—announced the initial combat phase...a week early.

THRUM!

The entire island was a hornet's nest that had just been poked.

The soldiers, engineers, and scientists had all been caught off guard, but after a split-second's hesitation, they took off running to their stations.

The first confused query—*Is this a drill?!*—came in to the Euro Sixth Army's central command. Countless others flooded in after. In an instant, calls saturated the voice modulation transmission network, and text requests for confirmation scrolled down the command center's display screen like a waterfall. The commander of the Sixth Army personally relayed the requests to Heurtebise's control plane in the form of a strongly worded demand for an immediate explanation.

Hikari spoke through Heurtebise's external speakers. 《Watch out! I'm going to lift you up!》

She picked up the nearest truck and turned the vehicle away, sending the quantum wave echo out of focus. Before the other trucks could realign themselves, Heurtebise's A.I. assigned them new tasks, and the trucks' guidance systems once again allowed manual input from their human drivers.

The heartbeat, which had been thundering like tens of thousands of soldiers marching in unison, evaporated in an instant, leaving behind only the noise of alarms and jet engines.

The assistant let out a sigh of relief. Then, the severity of the false start sank in, and his face turned pale. He reached for the transmission switch. "We'd better let them know it was a mistake and get those alarms turned off."

Clausewitz gestured for him to hold off. "Wait!"

"But they told us to reply immediately!"

"Wait two minutes until we can be sure we didn't accidentally summon the enemy. Don't take your eyes off the sensor readings!"

All eyes went to the display screen.

"What if we stop the alarm," Clausewitz said, "and as soon as everyone relaxes, the enemy appears? Even if we start the alarm again, everyone will be out of step. We should remain in panic mode for now. Let them stay angry with us until we're sure this really was a false alarm."

Everyone was on tenterhooks. The requests to confirm or deny the starting order devolved into enraged shouting and vicious threats. Each time a new transmission came in, the young soldiers at the comms station trembled and looked to their commander with pleading eyes. By the time two minutes had passed and the lieutenant colonel ordered the all-clear, the control staff were all feeling heavyhearted.

As the assistant reported the false alarm, his only thought was how they were all going to be held responsible.

The alarms quieted. The aircraft shuttling personnel and supplies had already made their escape. The only remaining sounds were the rumble of the trucks' engines, the Eva's graviton floaters, and—

THRUM.

Clausewitz and his assistant looked at each other. "What?" they said in unison.

The heartbeat had been faint, but both had heard it.

"Why is the fake heartbeat still going?" Clausewitz asked.

The lieutenant colonel read the status window for the

telemetry data sent by Heurtebise and the trucks but saw nothing unusual. "Hikari?" he asked.

Within a small sub-window on the display, she was shaking her head. 《It's not me, and it's not the trucks, either!》

THRUM.

"Then...what is it?"

"Is that...an echo?" a soldier asked. The sound seemed to be coming from a different place than before.

Everyone who'd been moving froze and turned to listen. The soldiers who were already at their stations looked uneasily around to find the source of the heartbeat.

THRUM!

"That's not an echo! It's even louder than before!"

Something leaped out of the ground.

"Torwächter!" someone screamed. "I repeat, a Torwächter is here!"

Torwächter—German for gatekeeper—was the Euro designation for the enemy that Nerv Japan had yet to assign a code name. It appeared on Japanese detection systems as "Victor."

They'd summoned Armaros' vassal. But that wasn't the biggest surprise.

Mouth agape, the same soldier shouted, "The Torwächter is making the heartbeat?!"

Heurtebise's graviton floaters were still in alignment. The graviton array resonated with the Victor/Torwächter's heartbeat and began beating in time. The sound made Hikari shiver with fear. This had happened to her before.

"No, not that," she cried. "Not that!"

Inside the Eva's control plane, Clausewitz said, "The Torwächter is making an imitation heartbeat? What the hell is going on?!"

《Kommandobrücke!》 Hikari shouted from the speaker. 《It's not an imitation. It's the original!》

"Wh...what?"

Another voice cut in. 《It's moving!》

The Torwächter held its arms crossed in front of its chest. Then it unfolded them to reveal a triangular object with a large cleft in the middle and anchors at each point.

It was the Center Trigonus—the vessel that contained Super Eva's heart. Behind the cleft shone a brilliant, fiery light that flickered violently in time to the heartbeat.

In the speakers in Toji's helmet, Ibuki Maya and the Hakone control center were coordinating the search for Asuka, but as the chaos unfolded around him, he was in no position to participate.

"Oh, come on!" he shouted. He recognized the Center Trigonus immediately. "Super Eva's heart?! *That's* what's causing the heartbeat? Hyuga? Maya-san? Are you seeing this?"

He hurried to the N_2 Flanker but ran backward so that his helmet camera could send video of the Victor back to Hakone, even if it meant a few stumbles along the way.

Shaken, Maya exclaimed, 《I don't believe it! That's the singularity—the window to higher dimensions and to the energy they hold. It's the one we stabilized into a heartbeat with the quantum wave mirrors inside Super Eva's chest!》

No one spoke in the command center in Hakone. They were all too stunned by the feed from Toji's camera. They were hearing Maya, too. It wasn't like the chief scientist to raise her voice, but she wasn't speaking for their benefit. She was talking herself through what she was seeing.

《The Lance of Longinus stole the singularity from Super Eva and broke the shell that contained it. But when the singularity didn't split the Earth apart, and we didn't measure any unusual burst of energy coming from the lance's orbit, I assumed it had exploded in the space they use to travel between their gates.》

"That's right," Misato replied. "Once the singularity was torn from Shinji, it shouldn't have remained stable."

Misato thought back to the disaster in North Africa. The Lance of Longinus had been orbiting the earth and extending itself toward a complete ring when the weapon suddenly changed course—like an 28,000-kilometer-long steel snake—and pierced through the Earth, through Super Eva, taking the heart away.

She angrily slammed her hands down onto the desk at her station. "That heart belongs to Shinji-kun!"

She wasn't speaking figuratively. Shinji's own flesh-and-blood body possessed no heart. In its place, medical imaging showed a hollow cavity. His blood circulated from the beating of Super

Eva's heart. With that heart stolen, only Armaros' Q.R. Signum scale was keeping him alive.

"While the singularity was beating within the reflecting mirrors, could it have stabilized into a heart-like state?" Hyuga asked.

《Hm? By its own choice?》 Maya seemed to think about it. 《Like how primitive organisms choose stability as if they possess consciousness?》

"Whatever the case," Fuyutsuki cut in, looking to Misato, "we are where we are."

"He's right." The commander nodded. "I don't think the Victor would've shown up with that thing in its chest if it made it easier to kill."

The opposite was far easier to imagine.

"Maya, what's your take on Asuka's disappearance?" Misato asked, shifting gears.

《It may have been one of Armaros' gates. She was sucked into the ground without a trace. In which case, searching for her here would be wasted effort.》

"Come back here right away. I feel bad for Asuka, but there's nothing we can do for her at the moment. I believe in her. That girl has luck on her side. She came back from the moon, didn't she?"

"Next subject," Misato said, turning to Hyuga. "Is Unit Zero Allegorica ready?"

"I'd say we're sixty percent there," he replied. "None of the remaining work is mission critical."

"As of this moment, Unit Zero Allegorica is designated active. Six, get moving!"

"Woof!" Six said.

"Arm the Eva with no restrictions."

"Woof! Got it!"

Misato clapped her hands. "All right everyone. Get moving!"

THRUM!

The enemy's heartbeat frightened Hikari, and at the same time, she had to suppress the Q.R. Signum's pulsing urge to seek it out. Her own Eva was producing a heartbeat, too, but hers was a mere imitation, overpowered by the real thing.

Nevertheless, Hikari managed to pick up the positron rifle from the ground at her feet. The fire control system loaded up, and the blue options of the practice menu were replaced one by one with a wave of orange live-fire modes. The Eva's reactor spooled up and began charging the weapon's capacitors.

"Ritter to Kommandobrücke, requesting permission to fire!"

Hikari felt sweat pouring from her skin into the circulating LCL. It was a strange feeling.

PART 6

NEON GENESIS

THE INVITEES

EVANGELION: ANIMA

NEON GENESIS
EVANGELION ANIMA

CHAPTER 28

LOST ON THE WAY HOME

As SHINJI AND TROIS raced through the darkness, Trois whispered, "I'm sorry."

Shinji looked over his shoulder at her. She was sitting in the plug seat, close enough that he could almost feel her breath. Yet even from this distance, he couldn't read her expression.

"You don't have to apologize. We'll keep trying as many times as it takes."

What else could he say?

After serval attempts, Super Eva had finally broken back in to the tunnel network. But now they couldn't find their destination. They were lost on the highway.

Inside Super Eva's plug, Shinji and Ayanami divided roles the same as he had with Quatre. Shinji piloted the Eva, while Trois controlled the Q.R. Signum that acted as his power plant.

Why isn't this working? Shinji wondered.

When Trois had piloted Eva-0.0, she'd lost sight of who she was. She'd traveled these tunnels many times, thoughtlessly following Seele/Kaji's commands. But now that her thoughts were clear, she struggled. She'd found a reason to live, and the Q.R. Signum's ever-encroaching darkness terrified her.

Unable to find an exit, Super Eva drifted at tremendous speed through the massive travel network that connected all the vast lands the Instrumentality Project had created.

Seele/Kaji had said that the Apple's Core, the moon, and the Earth all constituted one land, no matter the distance separating them, while Kaworu had called this tunnel network the space below the stage, where the stagehands scurried to and fro. Super Eva felt no sense of movement within this dark space but was aware of the countless paths flowing past in rapid succession.

Why can't we exit to normal space?

Shinji could think of two possible reasons.

First, Seele/Kaji might have followed through on his threat to cut them off and was somehow preventing them from opening an exit portal.

But during the fight with the Victors in these tunnels, Trois had felt that anyone who entered this space couldn't be blocked from leaving, otherwise, the Victors would have trapped Super Eva here. Besides, however Kaji blustered about cutting off the only route to the Apple's Core, Shinji could sense that Super Eva had returned from that long, lonely tunnel to the main network.

It was probably an empty threat. I'm not even sure Kaji-san has the power to do such a thing.

The second possibility was that Trois wasn't letting the Q.R. Signum sink as deeply into her as Quatre had and that she didn't possess full control over the abilities the scale could grant her.

But it's not like I can just come out and say, "Hey, Trois, let the darkness consume you a little more."

Every time Shinji drew power from the Q.R. Signum, he could feel the darkness trying to eat him away. Right now, Trois was taking on the majority of the burden. She didn't complain, and Shinji couldn't read her expression, but she must have been hurting.

The skirt of her black chiffon dress swayed in the LCL.

Shinji didn't know why, but Trois was wearing the same minidress Quatre had taken from her room. The dress must have stayed with the mutant Eva-0.0 this whole time.

Whatever the particulars, Trois wasn't wearing any mental shielding gear while she accompanied Shinji in the Eva—which was also his body. But he was experiencing no cross-contamination of thought.

Which meant that her presence was weaker than Quatre's had been, though both were Ayanamis.

Shinji thought back to the promise he'd blurted out in the heat of the moment. *I'll find Trois' color. But...can I do that? I can't even get my own crap together.*

Shinji thought he sensed something cut across Super Eva's path through the otherworldly space—something very familiar.

Something red.

"Asuka?!" Shinji reflexively called out, startling Rei Trois.

"Crimson A1 is here in the tunnels?" Trois asked. "But Quatre thought Asuka went straight back to Hakone from Africa."

"She did. But a lot of time passed while we took our little tour of Eden. I wouldn't be surprised if something's happened on the Earth side."

Shinji could have said he might have been mistaken about Asuka's presence here, but he was certain he'd been right.

His eyes stared at a single point on the virtual display. From behind him, Trois realized his consciousness was shifting out of the entry plug.

"Stay here," Trois said, sounding oddly peevish.

"Why?" Shinji asked.

But Trois didn't know the answer herself. "Never mind," she said, and that was the end of it.

She told herself her emotional reaction had nothing to do with their current situation, but it wasn't like she'd never felt that way before. In fact, she'd felt a similar way when she'd lost Gendo.

Having obtained a target, Super Eva began pursuing the red presence.

In this mysterious space, which provided no sense of speed or distance, the Eva changed course like a train switching rails.

CHAPTER 29

THE GAP BETWEEN

I N HER BIO-TUNING ROOM within the UN giant-transport airplane, little Mari suddenly looked up. "Who's there?"

The only sound within the plane was the rumble of its engines and the roar of the wind.

News had already arrived that the Euro's planned ambush in Novaya Zemlya had turned into a surprise engagement with the enemy, and the transport plane had accelerated to high speed. The majority of the crew needed new orders, and the personnel had crammed into the cafeteria—now an impromptu war room— for an all-stations emergency briefing. Everywhere else, the plane was deserted.

Mari's plugsuit gloves were oversized—a preventative measure to keep the girl from impulsively scratching herself with her claws—but they also made it hard for her to hold on to anything. Still, she skillfully managed to set her milk cup down on the table without a spill.

The U.S. Eva pilot hopped down from her chair and left the white room.

Several IV tubes and data cables trailed behind her and connected into a four-legged robot taller than she was—about an average adult's chest height. The robot activated and followed her from the room. As the machine moved, several IV bags dangled from its underside.

The robot's walking motors whirred, and the roar of the outside wind made the plane's interior sound like a school gymnasium during a downpour. Atop Mari's head, the ears that weren't her ears twitched.

Those animal ears were a sign that the spliced-in animal DNA was gradually taking over her body. The claws were another. Each time she piloted the U.S. Eva, the transformations progressed a little bit more. The Nerv U.S. medical team was concerned that a tail might appear next.

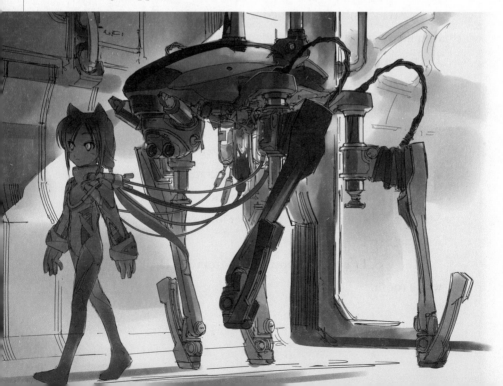

Like other Nerv branches, Nerv U.S. had struggled to find compatible pilots.

But they'd taken a different path. They'd researched methods to remove any say the Evangelions had in deciding if a pilot was compatible or not. The answer they found was de-evolution—to return the Evangelions to an earlier form, before they had an element of human consciousness. Consequently, the U.S. Eva, which could scarcely remember how to walk upright, accepted a pilot who'd undergone the same treatment. As a side benefit, the giant had acquired an extremely powerful, explosive aggressiveness.

Each time the girl entered her Eva, she risked becoming something that could no longer be called human. The tubes and cables served as a literal lifeline connecting information from her brain to the medical staff. But she didn't particularly care what she became.

Over the course of several years, she'd formed a bond with the many animal species that had been introduced to her. They were a part of her, and she now thought of herself as a "pack."

That word, in particular, made the people around her uneasy. She'd already begun to forget human sensibilities and language. Would she one day become a beast who only obeyed her instincts?

In her home country, religious fundamentalists who denied the very existence of evolution were no mere minority. The Nerv U.S. staff was more secular, but even they felt that if she continued regressing, it would be exorcists she needed, not scientists.

Mari's ears led her directly to the source that had aroused her curiosity. "Who's there?"

In the twenty-degrees-below-freezing cargo hold, Momo, the golden retriever, was shivering and whimpering in a gap between the cargo nets.

Had this dog gotten separated from her sister, Azuchi, in Hakone's Daikon airport and boarded the plane by accident?

Pulling her cables behind her, Mari slipped into the gap and put her face up to Momo's nose. She sniffed.

At first, Momo was frightened by the girl's sudden approach—and by the robot that loomed over her shoulder. But even before then, the dog had been confused. Was this little girl really a human? If not, what was she?

Before the dog could shrink back, Mari licked Momo on the nose.

"You've got a curious streak, don't you?" she asked.

The girl's assertive smile was undeniable. Momo couldn't help but wag its tail. The dog hadn't been afraid of this one little girl... It had been afraid of the many sets of eyes it felt watching.

CHAPTER 30

THE BATTLE
ON THE NORTHERN ISLAND

THE COMBAT RADIO FREQUENCY filled with shouting voices.

The enemy's unanticipated early arrival had thrown the battleground into chaos. Cargo trucks and freight containers had been abandoned where they were, rather than withdrawn from the area of active fighting as they should have been, but the troops themselves were largely in position and ready.

The Victor's black figure rose above the horizon. It was still more than ten kilometers away, yet its heartbeat traveled the distance loud and clear. The gravitational waves were solitons, which didn't attenuate like normal sound waves. Even though the sound wasn't particularly intense at the source, the heartbeat traveled far.

It overpowered Heurtebise's imitation.

THRUM!

Toji would never forget the first time that heart had begun beating.

An unknown, unstoppable enemy had been advancing upon Nerv HQ, and Shinji and Eva-01 were mortally wounded and dying in a hangar. The scientists and engineers were performing what amounted to an elaborate funeral, to allow the Eva and its pilot to pass on in peace, rather than in a runaway reaction that might very well have taken a good chunk of the world out with them. But then came the heartbeat, full of vigor, announcing their rebirth. For no tangible reason, everyone present was electrified—almost delirious with excitement—as they waved their arms and drummed along to the beat with whatever was handy.

Now that heart beat in the chest of their enemy. It was a teeth-grinding humiliation.

THRUM!

In the seat of the N_2 Flanker, Toji shouted, "This is an outrage... An outrage!"

Toji had only come here as an early observer, and he didn't know what to do now that the battle had begun. After a moment's indecision, he lifted off from Misha's Frying Pan. Directly in front of him, he saw the pure-white Heurtebise pick up the positron rifle and take aim.

Each heartbeat reverberated through his graviton floaters. He turned the plane and headed north. As if she'd been waiting for this moment, Hikari fired.

Heurtebise's positron rifle glinted in the sun like a brass instrument. A brilliant flare blossomed from the muzzle, and moments later came the shock wave and the roar.

Visible on the horizon twelve kilometers away, the Victor blocked the positron shell with its invisible, A.T. Field-like power shield. The antiparticles struck the shield at near light speed and released a tremendous burst of energy that scattered across the shield's surface, either dissipating or turning into steam. The soldiers in the basin saw a blinding flash, followed by a loud bang.

So it was with battles between giants. To the human senses, the colossi lagged behind the beat, and the result felt like slow motion. They weren't actually slow. The human mind could easily understand that airplanes flew fast despite appearing slow from the ground, but because the giants had a humanoid shape, the subconscious couldn't help but assign them a human scale, thus creating a gap between perception and reality. The giants seemed to move as if underwater. This disconnect between senses and perception could be jarring and nightmarish.

Even when Heurtebise's second shot fizzled on the Torwächter's shield, Lieutenant Colonel Clausewitz of the Euro Sixth Rapid Response Unit wasn't about to become pessimistic. The plan hadn't assumed any other result.

"That's the way, Hikari!" he shouted. "Keep shooting. Lure that bastard into the trap! Stick to the plan."

《Yes, sir!》 Her voice crackled. Steam from the second shot of her positron rifle had caused significant interference in the radio spectrum. But she got the message and proceeded as planned.

The enemy's early arrival had thrown the multinational forces into extreme confusion, but they'd recovered surprisingly fast and had deployed in an orderly manner.

The first wave of troops to arrive on Novaya Zemlya had been about to begin their second practice exercise. They were ready.

The rear guard, who'd only just arrived, were still near the airport on the island's southern side, and their reaction was far more chaotic.

Even though the graviton wave mirror trucks—the linchpin of their strategy—had malfunctioned and summoned the enemy a full week ahead of schedule, Clausewitz remarked, "All things considered, I think we can say we're performing admirably."

When the Lance of Longinus first began encircling the Earth, the weapon had cast a light upon an area from North Africa, across Europe, and into Russia, and had turned 1.9 million people into crumbling pillars of salt. But that was just the first taste of the apocalypse. The disasters that followed had claimed a far greater toll, even in Europe alone.

But now the Euro forces needed to make the bringers of destruction pay for what they'd done—no matter the cost.

This wasn't merely a question of national pride. They needed to do something before humanity fully gave way to despair.

THRUM!

The black Torwächter's stolen heart kept beating as the giant turned toward Heurtebise and began its advance. When Super Eva had last faced this enemy, the Torwächter had wielded an ornate, ringed staff, but this time, the giant had shown up empty-handed. The reason would soon be apparent.

The Torwächter reached behind its back, grabbed the edge of its obsidian-like rear plate, and snapped off a sliver. At the moment of separation, the end of the thin handle transformed into a large, jagged spindle-like weapon.

"Is that a hammer?" Clausewitz's chief assistant asked. "An ice axe? Those angles are strange, but if that's supposed to be some kind of blunt weapon, it won't have much range."

"Or maybe there's more to it than meets the eye," Clausewitz said. "Let's make the Torwächter use that weapon so that we can get some data. UAV Team 3-Alpha-East, do you have any autonomous decoys ready to attack?"

Within moments, gunfire rang out from the ground. Several unmanned mobile howitzers began firing from the trenches. Once fired, their 150 mm caliber shells discarded their sabots to reveal a long, slender, pointed spear of depleted uranium. The projectiles struck the Torwächter's shield and were instantly obliterated into smoke and debris.

The Torwächter responded with a wide swing of its arm and a flick of its wrist. The weapon's handle bent, and the thirty-meter-long spindle thrust forward. Cutting through the air, it made an eerie, low-pitched sound that could be heard throughout the battlefield.

"It's an atlatl!" Clausewitz shouted. The spindle launched forward, attached to the handle by a cable. "A spear-thrower! Except the thrower and the dart are connected by a sling!"

The giant swung its arm again.

Attached to the sling cable, the spindle's parabolic trajectory transitioned into a large, sweeping circular motion. Another swing, and the projectile accelerated, around and around. Suddenly, a huge crash shook the air.

"It broke the sound barrier!" Clausewitz said. The jagged mass created clouds in its wake and then passed them on the next revolution.

The spindle struck the howitzers' position, and its overwhelming kinetic force—and the enveloping shock wave—smashed through the armored vehicles and the ground beneath them. But the spindle didn't stop. It simply bounced upward and continued circling at supersonic speed.

Other nearby howitzer emplacements began to fire, joined by guided rockets belching flame.

"Who else started firing? Stop them! If that giant turns course..." They wouldn't be able to lure it into the trap.

But Clausewitz needn't have worried. The black giant responded by lengthening the thread. In a single swoop, the spindle scattered the howitzers that had joined the attack like they were toys. Armored vehicles and chunks of dirt and rock flew upward and began falling in all directions.

The brutish weapon circled freely at any length within a 1.4-kilometer diameter.

The Torwächter walked forward. The whirling spindle made the air howl and the ground rumble. Both the giant and its weapon approached the center of the battlefield. The spindle's shock wave carved arcs across the ground, and dust and debris rose like a curtain. The airborne Heurtebise could hardly see the Torwächter through the haze.

Impressive to be sure, but still only brute force.

"We shouldn't take this thing lightly," the assistant said.

No one offered disagreement. And yet, there was something absurd about having to fear such a primitive weapon, while the Torwächter's shield—and regenerative abilities—shrugged off humanity's weapons, which possessed far greater range and firepower.

Nerv Japan claimed to have destroyed the other Torwächter. They hadn't offered any proof, but previously, the pair had always appeared together, while today only one had come. *Does that mean the report was true?* Clausewitz thought. *If so, I'm thankful. Especially since those two plates together could have opened a gateway to another space—a source of enemy reinforcements, or our worst nightmare...another salt pillar massacre. Only having to face one plate is good news, but today it's behaving differently. That damn giant tore off a piece and made a weapon out of it.*

"Anything goes, huh?" Clausewitz said and then clicked his tongue. "What the hell *is* that plate, anyway?"

Whether attached to a Torwächter or Armaros, the plates never separated from the ground. They matched their bearer's movements, emerging from the earth or submerging into it as needed.

Nerv Japan had come up with an oddball theory. The largest of the giants, Armaros, previously had two rear plates that connected to the ground. After the Japanese Eva destroyed a Torwächter, Armaros was seen with only one plate. And the Torwächters could use the Earth's surface as a warp gate. Connect those two facts, and...

The assistant must have been thinking the same thing, because as he double-checked Heurtebise's status windows, he said,

"The Japanese claim the plates don't have an end on the other side of the ground. If you followed Armaros' plate, it would lead you through the tunnel network to the Torwächter's back. They made sure to clarify that this is only conjecture, but the circumstantial evidence is there."

"Our strategy stays the same," Clausewitz said curtly, "but I'll take that into account. For now, my biggest concern is that weapon it's swinging around. It's going to be even more trouble than it looks. With one swing, that spindle could take out half our mirrors. Remove the option from the formation list for the graviton wave mirror trucks to surround the target in concentric circles. And let's see if we can sever that sling with some long-range fire. In three, two, one..."

The A.I. chimed. 《The Torwächter is speeding up and is now entering the mirror array.》

NEON GENESIS
EVANGELIONANIMA

CHAPTER 31

A PERSON IN SPIRIT

As the pitch-dark space of the tunnel network raced by, something grabbed Super Eva's hand. Shinji was startled but not afraid. The hand was warm.

《Shinji! I found you!》

The voice seemed to come from overhead. Shinji recognized it immediately.

"Asuka?!" he asked.

When Super Eva turned to look over his shoulder, he expected to see the red giant, Crimson A1, the mix of Asuka and Eva-02. So he was surprised when he saw Asuka's human face. There in the strange corridor was Asuka, outside her Eva, unclothed save for countless red shapes swirling around her, so fast that they were a blur, like a robe of heat and wind.

Shinji didn't understand what was happening. He began to consider the real possibility that he was hallucinating.

Asuka rushed toward him, though he couldn't get a sense of where she was in relation to him or how big she was, either. He caught her and felt his arms around her—and her at his chest.

Whether that was his own chest or Super Eva's, he couldn't tell. It felt like both.

"Trois...I think maybe I'm hallucinating."

"No, that's the Second—" *Child,* Trois was about to say, but she started over. "That's Asuka. I see her. But physically, I can't make out where or what she is."

Right now, she was human-sized, and she happily buried her face in his chest, with her hands on his shoulders.

Wait, this isn't right. This isn't like her.

《You were the one crying, telling me not to go anywhere— but then *you* left *me*. You've got some explaining to do!》

Ever since the Q.R. Signum had replaced his heart, the entry plug had felt chilly, no matter how warm he set the LCL. But now he felt warmth spreading through it. Was this happiness? A feeling of security?

Asuka noticed Ayanami Trois sitting behind Shinji.

"Cinq!" Asuka said. But that Ayanami was no longer in this world. "Cinq...you got home ahead of me. I see you melded into Trois. Oh, Cinq, I'm so sorry I left you."

But rather than correct Asuka, Trois replied, "It's all right."

Startled, Shinji turned to Ayanami.

She really was Trois, and yet her gentle expression belonged unmistakably to Cinq.

Cinq's memory—or was it her consciousness?—spoke through Trois' lips. "I can only see myself in the connections I have with others. That's what limits me—but it also gives me a sense of values. I made the right decision, and I feel fulfilled. You mustn't feel bad for me. And that goes for you, too, Trois. I was able to express who I am."

Shinji didn't notice that Trois was crying into the LCL. Cinq's words had provided salvation from her guilt over Cinq's birth and death.

Trois was the one who'd come up with the plan to form a mental link with her three clones to create an orbital Angel interception network. Ultimately, Cinq's death flowed from that decision.

"Trois," Asuka said, grinning. "You look good in that dress."

Who was this straightforward, sincere girl? Who was this person who'd found Cinq within Trois and who looked straight into Shinji? Was this who Asuka had kept hidden beneath her pride?

"Whoever picked that out must have had a good eye," Asuka said.

At least she still knew how to brag. Shinji wanted to believe this was Asuka and not an illusion. She separated from his chest but kept both hands on his shoulders as she mounted the front of the pilot's seat. The red forms continued swirling around her body like clothing. The skirt—if it could be called that—billowed around her legs.

"Shinji," she said, "I flew all the way to the moon by myself. I guess I came home with a crowd, but still, don't you think I'm incredible? Tell me I'm incredible."

She batted her long eyelashes at him, but it sounded like an order.

Shinji's expression had been frozen in shock, but now it shifted to one of confusion.

Asuka had come home from the moon—but her data had merged with that of her Eva. He'd thought there was no hope of reconstituting her alone.

Yet here she was, right in front of him. Smiling. *Is this really her?*

He began to think about everything that had happened to them, and he started to grow emotional. *No, I can't let myself cry now.*

He knew she'd make fun of him for it later.

"Yeah, Asuka," he managed. "You're incredible. I...I've got a lot of respect for—"

She pressed a finger to his lips. "Respect feels too distant. You can keep it."

Shinji didn't care anymore why or how she was here. Her presence was enough.

She'd made it to the moon by herself, she'd battled an Angel Carrier in low gravity, she'd discovered the moon's Ark, and she'd made it home to Earth even after losing her body.

Now she'd reclaimed her *self*, in body and mind. Astounding.

What could a guy even say to that?

"Asuka, you're...you're one crazy son of a—"

"Watch it."

Probably not that.

Shinji couldn't believe they were talking like this again— sharing words, sharing apologies...

Asuka suddenly looked into the far distance, as if someone had called her.

She stiffened and then looked toward Shinji.

"Asuka?" Shinji asked.

Her smile had vanished. Her stare was piercing, her voice wary. "It wasn't you. Then who?"

The flow of LCL in the plug reversed, as if blown by a gust of wind.

"You didn't bring me here, Shinji! It wasn't you!"

In an instant, she'd separated from him. Then she was outside Super Eva once more.

"What?" Shinji asked. He felt like he'd been pushed away.

The whirling red wind hid Asuka behind its veil, and the vortex grew wider and bigger until it was as large as an Eva. It flew away through the tunnels.

Then Shinji and Trois heard the sound, coming from the direction Asuka had gone.

THRUM!

They both froze.

"That's your..." Trois whispered.

Shinji looked at her over his shoulder. "My heart? How?!"

NEON GENESIS
EVANGELION ANIMA

CHAPTER 32

THE CLOSING MIRRORS

*T**HRUM!***
    Super Eva's stolen heart pulsed in the center of the circle of dust and debris stirred up by the spindle's sweep. The heart's current owner, the Torwächter, advanced toward the sound of Heurtebise's imitation heartbeat.

Were Armaros' retainers driven to steal the heartbeat's source? Or did the imitation heartbeat simply offend them?

Hikari's eyes darted between her Eva's visual feed and the map with the deployment diagram. The dot indicating the Torwächter's location crossed a demarcation line on the map.

"Th-the target has entered the mirror array!" Hikari stammered. "Heurtebise to Kommandobrücke—I'm switching the graviton floater mode."

The graviton floaters stopped making the imitation heartbeat and prepared to generate gravitational distortions. Losing the sound of the heartbeat it sought, the Torwächter slowed its advance, as if unsure, which was just what Hikari wanted.

From the control plane, Clausewitz announced that the trap was ready.

《Mirror convoy, close the circle! Ritter, begin!》

The sixteen armored trucks, with trapezoidal arrays of quantum wave mirrors mounted on gimbals, raced across the barren land. The convoy overtook Heurtebise and began to spread out.

Heurtebise's graviton floaters hummed. The majority of the energy created by gravitons escaped out of our dimension through gravitational waves. But when positioned right, the graviton wave mirrors could reflect and focus those waves into a single point in space.

The Torwächter continued swinging the spindle. As the giant took another step, the space beneath its foot warped slightly and snapped violently back into place.

This was the limit of the N_2-based graviton technology. By producing gravitons in greater quantity, the effect could be used to make Heurtebise and the N_2 Flanker fly, but those were fixed targets upon which the floaters could be applied in great number. Gravity-based weapons that could blast away or even knock over a distant target remained the stuff of science fiction.

But graviton technology still had its uses. The gravitational alteration could pass through the Torwächter's shield. The effect wasn't strong enough to push it over, but the Torwächter stumbled on the small distortion and staggered forward.

Clausewitz spurred her on. 《Again, Hikari!》

"Yes, sir!"

Evangelions and Torwächters were able to stand on the ground. In other words, they were physical objects affected by gravity, and their A.T. Fields and power shields couldn't block the force, either.

The Torwächter tripped on another distortion and lurched forward, just barely regaining its balance.

《Careful! The Torwächter lengthened the sling! The spindle will hit you on the next revolution!》

Hikari's eyes widened. She looked to her left where the jet-black projectile raced toward her.

She swung the positron rifle around and managed to shoot at the last moment, but she missed. The spindle had bounced and changed course, smashing into her rifle. The weapon was instantly destroyed.

The impact jolted through Heurtebise's left shoulder and opened a deep crack in the Eva's armor.

"I can't block it with my power shield?" Hikari asked. The surprise hit even harder than the feedback pain.

In Heurtebise's control plane, Clausewitz's assistant said, "Huh? The spindle pushed right through Heurtebise's shield. We're not just dealing with kinetic force here."

"It's not over yet!" Clausewitz said. "Heurtebise's major organs have taken only minimal damage."

《Heurtebise to Kommandobrücke. Return the dummy plug's control levels to how they were before. I...I can't draw enough power on my own.》

The fear in her voice startled Clausewitz, but now that he thought about it, this was the first time she'd been in a real battle while in full control of her faculties.

"Stay calm. I know you can do this!"

《But, sir!》

"If it'll make you feel better, I'll ready the dummy plug for deep submersion. I'm also working on getting you a replacement for that rifle."

He'd promised to release Hikari from the dummy plug's control, but the dummy plug was still operating—just at a much lower level. Completely shutting off the dummy plug would allow the Q.R. Signum to infiltrate the pilot's psyche, just as the scale had done to Japan's Rei Quatre. The dummy plug was shouldering that burden in Hikari's place.

But Hikari couldn't draw as much power from the scale as she had before—and not just because she'd given one of her two scales to Japan's Super Eva.

Back to the matter at hand, Clausewitz reminded himself.

"Russian railgun howitzer battalion, are you ready?"

The moment he finished speaking, his screen flashed bright white.

The railgun shell struck the Torwächter's shield and created cascading, rainbow-colored electromagnetic smoke clouds.

The transfer of kinetic energy was so terrific that the shell wasn't merely obliterated, it ionized. The black giant's shield held strong, but the impact sent the Torwächter reeling backward. Yet the giant managed to stay on its feet. It counterattacked immediately, smashing the spindle into the side of the well-hidden forty-ton howitzer. The mobile railgun was utterly destroyed.

The camouflaged tank crumpled like a cardboard box, and the 350-meter-long railgun tumbled across the ground, like a thin strip of paper tossed about in the wind. It crashed into a quantum wave mirror truck. The trucks' A.I. system recalculated the formation to compensate for the loss, and the remaining vehicles assembled into the new formation.

Though the gravitational distortions had felled Super Eva on the first attempt, the Torwächter had been tripped up almost ten times now and still stood. But it was easy to calculate how to stabilize—or destabilize—a biped. Medical researchers and roboticists had been performing those calculations for a long time.

Heurtebise and the mirror trucks created another distortion point.

This time, the air pocket burst behind the Torwächter's back, and the black giant staggered forward. The large, circular motions of the giant's hand faltered, and the sling flung the spindle high into the sky, then straight down. The projectile sank deep into the ground, dislodging a chunk of frozen soil larger than an Eva.

《Hikari,》 Clausewitz said, 《can you break through that thing's shield?》

"I can do it!" she replied, not knowing whether or not it was true. But she at least had a chance.

Though she was frightened, she counted on her shield's protection as she propelled her Eva forward. Heurtebise discarded the broken rifle and drew its legside sword. The Torwächter tried to right itself, and she sent another gravitational echo bursting at the back of its leg. The Torwächter went down on one knee. Heurtebise thrust its sword.

CLANG!

At the blade's tip, the two giants' power shields clashed.

Hikari shouted a war cry and pushed the sword forward with all her strength.

She noticed something strange. Her sword's tip was shaking. No...the shield is?

Hikari looked beyond the fiercely flickering light of the shields. There was the Torwächter's chest.

The heart is beating faster.

A rapid-fire *BA-THUMP BA-THUMP BA-THUMP* overlaid a waterfall-like roaring. From the heart, restless lights flickered and wispy smoke rose. Hikari was immediately reminded of a large pot that had begun to boil over.

What's happening to the heart?

Beneath the two giants, the ground burst open, and the spindle flew out. Caught by surprise, Hikari couldn't move out of the way in time. The spindle struck Heurtebise and split its armor open from abdomen to chest.

The air shot from her lungs, her head rocking back. She saw white shards of broken armor scattering. Beyond them, the Torwächter pushed its left palm toward her, and the air distorted.

FWUM!

Heurtebise's giant body was thrown backward.

An invisible wall had struck her. The Torwächter had attacked by pushing its power shield against her.

Oh, I didn't know we could do that...

Toji was a fair distance away but close enough to see what had happened with his own eyes. "Hikari!" he shouted. But then Clausewitz spoke over the shared frequency without encryption.

《Break, break, break! We're firing from the west. Heurtebise, don't move!》

Now came the important question—what happened to the Torwächter's power shield when the black giant was using it as a weapon against Heurtebise?

On patrol west of Novaya Zemlya, the Russian fleet had been waiting for this moment. The fleet-wide FCS synchronized the ships' railguns into three volleys, each separated by only a miniscule delay. The first obliterated any obstructing terrain. The second cleared aside the air and debris. The third passed through the dense air and smashed into the Torwächter with maximum kinetic force.

All that was visible of the first two volleys were the trails of scorched atmosphere left in their wake, but the shells of the third volley converged on a single point and blossomed into a tremendously bright explosion that blotted out everything else.

The shock wave slammed nearby Heurtebise against the ground, pinning the giant there as debris and air particles battered its shield.

Hikari thought she heard voices cry out in awe from all over the island.

Indeed, the artillery soldiers watched through their spotting scopes, the commanders of each squad watched through the main screen, and the crew of the observation planes watched through composite resin windows. All were waving arms and pumping fists in victory.

The battlefield was strewn with debris, white, gray, and black.

But in the center of it all, the smoke cloud dissipated outward, as if something was brushing it aside—and something was. The Torwächter had spread its shield.

The bastard was still alive.

But the sight of what emerged from the smoke left the attackers speechless.

The Torwächter's left arm had been ripped away, and both legs were missing from the thighs down. Yet the giant hadn't fallen. Extending from the ground, the Torwächter's rear plate hoisted the legless giant to its original height.

"Wait," Clausewitz said, flabbergasted. "How is it still moving?"

The Torwächter *was* still moving, albeit slowly. Conveying the one-armed, no-legged giant, the rear plate pushed through the debris as it slid along the ground toward Heurtebise, who was still flat on its back. The black giant looked like a torso strapped onto the bow of a broken ship, like a figurehead.

Nerv Japan's report had theorized that Armaros' rear plate connected through hyperspace to the Victor's rear plate. No more than ten or so present on the island had seen the report, but in that moment, every single one of them was thinking about what they'd read.

With a barely audible *pwssh*, Hikari's plugsuit injected sedative into her body.

From the command plane, Clausewitz called out, 《Hikari, are you all right?!》

"Y-yes...but I used the sedative, and..."

《Don't worry. Just hang on. I'll increase the dummy plug's control. The Q.R. Signum will become more active, which should speed up Heurtebise's regeneration. Just take it easy. We'll pilot you from here.》

The dummy plug had only just begun interfacing and optimizing with the Eva's damaged organ systems. Heurtebise's body was still limp, but the N_2 reactor and the graviton floaters got to work. The weary giant lifted from the ground and started to move...slowly.

The pain in Hikari's chest had begun to subside. Between the sedative and the dummy plug system, her consciousness was growing hazy. But she needed to speak.

"Clausewitz, sir... The heart. The Torwächter's heart is beating faster, and..."

《What is it?》

"It feels dangerous...even though...it's my class rep's—my friend's heart."

The Torwächter continued to slither toward her.

But as its quarry began to fly away beyond its reach, the mangled Torwächter froze, no longer pushed by its back plate, like a child left behind.

Brightly shining particles rained like blood from the Torwächter's gaping wounds. The particles came from the same radiant light that spilled from the higher dimensions with each beat of the Center Trigonus's heart.

"The heartbeat..." Hikari said, "it's..."

The heartbeat's sound had been drowned out by the battle, but now that quiet had fallen again, the Euro and Russian soldiers noticed the black giant's hastened pulse.

BA-THUMP BA-THUMP BA-THUMP.

As glimmering blood gushed from the Torwächter's wounds, the light behind the crack of the Center Trigonus flickered even brighter. Crudely grafted onto the Torwächter's chest, Super Eva's chest cover glowed red with intense heat, searing the black giant's flesh.

Was the heart about to explode, taking the giant with it? That might be cause for celebration if that were the extent of the destruction.

The soldiers felt an instinctive alarm. They were standing in front of a dam about to burst.

"Damn it," Toji said from the cockpit of the hovering N_2 Flanker. He pounded his fist on his cybernetic leg. "I think I understand now."

Super Eva's heartbeat inspired hope in humanity to keep fighting, even when confronted by colossal forces that could easily squash them. The heartbeat signified the will to exist. It was a force that fought, at any expense, to remain on the world's stage even after the curtain had fallen. Armaros feared that heartbeat. He'd stolen the heart in desperation.

"He fears the heart, and so he hates it. He wants humanity to destroy it!"

BA-THUMP BA-THUMP BA-THUMP.

"And as if that wasn't bad enough, when that thing blows, from what Maya-san says, the blast will wipe out this whole island—and beyond. With all these soldiers dead, our will to survive will weaken. What a fine way to teach us a lesson, huh?"

But what could be done? If the soldiers evacuated, and they tried to call down Aten's Hammer instead, the Torwächter might escape, leaving humanity no better off than when this had started. Let up now, and they'd lose their opportunity to destroy the Torwächter.

In the control plane, Clausewitz said, "We just have to keep fighting."

Everyone else was thinking the same thing.

The flow of the Torwächter's glimmering blood slowed, and that was when the soldiers realized there was a second black giant.

Pressed tightly against the back of the propped-up Torwächter, so that their two shapes matched, the second giant reached two arms around the front of the first and soothingly held the raging heart. The heartbeat calmed.

Then the second giant moved out from behind the silhouette of the first and revealed its own rear plate.

"A-alert!" Clausewitz stammered. "All forces, alert! A second Torwächter has appeared! I repeat..."

But Toji was the most surprised. "That's impossible! The other one... Shinji said he'd defeated the other half!"

The Euro and Russian forces began firing at will. Amid the rising smoke, nearly every shot missed. The chaotic barrage obscured the new Torwächter from view. The giant seemed to have deployed its power shield, but the thick smoke, electromagnetic interference, and heat blocked all sensors.

All Toji saw was the very tips of the two giants' rear plates touching together.

"Damn!" he said. Using the military advisor protocol, he cut into the combat radio frequency.

"Nerv Japan observer to all forces. This is an emergency! All units near the Victors—er, the Torwächters—withdraw immediately!"

But the Euro's control plane wasn't hearing any of it.

《What idiot is shouting on this frequency?!》

The cause of Toji's panic was about to become clear to them.

"Kommandobrücke to Heurtebise," Clausewitz's assistant said. "Hikari, can you stand up?"

The giant's white legs were unsteady, but with the help of the graviton floaters, Heurtebise stood. Its chest armor had regenerated but little else.

The damage extended to the Eva's internal organs, though everything that was supposed to be on the inside had at least stayed that way. All that could be done now was to apply pressure with the restraint armor and pray that the wounds would heal faster than the Eva's movements tore them open.

Within the transmission window, Hikari shook her head, as if shaking away the last of the pain from in her skull.

《I think...one of the railgun shells...clipped my wing. The floaters aren't damaged, but...》

Clausewitz watched at the neighboring display. "Frontline units, retreat!" He'd just seen the two Torwächters' rear plates separating. "Front lines, retreat!"

"Is that an order?" the assistant asked.

"Get the hell out of there! Leave your equipment and run!"

He'd reached the same conclusion as Toji.

"The gate is opening!"

The two plates separated. Between them, visible through the smoke, the gateway widened like a blackout curtain, unfolding in midair.

Above, Hikari watched from Heurtebise.

The second Torwächter finished opening the gate and then leaped out from the cloud.

Hikari gasped.

Two long, ponytail-like wings fluttered in the air. A silhouette appeared, bearing dynamic curves that flowed in and out from chest to toe. It was an assertive, feminine form.

"Asuka?" Hikari said. "What are you doing here?"

A black stain had spread from the Victor's plate attached to her back, blotting out much of her signature red color.

"Wh-wh-whaaat?!" Toji sputtered, also taken by surprise.

Just minutes ago, he'd received word that she'd disappeared off the shore of Kanto Bay.

Just what the heck is going on here? he wondered.

But he didn't have time to think about it.

A crowd of white hands emerged from the darkness to clutch at the edges of the gateway. A moment later, seven Type-3 Angel Carriers spilled out from the other side.

CHAPTER 33

T HE BATTLEFIELD was in chaos. The video feeds transmitted to the UN giant-transport plane began to shut off, and the ones that remained provided little useful information. But the U.S. crew didn't need the cameras—their plane could see the operational area with their own super-telephoto lenses.

The crew gasped when they saw the ten giants—nine against one.

Even with the support of the militaries' combined firepower, the fight was ludicrously unbalanced. Was there any point in joining in?

Mari watched Asuka/Eva with rapt attention.

"That woman... She's sublime. Even with all those others mixed in, she shines right through, pure and true."

The girl was seeing something beyond human perception.

But she had no way of showing this to the others, and they heard her words as just another nonsensical and unsettling utterance.

"A woman?" an officer said. "That's not a woman. Nerv Japan calls it Crimson A1. A pilot named Asuka got her data mixed together with her Eva, and that's what came out. Hm? Mari?"

Mari abruptly turned and took off running toward the entry deck, with her bio-tuning robot hurrying after.

"Asuka-chan is cool! Cool, cool, cool!"

Mari had found her reason for existing—and an ideal to seek.

"I want to be you!"

NEON GENESIS
EVANGELIONANIMA

| PART 7 |

NEON GENESIS

DIVERGENT PATHS

EVANGELION: ANIMA

CHAPTER 34

RESOLUTION AND EXECUTION

THICK, BILLOWING SMOKE rose from the smoldering earth of the battle-ravaged arctic island of Novaya Zemlya.

A window to another place stood open. Seven Angel Carriers had arrived from the other side. One group dominated the sky, white wings thundering, while a second group landed on the ground.

Two Victors—or Torwächters, as the Europeans called them—had opened the gate. The first Victor carried Shinji's stolen heart, and had been gravely injured by the Euro and Russian forces and the Euro Eva, Heurtebise. But the Eva had also taken a deep wound.

When the gateway opened, several units on the front line went radio silent.

A tepid, sweetly scented wind blew out from the other side.

Soldiers who'd properly protected themselves with CBRN gear sent panicked reports as they watched their less-prepared comrades transform into pillars of salt—some of whom dutifully radioed in their own disintegration during their last seconds of life.

Heurtebise's control airplane closed off all external air intakes. From the comms station, a radio operator said, "Kommandobrücke to all mirror trucks, check that your personal equipment is airtight, pressurize your cabins, and switch to interior air recirculation!"

Despite being badly shaken by these events—or perhaps *because* they were shaken—the operators carried out their duties by the book, and they disseminated the instructions that had been prepared for this eventuality.

Good, Lieutenant Colonel Clausewitz thought as he watched his crew.

"Hikari," Clausewitz said into his headset, "you'd better arm yourself with Dora while you have a moment." He paused. "Hikari?"

A message came in from the joint forces headquarters by way of the Sixth Army command center. They'd lost contact with three artillery units near the Torwächters. The joint commanders wanted to know if Heurtebise could buy any time for rescue efforts to be staged.

Clausewitz plucked the headset from his assistant, who, to his credit, remained resolute despite the chaos.

Speaking into the microphone, the lieutenant colonel minced no words. "Sorry, sir. Everyone in those units has been turned into a pillar of salt."

Several members of the observation team had also ceased transmitting vital signs.

The team had been installing sensors across the battlefield when the shooting started, and they'd taken refuge under the closest shelter. A nearby sensor was now reporting the presence of sodium chloride, equal to the mass of several human bodies. A saw-toothed line on the graph captured the moment of their deaths.

Clausewitz could apologize to the dead later.

He tossed the headset back to his assistant. "Something's wrong with Hikari."

"Is she not responding? I'm not seeing any abnormal readings—or at least, not any more than you'd expect from those injuries. The regeneration is proceeding well, and—"

Before his assistant could finish, Clausewitz adjusted the microphone on his own headset and spoke loudly and slowly.

"Ritter! Schaft! Hikari! Get Dora! The eighty-centimeter armor-piercing cannon! We can't bring it to you—the cannon weighs 550 tons, and we don't have anything that can move it on this terrain!"

This time, Hikari replied, but her voice was trembling. 《Y-yes, commander. Heurtebise...acknowledged. I'll go... I'll go get Dora.》

"What's wrong, Hikari?"

A pause. She was considering whether to answer.

《The second Torwächter... The one who came to open the gate. It's... She's my friend. And the Eva beneath that plate is Heurtebise's sister.》

"Are you telling me that's Asuka Langley and the first production model Evangelion, Eva-02?!"

An operator from central command came on the line. 《The outer territory observation UAV squadron is launching.》

At timed intervals, small scouting drones began taking off from just beyond the outer ring of the battlefield. They were light gray and resembled miniature fighter planes.

"Are you sure it's her, Hikari?" Clausewitz asked.

《I...》 she began weakly. But then her voice rose into a loud, tearful cry. 《I wouldn't mistake her anywhere!》

Startled by the noise, the staff at the nearby stations looked up in surprise.

Acting in parallel with the main combat operations, the plan was to fly the squadron of scout drones into the open window to determine the location on the other side. The gateway had previously shown glimpses of a glasswork cubic structure—the Ark. These reports had been corroborated by spies on the ground in the Hakone Caldera. Now that Armaros had moved the Ark from North Africa's Atlas Mountains, the Europeans hoped to learn its new location.

By this time, Nerv Japan had passed word on to the Europeans that the Ark didn't offer salvation, but rather was a high-density repository for the information of all life, so that the Instrumentality Project could be more quickly rebooted after each failed attempt. But the European military had been searching for the Ark in the Mount Ararat region because of the area's connections to religious stories, and they weren't convinced that what Nerv Japan had found was, in fact, the same Ark they sought.

Europe's religious constituencies contained a great many people who looked to the Ark for salvation.

But even if Nerv Japan was right, Armaros had specifically moved the Ark to keep its location hidden from humanity. Whatever else Armaros was, he was the enemy, and the Ark was important to him. All the more reason to seek it out.

No one knew how many more lives would be lost on the battlefield this day.

Because of this, humanity needed to start focusing on the next step.

The ground forces launched an attack to draw the enemies' attention away from the scout drones. The Angel Carriers had spread out, with their backs to the gateway, and the swarm of bullets struck their A.T. Field-like power shields and disintegrated.

Over the radio, Hikari muttered, ⟪It's all so strange. Heurtebise isn't asking me to rescue Asuka. Asuka is acting of her own free will. She's not being compelled.⟫

"Hikari," Clausewitz repeated, "get Dora. And stay at range. We need you to figure out which Angel larvae those carriers are hiding!"

Hikari usually had no trouble focusing on her tasks, but now that the dummy plug had taken greater control, her consciousness was melding into the Eva. She was gaining new, extraordinary senses, and she was beginning to act in previously inconceivable ways.

"You need to keep your head in the fight, or you'll get yourself killed. There's too many of them!"

"Understood," she said, but she was clearly more concerned about Asuka/Eva turning out to be the Torwächter who'd opened the gateway than she was about the seven approaching Angel Carriers.

The attacks of Heurtebise and the Russian naval railguns had fatally injured the first Torwächter, reducing it to a torso, a head, and one arm—the same arm that had been swinging the spindle-shaped weapon. The giant had turned into a grotesque statue, propped up only by the black plate that grew out of its back, no longer contributing to the battle except as a raggedy scarecrow, while Super Eva's heart raged out of control. But the second Torwächter—Asuka/Eva—had come over and calmed the heart. Rather than self-destruct, the broken Torwächter had begun rapidly reconstructing its missing limbs.

A volley of guided munitions sailed toward the wounded Torwächter, but Asuka/Eva neutralized them with her A.T. Field. Though partially concealed by explosive flashes and billows of smoke, the Torwächter's recovery seemed to progress differently from the way Evas or even Angel Carriers regenerated. The giant's black armor was reassembling, as if guided by unseen hands, but only the Torwächter's external layer was being reconstructed, not the body underneath.

In the control plane, the observers from the science teams turned to each other in confusion. "Where's the Torwächter's Q.R. Signum?" one asked.

Previously, the Torwächters had arrived, opened a gateway, and then quickly departed. The location of their Q.R. Signum scale—or scales—remained unknown. The working assumption was that the black-and-red scale must have been hidden somewhere internally. But now, a gatekeeper's body had been shredded apart in plain sight, and there was no sign of a Q.R. Signum inside.

The resident theoretical physicists' minds raced. *Supposing the Torwächters don't possess any Q.R. Signum scales at all, what does that mean?*

Rather than being merely linked to Armaros, are the Torwächters his shadows?

The ground rumbled.

The Angel Carriers on land planted their feet firmly, and the ones hovering in the air descended to a few meters above the ground. In time with the Torwächter's heartbeat, they began slamming the butts of their staves on the ground.

Each strike shook the earth. Even amid the explosions and gunfire, the rhythmic rumble announced the heartbeat—and their presence—far and wide.

So far, the battle had been a messy free-for-all. The ten giants seemed to move with no apparent order, and the soldiers fired their cannons and missile launchers at will. But when the seven carriers began striking the earth in unison, the armies from each nation could sense something bad was coming, and their chaotic barrage temporarily subsided.

The armies shifted from offense to defense while new orders filtered down from their commanders.

During the lull, the joint command officers took a moment to assign each Angel Carrier a number from one to seven. Any allied forces with electronic sensors and line of sight—from fire control teams stationed around the edge of the battlefield, to warships, to Heurtebise's control plane—shared their information with the rest of the military, and each carrier, along with its number, appeared in real time on the strategic map.

The fundamental strategy employed when eradicating Angel-class enemies—whether they appeared alone or in groups—was to focus as much firepower as possible on one target at a time. In practice simulations, this seemed to be the best approach. However, in a real battle, with this many targets, while the military evaluated the effectiveness of a given attack, the other carriers might already be striking back. To allow for better response time, the attacking forces were split into groups that would attack in a predetermined order. When assigned a target, the groups would focus on that target, regardless of what the enemy was doing, while groups without a target would be free to defend themselves against whatever was attacking them.

"If you identify an Angel Carrier carrying Zeruel in its cocoon, take that carrier out," Clausewitz ordered, "even if you're under attack from the other carriers."

The Angel Zeruel was capable of firing long-range attacks in quick succession. The human forces relied on striking their enemies from superior range, so an Angel that followed the same tactic posed the greatest threat. As long as the military didn't need to defend a specific point, they could fight the other Angels on the run.

CHAPTER 35

THEIR OWN REASONS

REQUESTS FOR INFORMATION flooded Nerv Japan's comms channels. It was, after all, their Eva-02—now the Asuka/Eva synthesis—who'd appeared as the second Torwächter, which Nerv Japan had also previously claimed to have destroyed. A careful response was required. Send the wrong message, and Nerv Japan might be deemed an enemy of humanity.

Toji was hard-pressed to respond to the cross-examinations coming from every nation whose military was present on Novaya Zemlya, and the major question fell on Commander Misato in far-off Hakone. That question being—if Asuka/Eva was taking hostile actions, should she be regarded as an enemy and destroyed? Since Misato was responsible for the entire organization, duty required her to answer *yes*.

With that in mind, she asked Toji, 《Can you lead Asuka outside the battle zone?》

The question, asked without hesitation, came as a relief. Misato wasn't simply giving up on Asuka. But that didn't change the situation.

"Honestly," he said, "I think it'll be tough."

Toji surveyed the battlefield through his head-mounted display.

"Soryu has attached herself to the Victor—I mean, the Torwächter—and I don't know why."

En route to Hakone from Kanto Bay, but listening in on the call, Maya offered her guess. 《It might be because of Super Eva's heart. Ever since she came back, Asuka has had trouble understanding surface-level concepts, like words and physical appearances, but I think she's perceiving things on a different level.》

"What do you mean?" Toji asked.

《She thinks the other Torwächter is Shinji-kun.》

With Heurtebise's hand, Hikari pulled the camouflage tarp off of the massive cannon lying sideways in the trench and bent to pick it up.

I want to be you.

"What was that?"

She sensed someone else was focusing their attention on Asuka, and she turned around to look.

A gray blur plummeted to the earth. The ground shattered, and chunks of rock flew outward, the shock wave scattering the surrounding dirt and debris. The enormous, falling object rebounded onto the shield of a low-flying Angel Carrier, and both slammed into the ground.

As white feathers scattered and fluttered down, a giant figure—something between a human and a four-legged beast—raked its claws against the carrier's shield, sending sparks flashing along the surface.

The U.S. Evangelion, Wolfpack, had entered the battle unannounced.

Mari had ignored her commanding officers' protests and ejected her Eva from the UN giant-transport plane. Right now, the U.S. crew were likely having a very bad day as they hastily exchanged friend-or-foe identification codes with the Euro and Russian forces.

A chain-like object flew out from the Angel Carrier's cocoon and launched toward the U.S. Eva's head. The chain was shaped like a double helix. It had to be the Angel Armisael. The U.S. Eva lifted its head out of the way of the first attack and stopped the second by biting down on the Angel with fanged jaws, stopping the whiplashing double helix dead in its tracks.

"Eliminator Torus!" Mari shouted. "Engage!"

Four conical structures were mounted on the U.S. Eva's back. One began to rotate, smoothly accelerating faster and faster.

The four cones contained American-developed super-directional N_2 explosive charges. The high-velocity spin caused a more compact N_2 reaction along the core and the outer ring, which then produced a secondary reaction in the middle. The result was a hyper-directional N_2 explosive, created within the barrel of the cannon that fired it.

《Mari!》 an officer transmitted from the giant-transport plane. 《Don't waste those! You only have four. And you're too close!》

"Bang," Mari said.

Once the core of the N_2 explosive had been compressed into the density of a micro black hole, the charge launched from the cannon and struck the Angel Carrier's tough power shield like a rock tossed into a pool of water. Small droplets of the shield splashed outward, and the N_2 charge sank straight through. The reaction on the other side was massive. A tremendous explosion completely obliterated the carrier's right-hand Q.R. Signum, shoulder and all, and even tore a hole in the shield of a second Angel Carrier behind it.

Before the second carrier's shield could close back up again, another explosion sounded. This one carried the classic, booming roar of cannon fire, though it, too, was terrifically loud. Crouching down, Heurtebise had shot its cannon from the hip. The weapon was too heavy to lift any higher.

The eighty-centimeter caliber shell zoomed forward, absurdly large even after discarding its rifled sabot, streaking past the first Angel Carrier and into the open tear of the second's shield.

The resulting reaction, however, wasn't an N_2 explosion like the others but rather a phase explosion. The soldiers on the ground looked up with awe at the cross-shaped jets of flame.

Backdropped by the flames and still clutching the Angel Armisael's double helix in its maw, the U.S. Eva realized, on some level, that even its mighty jaws couldn't physically snap the Angel in two. So it gave up trying and instead looped the helix around the carrier's remaining Q.R. Signum scale, yanking the Angel to the ground. Too strong for its own good, the helix crushed the scale. The Eva kept pulling, dragging the Angel out from its cocoon. The larva couldn't support its life on its own. It crumbled to dust before it ever had the chance to infect the Eva.

The second Angel Carrier was badly damaged, but it still moved. A mobile railgun howitzer roared, landing the killing blow.

The crew of Heurtebise's control plane cheered.

"Amazing!" Clausewitz's assistant said. "Those carriers didn't stand a chance!"

"That was only the first two," the lieutenant colonel replied. "As for the reckless Eva on four legs—is that the American one? Why do they call it Wolfpack if there's only one?"

"What if there *is* more than one?"

Heurtebise had immediately supported the U.S. Eva in battle because Hikari's psyche had spread into the Euro Eva-02. She'd sensed the U.S. pilot's peculiar focus on Asuka.

Unconsciously, Hikari decoded the U.S. Eva's control signal and cut into her communications.

"What do you mean, you want to be Asuka?" she asked. "You're coming on a little intense. You look like if you don't slow down, you just might eat her."

《Oh, really?》 the U.S. pilot replied.

"Your voice... You're a girl?"

《Eat her, huh? I hadn't thought of that. You must be smart.》

"You're kidding, right?" Hikari said.

But she felt many pairs of beast-like eyes staring at her. Their consciousnesses overlapped with the girl's.

They're...a pack?

Though different in scale and degree, their presence reminded Hikari of that night in North Africa, when Asuka had been lost within a vast sea of organisms.

"You can't be here," Hikari was saying, but she hadn't meant to. She hadn't even thought it.

What?

Someone else is watching. Someone far bigger than this girl.

Hikari felt as if a tremendous weight was pressing on her back, compelling her to speak the words.

"You must not be here."

As soon as the words stopped, Hikari blurted out as quickly as she could, "Kommandobrücke! Lieutenant Colonel Clausewitz! I feel a strange presence."

《What is it?》 Clausewitz asked.

"I think it's another message." She began to breathe heavily. "You who should not be... The human form must not... The form of... To give the form of... To degenerate into the lower forms of life... Your sins are heavy."

《Another message from the black giant?! Hold on.》 There was muffled conversation in the background. 《We're monitoring the message from responsive subjects back home. You don't need to concern yourself. Leave everything to the dummy plug.》

In Nerv Japan, the Ayanamis had previously spoken as Armaros' voice. The dummy plug wasn't robbing Hikari of her consciousness to the extent the clones had experienced, but Armaros' powerful thoughts came out through her lips and words just the same.

"Withdraw...stray wolf. The song of Instrumentality cannot be woven into those who have degenerated into beasts. Know this—your soul will bear the scar and will not be reborn into the next world."

Every remaining Angel Carrier stared at Wolfpack.

The soldiers stopped their attacks as they tried to figure out why the Angel Carriers had gone still. But then, in the next moment, the five white giants rushed the U.S. Eva at once.

Mari was unmoved by Armaros' message. "So what?" she muttered. "Who cares about tomorrow. I see what I want to be. And you're all that stands between me and her."

Moving not by calculation, but by instinct, and not heeding the warnings from her control plane, she launched her second Eliminator at the nearest target.

"That's all that matters."

NEON GENESIS
EVANGELION ANIMA

CHAPTER 36

STRAY CHILDREN

MISATO'S VOICE came over Toji's headset.

《Toji—I mean, Acting Deputy Commander Suzu-hara—I have bad news. We no longer have an ETA for Rei Six at Novaya Zemlya.》

"No one was able to find Momo, I take it?"

JSSDF Lieutenant Colonel Kasuga had left his golden retrievers, Azuchi and Momo, in Little Rei Six's care. But Momo had gone missing, and as a result, Eva-00 Type-F Allegorica's launch had been delayed, despite the engineers' rush to get the flight configuration ready on time.

A missing dog hardly justified not leaving for the mission, but even though Six had the knowledge of a seventeen-year-old, her body—and more importantly, the structure of her brain—was only that of an eight-year-old. Her priorities were different from anyone else's. With her dog missing, she couldn't concentrate on anything. And getting angry with her or yelling at her wouldn't do any good.

《No, we didn't find Momo. Thankfully, she came to the

decision for herself. She gave up looking, and we sent her out on a suborbital flight path.》

Then what's the problem?

"That's a simple parabolic trajectory," Toji said. "Whatever else happens, what goes up has to come back down. Right?"

Hyuga answered. 《Her graviton floaters kept accelerating after she reached the proper trajectory. And with all the electromagnetic interference, we can't measure how long they've been like that. Actually, we can't get any signals to bounce back at all. I don't know if maybe her Eva got turned the wrong way and the receiver... Oh, damn it! It's another message from Armaros. Why'd he have to send it *now*?》

"What?"

So, Six must have lost consciousness.

Whenever Armaros sent his messages, Six lost consciousness and acted as his speaker. The last time Toji witnessed this was when Super Eva had flown for the first time. Her eyes lost their focus, and she became unresponsive to any stimuli, acting like an automaton that could only construct faltering speech. After some time passed, she regained consciousness. Would she awaken this time, or would she stay under?

"What about the autopilot program—" Toji began, but he cut himself off.

It would already be available, of course. But whether or not the Eva would use it—or use it properly—was another question. Evangelions were highly capable weapons but not always the most reliable at following procedure.

So, what, she's going to be lost in space?!

"Can't anything go right?"

His frustration and anger sent conflicting signals into Toji's cybernetics. His left arm trembled and creaked.

Rei Quatre had gone rogue, Hikari's sister—Kodama—had transformed into a pillar of salt, Rei Cinq had died between the Earth and the moon, and Shinji and Trois were missing. The ground under Tokyo-3 had sunk, stranding Hakone Caldera, and Asuka had come home completely changed…as an enemy. Would Rei Six be next?

It had been one loss after another.

Can't anything good happen in this world anymore?

Seeming to read Toji's mood, Misato tried to sound optimistic.

《We still have hope. We don't have any usable satellites in orbit, and our terrestrial omnidirectional signals can't reach beyond the electromagnetic disturbance in the atmosphere. But get the stratospheric airplane network to turn their antennas upward, and we'll broadcast signals to try to activate her plugsuit's stimulant and AED systems.》

If the Earth and the moon hadn't gotten all screwy, it wouldn't be any trouble to figure out what the hell is going on out in orbit. But they did, and it is. Misato-san is just putting on a happy face for me.

Toji removed his helmet's face mask and head-mounted display and slapped himself hard on the cheek.

So, what, you're going to make her worry about you now? Doesn't she have enough to do without babysitting you? You get pissed because you're seventeen and everyone still talks to you like you're a child? Well, this is why! Even if you're just an "acting" deputy commander, you're still part of the command team—so do your job, Toji!

《What was that noise? Did you hit a bird?》

"It was nothing."

That's right, it is nothing. Six won't let herself get killed this easily.

Without warning, the Flanker's nose and the plating on the left side of its cockpit were shredded apart like a paper balloon.

Oh, crap!

Super high-speed munitions rarely ricocheted. When they struck their target at a shallow angle, the fast-moving projectiles tended to turn inward. But sometimes—this time—it happened. One railgun slug had happened not to disintegrate or ionize on contact with an Angel Carrier's shield and had ricocheted toward Toji's airplane. Even after the N_2 Flanker's gravity field had sapped the majority of the slug's momentum, the projectile had split apart and pierced through the Flanker's airframe.

The stray railgun slug had damaged the N_2 Flanker's nose and the floaters on the port side of the cockpit. The plane tilted and, unable to recover, went into a spin.

"Toji!" Hikari shouted from Heurtebise. She'd flagged his Flanker on her display and had been keeping track of him. She noticed his airplane's distress immediately.

The Flanker kept spiraling down, but Hikari saw no sign that Toji had ejected. Then the plane disappeared behind the smoke clouds.

Hikari let go of her cannon.

The air warped around Heurtebise as the Eva grabbed the cross-shaped spear in front of it, dislodging the weapon from the ground. Hikari roared as she charged the nearest enemy.

The quantum wave mirror trucks couldn't keep up with her. The crew in her control plane frantically called out to her to make her stop, but she ignored their commands.

The 550-ton, eighty-centimeter caliber cannon slammed breach-first into the ground. The impact detonated the loaded charge, and the eight-ton shell flew out from the barrel at a low angle.

The shell zoomed past the sprinting Heurtebise and struck the shield of an Angel Carrier, whose larval Shamshel was reaching out from its cocoon with two tentacle-like appendages. The shell failed to penetrate the shield but sent the carrier flying backward.

Hikari saw a small crack in the Angel Carrier's shield, and she thrust the spear deep into the cocoon, vaulted over the carrier, and kept running into the smoke cloud.

The carrier hadn't died, but the U.S. Eva was about to have a turn. As the carrier tried to get back to its feet, Wolfpack crushed the giant's head with its powerful forelegs and then smashed both Q.R. Signum scales. The Angel Carriers had surrounded Wolfpack, but when Heurtebise took one down, the U.S. Eva seized the opportunity to break free.

Mari didn't understand why Wolfpack had suddenly become so much stronger than before, but she didn't care. It was only fair, considering the other side had two Torwächters—one of which was the Asuka/Eva synthesis Mari wanted to meet. Asuka/Eva embodied the perfect synthesis of numerous creatures, and Mari wanted that for herself—even if it meant, as Hikari had said, eating her.

The U.S. Eva ran into the thick smoke cloud after Heurtebise. Behind her, the fallen Angel Carrier was still writhing on the ground, but the nearby howitzers spat fire, turning the enemy into chunks of meat.

But striking out on their own inside the cloud, the two Evas wouldn't have any more support from the cannons.

Heurtebise ran through the smoke. The clouds were too thick for her sensors to penetrate. Just before she made it out the other side, a spear-like object pierced her right-side wings at her waist. She kept running. Overhead, her shield repelled a corrosive liquid, and she pulled the spear-like object from the ground by sheer force.

The object turned out not to be a spear but a long leg that extended above Heurtebise's head, where the four-legged larval Angel Matarael had lifted its own carrier. Catching up, Wolfpack leaped onto the Angel Carrier and knocked it down.

An intensely bright, long-range attack zoomed through the smoke and struck Matarael's body. Luckily, the attack narrowly missed Hikari and Mari—but something was out there, waiting for them. Hikari recognized the Angel's attack from a report she'd read, and she wasn't surprised when two long, thin, razor-like ribbons snaked out and sliced through Matarael's remains. A carrier bearing Zeruel's larva was somewhere within the hanging smoke.

But where?

Toji felt an impact but not a fatal one.

Had his plane miraculously come down for a soft landing? He couldn't see outside to tell what had happened.

His injuries announced themselves slowly.

The cockpit was surrounded by a box of armor plating sometimes called the "bathtub." But the bathtub had been bent, and the metal pressed Toji into his seat, pinning him there. The twisted frame had completely crushed his cybernetic left arm. If he'd reflexively triggered the ejection seat before the crash, he might have been even worse off.

"Ow, ow, ow... I'm glad it wasn't my right arm, but an artificial one can still hurt like hell."

The liquid-crystal polycarbonate canopy was warped, and its clear surface had turned completely cloudy and white. When Toji tried to lift it, sharp pains shot through his chest and stomach, and he couldn't put enough force behind the action. The canopy didn't budge. But someone outside must have heard him making noise because the canopy peeled open like the lid of a tin can, and Toji could see outside once more.

Long, beautiful hair flowed above him. Between the pressure on his body and the sharp pain, Toji's thoughts were a little hazy. The hair reminded him of when he was young boy, gazing up at the giant, carp-shaped windsocks in the field by his elementary school. Their bamboo poles, thicker than his own legs, had swayed and creaked, and as the carp banners danced about, his eyes caught flashes of sunlight between them.

"Oh, Soryu, did you catch me? Thanks."

Holding the plane level, Asuka/Eva turned it back and forth. Was she looking to see where it was broken?

"Ouch. Ah, darn it. Don't bother. This plane wouldn't fly even if you threw it. So, do you want to tell me why you're with the enemy?"

Toji couldn't tell, but he thought Asuka/Eva was looking at him with worry.

"Didn't you know?"

The sounds of a vicious battle continued around them. There were flashes of lights, shock waves, falling debris, but all that felt distant now. Amid the turmoil, Asuka/Eva stood tall and graceful.

As Toji wheezed for air, he thought he understood the nature of her behavior. Even with the black plate attached to her back, she wasn't part of the enemy's faction but remained her own self with her own perceptions and cognizance. Had she *chosen* to put the plate on?

"Look, Soryu," Toji said, "ever since you became one of the big fish, I know it's been hard for you to see the little things. But even though Shinji's heart is beating inside that Victor's chest—that doesn't make the Victor Shinji."

Toji was still by no means safe, but for whatever reason, he didn't feel tense anymore. He could feel his body begging to black out.

I guess all we've been doing is nagging you about the little things. Probably makes it hard to listen. Probably...

Heurtebise came attacking out of nowhere. Asuka/Eva seemed startled but put up her A.T. Field just in time to deflect the spear.

"Asuka!" Hikari shouted with rage. She'd seen Asuka/Eva holding the broken N_2 Flanker and had immediately flown into a blind fury.

"Let Toji go right now!" she shouted.

Far behind her, Zeruel's long-ranged attacks continued to thunder. Maybe Mari was having a harder time finishing off the Zeruel carrier.

Asuka stood in front of Hikari. Beyond her, deep in the smoke clouds, Super Eva's heart was beating. The Torwächter was still out there, and Asuka was protecting it. The other conventional forces were surely firing upon the injured giant, but judging from the steady heartbeat, their attacks were having no effect. Maybe the Torwächter had repaired itself enough to redeploy its power shield.

Hikari glared at her good friend through Heurtebise's eyes.

Asuka/Eva shrank back, gingerly offering the broken plane.

"Let him go!" Hikari shouted again.

Startled into submission, Asuka/Eva gently placed the N_2 Flanker on the ground. Then she said, "Ah..."

It was the first time she'd spoken since taking this form.

"Ah," she pleaded. "Ah..."

Ah. A. The first sound born in every language—and the prideful girl's first initial.

A, for Asuka.

"Stay away from me!" Hikari yelled.

Having been rejected by her friend, Asuka backed away into the smoke and disappeared.

Hikari was breathing heavily. She knew she wasn't being sensible.

But all she could think of now was Toji. She just didn't have any worry to spare for Asuka. And the moment Heurtebise had swung its weapon at Asuka/Eva, Hikari had felt her body become heavy. She could still hardly move at all.

She felt like Asuka's mother was accusing her of bullying her daughter.

Heurtebise had been born alongside Eva-02. That is to say, the two units were created together, but only one had *become* Eva-02. Heurtebise had been discarded. Though no one would believe Hikari if she'd said it, she sensed the soul of Asuka's mother dwelling inside Heurtebise, just as it dwelled within Eva-02. Though, in Heurtebise's case, what Hikari sensed might only have been a lingering trace.

Heurtebise was moving again. The Eva knelt and lifted up the N_2 Flanker.

Oh, that's a relief. Toji's vital signs are still all right.

"I'm sorry, Heurtebise," Hikari said.

She'd betrayed her Eva's trust. The presence within Heurtebise might never lend Hikari her strength as it had before.

"I'm sorry, Asuka."

NEON GENESIS
EVANGELION ANIMA

CHAPTER 37

DEADLOCKED

I'LL SEE IF COMMAND will give the go-ahead for a regroup," Clausewitz said with a sour expression.

He was responsible for failing to manage Hikari. But assigning blame wouldn't change anything now. The only option was to break off and regroup. Neither side in this fight could currently hold a battle line.

A great, unpredictable—and unpredicted—battle had erupted within the basin. Now, on its northern side, a change came, small at first.

A sharp, flat piece of metal, not unlike a sword blade, poked out from the ground and began to slide around, like a submarine's periscope gliding across the surface of the ocean.

The blade grew taller, grazing an armored truck and plowing through a barricade of stacked forty-foot containers. It kept moving toward the center of the deadlocked battlefield.

The soldiers nearby could do nothing but watch. The sword glided right past them. They *felt* the blade's vibration on their skin—a strong, unsettling growl—and they knew, instinctively, not to touch it.

Radioing in to the control plane, an officer shouted, 《Some kind of sharp, blade-looking thing appeared on the north side of the Frying Pan and is sliding across the ground at high speed toward the center of the battlefield. Can you confirm what it is?》

Clausewitz didn't know. But a squadron of U.K. observation planes, loitering beyond the northern edge of the basin, performed a scan of all objects on that side of the battlefield. After filtering out the soldiers, stationary weapons, combat vehicles, and transport vehicles—and anything else that either gave an IFF response or was registered in the database—the field of dots were reduced to a single unknown.

"What is that?" Clausewitz asked as he stared at the camera feed.

An...arm?

An arm, holding a sword aloft, had appeared out of the ground.

The hand flipped the sword around, so that the tip pointed straight down, and then stabbed it into the earth with a *wham*.

The arm's muscles bulged, and its forward momentum halted. Using the sword as a handhold, Super Eva hoisted himself out of the ground and leaped onto the battlefield.

The giant opened his mouth and let out a fearsome roar, shaking the very air. His message was clear to everyone present.

Give me back my heart!

After traveling to another planet, and drifting through the extradimensional corridors, Super Eva's own stolen heartbeat had led him here, back home to his turbulent planet.

But just as he arrived, his heart was leaving.

Abandoning the Angel Carriers, the wounded Torwächter accompanied the spurned Asuka/Eva back into the tunnels. Shinji and Trois had come too late.

"Where are we?" Shinji asked. "And what the hell is going on?"

A loud explosion rang out, the impact rippling through his body. His head spun.

Having suddenly emerged onto a battlefield on an island at the edge of the Arctic Ocean, Super Eva took a fierce volley of friendly fire. He brandished his twin swords, Kesara and Basara, and Ayanami Trois, riding inside with Shinji, deployed the Eva's shield. Blindingly bright bursts immediately covered the shield's surface. Returning to Earth in an unfamiliar location would have been disorienting on its own, but appearing amid a massive battle was bewildering. For Shinji, the experience was a lot like vertigo.

After about thirty seconds, the friendly fire temporarily stopped. Shinji was trying to regain his balance when two razor-like ribbons shot toward him through the smoke. At that last moment, he raised his swords to block them. Sparks flew. He'd managed to guard himself, but the force of the impact pushed Super Eva's more-than-four-thousand-ton mass nearly two hundred meters backward. Then Zeruel's ribbons were gone, retracted back into the smoke cloud.

An Angel?!

Shinji shouted to Rei Trois behind him. "Is there an Angel Carrier here?"

He was hoping she could sense what was out there, but she didn't reply.

He looked over his shoulder. Ayanami's eyes were unfocused. She was fighting against something trying to steal her consciousness. Her fingers dug into Shinji's shoulder.

"Trois?"

"Wait, I'm getting something. A message...from the heart's owner? No, from the heart itself? My name is..."

Trois received the Torwächter's message just as the giants disappeared into the gateway.

"My name...is Shinji."

CHAPTER 38

OJI AWOKE in what seemed to be a quite well-equipped ICU room. *No, wait. I recognize this layout. This place is the same size as the standard modular barracks units.* Between the curtains to his side, he saw a row of operating tables.

A field hospital.

As he turned his head to look around, he saw Cyrillic letters.

"This can't be good."

He tried to scratch his head, but his left hand was oddly heavy.

The bedsheet fell from his arm, and his eyes went wide. His breath caught in his chest. What he saw wasn't his cybernetic arm but a terribly pale, emaciated flesh-and-blood arm fastened to his shoulder.

"What the hell is this?!"

A man's voice answered from the other side of the curtain.

"Don't you recognize it? That's your arm, Toji. We grew it for you three years ago but gave up on reattaching it after what happened. They didn't have any spare cybernetics here for you."

Through the curtains came...

"Kensuke," Toji said.

"We didn't reattach your limbs back then because of the whole 'once Toji's body becomes whole again the Angel Bardiel will reawaken and kill us all' thing. I bet you thought your arm and leg were still somewhere in the medical research lab in HQ, providing very valuable data on the efficacy of preservatives."

"What are *you* doing here?"

"Anyway, that's why we haven't reattached your leg. I've got that baby right here." Kensuke patted a cylindrical container on the bedside table. The faint hum of a circulation system emanated from within. "And just so we're clear, I didn't steal your limbs or anything. We just took them back." He cleared his throat. "We'd shipped them off to Nerv Germany as part of a trade. We got details on their synchro-equalizer tech, and they got a living sample of Angel infection to study. The security intelligence department's technology division has been making these kinds of backroom deals for the science department since before I joined them."

"I never heard about any of that." Toji sighed. "I can't figure you out anymore."

"I'm only doing what's logical," Kensuke replied.

"How have you changed so much? You didn't used to be so... clandestine."

Kensuke offered a wry grin and shrugged, as if he'd been expecting this reaction.

"That's exactly it, Toji. Am I the only one who's never allowed to change? I got tired of you and Ikari going ahead without me while I played the comic relief. If I couldn't follow the same road as you, and I was miserable where I was, why not find a different path? Is that so wrong?" Kensuke shook his head. "Anyway, don't make me get into it now. I'd almost forgotten how lousy I used to feel."

Kensuke picked up a water bottle and twisted the cap off. "I'll admit, I go too far sometimes, but I'll make things right. I know I really did something bad to Hikari."

Kensuke's team had, without permission, handed Hikari's family over to Germany. Toji had every right to be furious. The past version of him would've punched Kensuke at least once by now.

Instead, Toji said, "Your right arm... Is that working for you?"

Kensuke's arm had been turned into salt near the Ark in North Africa. His replacement was a basic robotic version—the kind typically donated to war-torn countries. The technology was limited so that local facilities could handle the installation and repair.

"It's definitely a step down from the one you had," Kensuke replied. "You almost walked out of here with one of these, you know."

Kensuke exited through the curtains. As he left, he stuck out his stiffly moving right hand and formed the rock-paper-scissors gestures. And then he was gone.

PART 8

NEON GENESIS

THE EXTENT OF THE SELF

EVANGELION: ANIMA

NEON GENESIS EVANGELION ANIMA

CHAPTER 39

▶ GIANTS, HUMANS, AND BEASTS

T HE UNEXPECTED WITHDRAWAL of the Victors only
made the battle more confusing.

Shinji tried to break away, but as soon as Super Eva took to
the sky, the Euro forces misidentified him as a Victor-class threat
and knocked him back down to the ground with an explosive
barrage.

"Gah!" Shinji groaned inside the entry plug.

Trois was still sitting behind him in the plug seat. She
explained what she'd figured out.

"I managed to pick up a time code from a radio transmitter.
The signal is weak, but we're somewhere in Moscow Time. High
latitude. Near the Arctic Ocean."

From the moment he'd arrived, Super Eva had been transmitting his unique, internationally registered signature code, which
identified the giant as Nerv Japan's Eva-01. Even if Super Eva
wasn't registered in the IFF databases of these armies, each country's strategic AI should have figured out who he was and flagged
him green. But the computer systems must have been confused,

too, and the friendly fire ebbed and flowed. This last volley had been particularly intense.

The biggest reason for Shinji and Trois' predicament had come directly before their arrival, when Asuka/Eva appeared with a black plate on her back and rescued the first Torwächter from certain destruction. The Russian and European militaries' trust in Nerv Japan had plummeted, not that the pair inside Super Eva had any way of knowing.

Currently, the allied soldiers considered Super Eva another of the black giant's underlings. Recognizing that he was in danger—though not why—Super Eva hid in the thick vapors that blanketed the battlefield.

The ground had been cratered and scorched. White and gray smoke rose from the smoldering earth, and black, electromagnetic clouds flashed with lightning, blocking all sensors from seeing anything within.

The clouds would likely offer little shelter from the Angel Carrier that had attacked him, but at least the bombardment from his fellow humans would ease. Their weapons weren't as effective as the Angels', but they still hurt like hell.

CHAPTER 40

THE WOLVES

"**I** SENSE ANIMALS," Rei Trois said. "A pack of animals, running around."

"Really? Where?" Shinji expanded Super Eva's eyesight far beyond the visual spectrum, and the black smoke appeared bright with heat. Something leaped out. It wasn't a pack of animals but one Eva-sized beast.

"Wh-what is that thing?!"

Shinji raised his swords to guard himself, but Kesara pulled on his arm and swung at the beast-like giant.

"Wha?"

Rei Trois was accessing the Q.R. Signum scale, Super Eva's current power source. Though she touched Armaros' scale only with her mind, she felt the repulsive black hands physically reaching out from the scale and through her chest to grip the swords with Super Eva's fingers.

The right arm swung Kesara wildly. The blade struck the beast above its shoulder, and its shield deflected the blow.

The sword recoiled, and the Eva beast leaped sideways, twisting its body to land with all four legs firmly on the ground. Its claws dug into the blasted soil.

Shinji got his first good look at the creature.

"That thing has a Q.R. Signum! Could it be a new kind of Angel Carrier?"

"Wait, Ikari-kun!" Trois said. "The AI is matching the insignias and code markings with U.S. military standards. Do you remember Armaros' message? He said something about beasts."

The song of Instrumentality cannot be woven into those who have degenerated into beasts.

Shinji and Trois had heard the black giant's message just before they'd emerged from the tunnel network.

"Are you telling me this is an American Eva? And it's powered by a Q.R. Signum, like Heurtebise? No one said anything about that..."

"Just wait," Trois said. "See what it does next."

"I'd like to, but—agh! The swords are swinging themselves again!" Shinji switched on his comms channel. "Transmission. This is Nerv Japan Eva-01 SE."

On the secondary display, an orange window popped open and read: TRANSMISSION ERROR.

"Damn it! I can't pick up the control signal to talk to whoever's in that thing. Maybe we can try sending an unencrypted message over the civilian call frequency."

"Don't bother," Trois said. "There are over eight thousand signals fighting to get through right now. Every frequency is saturated."

Trois was keeping her pain to herself. She looked at Shinji's back. His muscles were tensed, and his body shook as he tried to keep the swords from attacking.

"Super Eva is your body," she said. "Why can't you control it?"

"It's like that old party game... What's it called? Helping Hands? It feels like that."

Kesara and Basara were trying to strike the same beast the voice had denounced.

When he'd confronted the mutant Eva-0.0 on the Apple's Core, the same invisible force had moved his swords—or rather, had moved Super Eva's arms.

According to Maya, Shinji wasn't merely an Eva pilot now. Super Eva existed in a state of uncertainty, and the Eva and Shinji formed one complete entity. It didn't seem possible that another being could interpose its will between them.

It's almost like there's another me.

In the tunnels, Asuka had told him, "You didn't bring me here, Shinji! It wasn't you!"

And then Shinji had followed Super Eva's heartbeat and emerged on this battlefield, where Trois conveyed a new message: "My name is Shinji."

A wide hole opened in the smoke, and a white, staff-like weapon thrust toward the U.S. Eva. Thanks to Super Eva's previous attack, the Eva beast was already on guard and had managed to roll sideways out of the weapon's path. The staff impaled itself in the ground, which exploded, forming a crater wide enough that Super Eva had to retreat to keep his footing.

Shinji didn't even notice when two other staves similarly impaled themselves.

A fourth came swinging down to the beast's new position. The U.S. Eva sprang backward, out of the way—but when the beast tried to advance again, it ran headfirst into an invisible wall. Shimmering colors, like on the membrane of a soap bubble, swirled across the wall's surface.

Super Eva and the U.S. Eva had been trapped in a four-walled space, with each staff at one corner.

Shinji looked up, searching for a way out. The four walls converged at a point far overhead. He struck one of the walls with his sword, but the weapon bounced off with a loud clang.

"They trapped that beast," Shinji said, "but now we're caught in here with it!"

A voice came down from above. 《No, it was meant for you as well.》

Outside the invisible pyramid, four pairs of wings beat away the smoke of battle and the steam of heated permafrost.

Shinji gasped as four Angel Carriers leaped into view.

The white giants circled the pyramid once, and then each placed a hand against one of the four walls. The carriers slowly pushed their way through the barrier, which rippled around them like the surface of a pond.

"They're trapping us in here where they can gang up on us!"

But that wasn't all.

"Ikari, look!" Trois said.

Inside the barriers, the carriers' arms—and then their

bodies—were twice, maybe even three times as large as they had been on the other side. Like light refracting through water, the carriers' bodies grew as they passed through the walls.

"Oh, come on!" Shinji cried. This was absurd.

The carriers grew nearly as large as Armaros himself. Once fully inside, each supersized giant stood with its back to one of the four walls, where they stared down at Super Eva and the Eva beast, who'd both retreated to the middle.

"Trois, their Q.R. Signums..."

The Angel Carriers' scales had grown proportionally with the carriers themselves, but that wasn't their only change. Before, dark-red patterns had glowed softly across the surface of the quantum resonance plates, but now those patterns were bright and shining. Shinji could tell with one glance that far more energy was pouring into those scales.

"I see it," Trois said. "Maybe this space allows the Q.R. Signums to receive an oversupply of Armaros' energy. That could be why the carriers got so big."

Shinji renewed his grip on the swords—which still wanted to turn toward the U.S. Eva—and pointed them at one of the Angel Carriers.

Cracks of all shapes and sizes had formed on the carriers' armor, and blood oozed out through them.

"Careful," he said. "It looks like not even the Angel Carriers can conduct that much of Armaros' energy without paying a price. What if they're like suicide bombers?"

The voice returned.

"Human... For the crime of taking non-human form—"

This time, the words weren't coming from Trois' lips but from Shinji's. He reflexively clasped his hand over his mouth.

"I-I didn't mean to say that!"

Was Armaros speaking through him as he had through the Ayanamis?

Another voice spoke inside the plug. It sounded like a little girl. The voice was lilting, its words clear.

《Don't worry about us.》

"Who is that?"

He'd heard Mari's voice—impossibly—not through a radio signal but as if she were present.

Well, it was hard to say what was impossible in this space.

It was as if the inside of the barrier conducted *everything* better—not just Armaros' energy.

A terrible, oppressive feeling came over Shinji as the gigantic Angel Carriers stared down at him from every side. They projected a message, which came out through Shinji's lips once more.

"Human child... Take dominion over the wild animals of the earth."

Shinji's eyes widened. He knew what was going to happen next. He could feel it in his body.

Realizing that he'd been unwittingly handed the role of executioner, he protested, "You're telling *me* to do it?!"

The four Angel Carriers held up their hands as if to punctuate the voice's message.

"You, in the American Eva!" Shinji shouted. "Keep away from me!"

And then Super Eva was charging toward the beast.

Kesara and Basara filled with a savage power, glimmering with anticipation.

As the immense, unstoppable power flowed through Trois, she cried out, "Ikari-kun!"

Super Eva was moving, but not by Shinji's will.

"It's me," he said, "but it's not me!"

CHAPTER 41

THE TOWER OF BABEL

After bringing the badly wounded Toji to the medical staff in Rogachevo on the southern side of the island, Hikari flew back to the battlefield. As she approached, she saw a tall, four-sided, pyramidal tower reaching up through the clouds that had collected above the battlefield. The four walls glistened like soap bubbles and met at a point at the very top.

"What is that?"

She descended below the clouds, where a confused battle raged.

The enemy had done the allies the favor of bunching together, but the Euro and Russian forces were failing to implement a cohesive strategy. The soldiers were scattered and moved without coordination.

What happened here?

Hikari pulled up the timetable and deployment map on the secondary display screen to try to get a read of the situation, but the text was garbled and unintelligible, and the map only showed a jumble of shapes.

Hikari wondered if some of her systems were malfunctioning.

Steeling herself to be chewed out for temporarily abandoning the battlefield, she turned to her control plane for help.

"Heurtebise to Kommandobrücke, this is Hikari! Lieutenant Colonel Clausewitz, are you there?"

His familiar voice came over her hydrospeaker, but she couldn't understand a word he said. Confused, she tested every kind of transmission coding through her Eva's senses. She thought that maybe the language support system of the Eva's onboard AI might have glitched out, but that didn't seem to be the case.

No one on the island could talk to each other. The most they could do was attempt to convey their emotions through noise.

"No one understands each other's language," Hikari said to herself.

Judging from the state of her display screen, written words or symbols couldn't communicate any thoughts, either. She had a feeling that even a basic diagram would have the same jumbled result. It was like everyone had forgotten any knowledge of language, in all forms, that they'd acquired over their lives.

Still in flight, Heurtebise suddenly listed off-balance, and Hikari quickly increased the power from her N_2 reactors. She spread her senses into the Eva's systems, where nonsense characters flooded the command line, continuously changing the settings.

"It's even effecting the control system?"

The ability to communicate, whether through word, radio signal, or electrical impulse, had been drastically reduced.

The exact opposite of what was happening inside the tower was happening in the outside world.

STAND-IN EXECUTIONER

SHINJI DIDN'T KNOW if the compelling force came from Armaros or from the Victor who held his heart.

Deliver the judgment.

Though he didn't want to, Shinji responded automatically to the command, and Super Eva slashed his swords at the U.S. Eva.

The beast jumped sideways, dodging the strike. At the same time, Shinji had also forced the blades off target, purposefully missing. This wild, unnatural motion threw Super Eva off-balance, and he tumbled to the smoldering ground.

The two Evas repeated this dance, again and again.

Dodging each attack, the beast circled the inside of the tower. Super Eva's misses weren't due to Shinji alone. The U.S. Eva really was good at evading the swords.

But sometimes Shinji couldn't turn the blades away, and sometimes the girl wasn't quick enough. Whenever both happened at once, blasts of air struck Super Eva's body, blunting his attack.

Does the girl in the American Eva know how to use her field like that? But you have to concentrate on the projection... I didn't think it was possible to send out more than one at once.

Shinji felt his body groan. This awkward ballet was wearing him down even faster than full-on combat.

Out of breath, Shinji forced the relentless swords to stay in place. He stared at the U.S. Eva through the virtual display. The beast—or beast *pack*, it seemed—stared back at him, its eyes gleaming. As the U.S. Eva dug its claws into the ground, Shinji thought he felt the gaze of countless eyes on him.

《Are you going to kill me?》 the little girl asked. At least, she sounded like a little girl. But her voice was completely calm, as if she viewed her own death as something abstract.

His shoulders rising and falling with each heavy breath, Shinji found himself wondering about this girl at the core of the pack consciousness. *Just who is she?*

《I'm Mari.》

She answered as if she'd heard his thoughts, and without any concern about the fact that he was attacking her.

"We're Shinji and Trois. I'm sorry about this, Mari." Lamely, he added, "Hang in there."

Despite Shinji's words, Super Eva lowered his center of gravity and readied his twin swords for the next attack.

"I can't exactly explain why I think this," Shinji remarked, "but I get the feeling you're about the same age as Six."

《Six? If you know Ayanami Rei Six, then could you tell her that I have Momo?》

"Momo?"

Did Six make a new friend? A lot must have happened in Hakone while I've been gone.

When he thought about how the world had gone on without him, he grew jealous for everything he'd missed. And jealousy made him feel small. Even more so when he compared himself to the girl, who seemed confident that they were going to escape these walls.

She isn't shaken in the least. I've lost count of how many times I've swung at her, and she's completely unruffled.

He realized why. *She has a goal.*

Shinji let out a deep sigh and steadied his breath. If he didn't want to be controlled like this, he had only one option.

"Trois, direct power to the wings."

Launching another attack, Super Eva dashed toward the U.S. Eva. Shinji focused his A.T. Field into the Vertex wings' field deflection elements, and they began to roar.

"More!" Shinji shouted.

The field continued to converge on the wings, until their roar turned harsh and discordant. At that moment, Shinji pushed off from the ground and flew over the beast. *I'm not going to be your stand-in executioner any longer!*

Each oversized Angel Carrier guarded one side of the enclosed space, while interference patterns rippled across the barrier behind them. Shinji picked one carrier and flew straight toward it, head-on, the white giant looming nearly twice as tall as Super Eva.

"Do you have a plan?" Trois asked, fearfully.

"Not really." Shinji didn't look back. This answer would have left anyone at a loss for words, let alone the taciturn Trois.

"What?!" she managed to gasp.

"As long as I stay on the defensive, I'll keep being controlled. I have to take an action before one is taken for me. Either way, it comes down to fighting them."

No matter how big the enemies might have been, defeating them was the only way out. There was no retreat.

The white colossus met their first attack by holding out its hand as if to say, "Stop." It fired a power shield and batted away Super Eva's swords, sending him careening down, head over heels.

They're not just huge, they're strong, too!

Shinji grunted in pain. Ayanami was sitting in the plug seat, while he stood beside it, holding the control sticks. He tasted blood. He must have bitten his lip.

Still in an uncontrolled backward somersault, Super Eva put his right-hand sword, Kesara, into his left shoulder pylon. As soon as he landed, the Angel inside the carrier's cocoon fired two beams of light, which he deflected with the field over his left-hand sword, Basara. One ricocheting beam blasted away an abandoned howitzer. The other struck the tower's wall, creating ripples in the membrane, but no lasting damage.

Fighting the pain of the impact, Shinji spared a glance to the secondary display. Kesara had scanned its opponent's field, and the pylon was baking in the new configuration.

Without pausing, Super Eva leaped forward and switched Basara to a two-handed grip. Advancing upon the colossal Angel

Carrier was a risky move, but Shinji wagered that, up close, the carrier might not be able to use its size to full advantage.

The idea wasn't terrible, until two long, slender arms reached down from the carrier's cocoon. One hand opened and fired a long, glowing rod, in an attempt to pin Super Eva down.

"Sachiel again!"

After defeat, Angels could be reconstructed from the Ark's data to emerge again from another cocoon. *Even when we win a battle, we still lose.* The thought made Shinji feel weary.

The rod landed between Super Eva's legs, failing to impale him. But his legs got tangled up, and he fell over. Shinji winced, expecting to be impaled by a second rod from the Angel's other hand.

He heard a roar and opened his eyes to see the U.S. Eva leaping overhead. Carrying its momentum forward, the beast sank its fangs into Sachiel's arm and wrenched the Angel's elbow joint backward, as if trying to crack open a crab leg. With a loud, sickening crunch, the larval Angel's arm snapped. The Eva let go, swinging away with the same speed it had charged.

"Th-thank—whoa!" *Thank you,* Shinji had been about to say, when a second oversized Angel Carrier came flying in.

The toothy mouth of a giant deep-sea fish emerged from the carrier's cocoon, dripping magma-like beads of flame. Where the beads landed, the ground melted into lava. Anything there burned up and sank into the molten rock.

"And Sandalphon." Shinji sighed.

Super Eva got back to his feet and followed after the U.S. Eva just to put some temporary distance between himself and the carriers.

Sandalphon's carrier continued to fly around, blanketing the ground in lava.

Trois pulled open the deployment map. "That's the carrier from the south wall. The ones on the north and east haven't moved. That girl must have attacked the south one, like you did."

"And my sword?"

"It'll be reconfigured in another...110 seconds."

Trois could no longer hide her pain. Nearly all the power she'd drawn from the Q.R. Signum was being sucked up by Kesara in the left shoulder pylon. Its thirst was limitless.

Trois had to delve deeply into the Q.R. Signum, and Armaros' shadow soaked more deeply into her. As Kesara was reforged, Shinji felt a throbbing, burning pain, as if someone were pressing a hot iron against his shoulder.

A bulge moved down Sachiel's broken arm as internal tissues pushed their way to the injury. When they retreated, the joint had been put back into its proper place, good as new. The oversized carrier turned and began firing flashes of light at the Eva beast.

Running on four legs, the beast weaved left and right, skillfully evading the Angel's rays. One shot was on course to strike the Eva, but something invisible crashed against the light ray, deflecting it.

Shinji watched the air distort as unseen shapes seemed to pass over the U.S. Eva.

"Are they autonomous?" Shinji asked. "Something with free will? What..."

Mari responded with a question of her own. 《You're a man *and* an Eva, but in the end, you're still only one person. Don't you get lonely being by yourself?》

There must have been more than twenty of the distortions. They moved in unison, spaced apart. Shinji watched them encircling her.

"They're like a pack of wolves," he remarked, not knowing the U.S. Eva's code name.

The strange-looking Eva and its pilot had both undergone genetic modifications to incorporate the DNA of various animals. But that didn't mean Nerv U.S. had known the Eva would end up like this. The fusion of beast and Eva/pilot had been designed to inhibit their perceptions of individuality, so that Eva-compatible pilots could easily be sourced.

The manifestation of the wind animals, which now raced across the ground around the Eva, was almost surely a result of the way energy flowed within this enclosed space.

Shinji tried to rationalize what he saw as remote projections of the girl's A.T. Field, which she'd formed into a pack of beasts. He found it hard to believe that each and every one of them had its own consciousness.

As Shinji followed after the curious Eva and its pack, Mari spoke again. 《What about that Torwächter? It called itself Shinji, too.》

"What?"

The AI chimed. On the secondary display, the sword's countdown had reached zero, and a new message appeared: REFORGING COMPLETE. INITIATE COOLDOWN.

Shinji returned Basara to his left hand. "Let's do this!"

The shoulder pylon's chamber opened, offering the red-hot blade.

Shinji readied himself, remembering what happened last time.

When he went to grasp the sword, Super Eva drew the weapon before he even realized what was happening.

My perceptions are lagging again!

Rei Trois was shaking. She covered her mouth to keep from crying out.

The black hand reached out from the Q.R. Signum and held the sword.

What is that thing?

Hot wind whipped around the forty-meter-long sword. Super Eva turned the weapon upside down and thrust it into the frozen ground.

The tremendous reservoir of heat poured into the earth, and the underground moisture vaporized and swelled. The ground erupted around the kneeling Super Eva, veiling the giant in steam. Sachiel fired several rays of light into this white curtain, scattering the base of the steam column, but Super Eva was no longer there. He'd flown upward with the rising steam and was now bearing down on the carrier, his sword at the ready.

Super Eva brought the blade down with all his might.

Kesara pierced the carrier's shield, but not all the way through. Its tip was suspended in air, the shield dramatically stronger than before the carrier had grown supersized.

"Damn you!" Shinji screamed.

All of Super Eva's heavily armored weight was behind the blade. Shinji turned his Vertex wings, putting their full thrust behind him. Sparks flying between the fields, he forced the sword the rest of the way through the carrier's shield and slashed sideways. Just barely, the blade reached one Q.R. Signum, destroying it.

But when two sharp rods pierced Super Eva's stomach and right thigh, Shinji realized he'd overcommitted to the attack.

While he'd been distracted, Sachiel had extended its arms out of its cocoon, opened its pile-driver palms, and driven the rods into Super Eva.

Super Eva had not only been stationary but had also partially routed his A.T. Field's power into his wings' propulsion, weakening the field. The Angel had used this opportunity.

But the carrier also had stopped moving, its attention on Super Eva.

Mari was ready. "Eliminator Torus, engage!"

Three of Wolfpack's back-mounted cannons had already been spent, but the fourth black cylinder began to spin. The super-directional N_2 explosive charge let out a blinding flash of light along its rotational axis, then burst in the hollow chamber. The charge imploded, spitting out the secondary N_2 reaction at such a high speed that the projectile appeared like a solid beam to the naked eye.

The secondary N_2 charge lost most of its initial velocity as it penetrated the carrier's thick shield, but it made it through. The charge exploded, shattering the Q.R. Signum and burning everything behind the shield—the Angel Carrier, Sachiel, and all.

The carrier was dead. Its shield instantly dissipated, and the explosion's leftover energy spilled outward. The blast threw Super Eva backward. His head visor slammed shut, protecting his eyes from the extreme heat, while his restraint armor burned. Before his visor closed, Shinji saw something that surprised him—not even the explosion had been enough to fully destroy the carrier's torso.

Super Eva hit the ground as if in slow motion, its mass trembling the earth as it bounced and rolled to a stop.

Shinji groaned in pain. The entry plug—and Super Eva— were sideways. The rod in the Eva's thigh had been dislodged in the blast, but when the heat subsided enough for his head visor to lift again, Shinji saw the U.S. Eva clamping its fangs onto the rod in Super Eva's stomach. With a sharp yank of its head, the beast pulled the rod out.

Shinji screamed in pain.

"Ikari!" Trois said.

One downside of merging with his Eva was that the feedback pain came directly into his mind. He couldn't disconnect.

《Get up!》 Mari said. 《There's still three left.》

"Damn it," Shinji moaned. "You're relentless." He smiled weakly to downplay the pain.

The beast seemed to sense some incoming danger and leaped away. Quickly, Shinji rolled to the side.

The ground jolted up and down. A pressure wave hit him, followed by heat. Something must have struck the place where he'd just been lying.

Shinji directed power into his Vertex wings, and Super Eva scraped across the ground as it rose, awkwardly. As soon as he got his feet under him, he pushed into the air. Now his view was merely askew, rather than completely sideways.

The ground exploded in a straight line, sending up a giant wall of smoke. Hot chunks of rock smashed against Super Eva's body. The Eva's senses picked up something that Shinji interpreted as a smell—ozone and polarized electricity.

"There's a Ramiel carrier, too?! Since when?"

Shinji was getting worried. He didn't know if his wounded stomach and leg would regenerate fast enough for him to fight back.

There was no way around it. Super Eva and Wolfpack were clearly outmatched.

"I'm sorry," Trois said, reading his concern. "If I were better at accessing the Q.R. Signum, it wouldn't be like this."

"Don't say that, Trois. The fight isn't over yet."

For the first time since they'd been trapped in the tower, Shinji turned to look at her.

"Trois!" he gasped.

Swaying in the LCL, the back half of her pale blue hair had turned pure black, as if engulfed in darkness. Her porcelain skin was a sickly ashen color, and her lips were stained with blood, like she'd bitten them more than once. Her shoulders heaved with each breath.

Armaros' darkness is devouring her.

Suddenly confronted with what he'd done to Trois, Shinji felt blood rush to his head.

"Ahh! Why?" he shouted in frustration.

"I'm sorry, Ikari-kun, I..."

Trois' eyes were fixed somewhere distant.

But Shinji's anger was directed at himself. And he didn't have to think long to understand why.

He should have known that if he left control of the Q.R. Signum entirely to Trois, she would do everything he asked with no concern for her own well-being.

He wanted to say, *Why didn't you tell me you couldn't handle any more?* But he resisted the impulse.

He touched his hands to Trois' cheeks.

She's cold.

Her temperature was much colder than the LCL. After a moment, her eyes focused on Shinji.

"Ikari-kun?"

Super Eva's flight remained stable, so long as he didn't get too far from the ground. He glided as low as he could as he evaded Ramiel's attacks.

Still facing Trois, Shinji patted his shoulders. "Trois, put your arms around my neck. Like a piggyback ride."

"Why?" Trois said, looking puzzled. "I won't be able to control the computer."

"Don't worry about that right now."

"But we're in the middle of a battle. I can't—"

"It's fine."

Trois' body had chilled, but as she leaned on his back, her weight and her heartbeat confirmed her existence. This was the moment Shinji learned that physical human contact—skin against skin—carried far more meaning than any knowledge he'd learned through the years.

Meanwhile, the battle was going terribly.

He never thought he'd have this much trouble fighting Angel Carriers when he'd defeated so many before. And there were still three left.

But he couldn't let it end like this.

NEON GENESIS
EVANGELION ANIMA

CHAPTER 43

▷ PLAYING THE HAND THAT'S DEALT

"IKARI-KUN," Trois said. "You need to reforge the sword."

He'd just attacked the Sandalphon carrier, but its shield had repelled his blade. The weapon's field was still attuned to the Sachiel carrier. But retuning the blade would force Trois to stare down the darkness once again.

Meanwhile, Sandalphon had turned a third of the ground within the enclosed space into a sea of lava.

"Isn't there anything else we can do?" Shinji muttered.

"Anything, like...?"

"We've got the same Q.R. Signum as they do in Super Eva, but unlike them, we're not drawing extra power. We've had to work too hard. I think our answer lies elsewhere."

《Shinji, Ramiel is about to fire,》 Mari said. 《What are you trying to say?》

Super Eva flew to the Sandalphon carrier, between him and the Ramiel carrier.

"I just mean that we need to start from what we *can* do, not from what we can't. Look, I'm talking to you right now without using any transmitter. I can feel your presence. What if we could somehow...transmit energy like we can talk?"

《Now!》 Mari interrupted.

A bright flash turned Shinji's display completely white.

Shinji had drawn Ramiel's fire and then put the Sandalphon carrier in the path of the blast. The Sandalphon carrier's back glowed brightly.

The particle beam pierced the oversized carrier's strong shield and through its lower body, exploding it.

"Yes!" Shinji said.

But the carrier's Q.R. Signum scales remained intact, and even without the lower half of its body, the giant could still fly. The larval Sandalphon had fallen from its cocoon. Separated from its carrier, the Angel should have crumbled to dust—but instead, the fish-like larva was swimming in the sea of lava. The molten rock was somehow a favorable enough environment that the Angel had survived.

The carrier turned to Shinji and began firing its shield walls. Shinji swooped down to evade them, but Sandalphon burned his legs.

"Ack! I think we just made things worse!"

They'd turned one enemy into two.

《Listen,》 Mari said, 《if you won't take this seriously...》

"I *am* serious! We'll figure out how this place works. But for now, let's just try that same tactic again."

"Reciprocal recognition, arising from our commonalities..." Trois remarked softly.

The carriers in the west, south, and east had moved, but the northern carrier remained motionless. The Angel inside its cocoon was Zeruel.

Mari and Shinji had seen the Angel attack from within the smoke during the chaotic battle. Shinji prayed the Angel would remain out of the fight.

Ramiel aimed at Wolfpack as the Eva beast leaped from island to island among the lava. Mari's job was to guide the Angel's aim onto Super Eva, but her Eva couldn't fly, and the lava had spread to the point where she was in serious danger of sinking into the molten rock.

《I want to ask you something,》 Mari said. 《Are you and the other Shinji the same?》

"Huh?"

《When that Torwächter left, it said, "My name is Shinji." It wasn't lying, and neither are you. Are you the same Shinji? A different Shinji? Also, Ramiel is about to fire.》

Now he knew what she was talking about. Trois had recited its message. *My name is Shinji.*

《Now!》

Super Eva narrowly dodged the searing flash of light.

"A torwhatzer?"

《When you showed up, you shouted, "Give me back my heart!" Didn't you? The Torwächter came here with your heart and left just as you came.》

"It did?!"

I knew it! My heart really was here!

Shinji's head was spinning, and not because of Super Eva's maneuvers.

Is something moving my heart around?

But who? It claimed to have my name. And Mari had said. "It wasn't lying."

What does this all mean? I'm Shinji, and the Shinji with my heart is also me?

The bright glare from the Angel's beam started to hurt his eyes, and he reflexively closed them.

If I were my heart, where would I go?

CHAPTER 44

▶ **FROM THE BUTTERFLY'S DREAM**

WHEN SHINJI OPENED his eyes, he was racing through the tunnel network.

When did I return here?

He looked over his shoulder to ask Trois, but all he saw were shadows flying past him.

The tunnels didn't recede into some far-off vanishing point but wound together into something like a black cloth, which itself flowed back up the corridor toward Shinji, to be sucked into the tip of the black plate on his back.

Shinji realized he wasn't inside his entry plug.

He *himself* was flying through the corridors—or rather, the corridors were a part of him.

Panicking, he looked down at his body.

It was dark black. His surface reflected the glowing particles that occasionally strayed into the tunnel system.

He felt the warm presence of someone next to him. "Trois?" he said, looking over.

It wasn't Trois.

"Asuka! What are you doing?"

The Asuka/Eva synthesis moved though the corridor next to him. She'd been facing ahead but now turned to look at him.

She, too, bore a black plate, which sucked up the corridor behind them. Her long hair waved in the darkness.

"Why do you look like a Victor?" he asked.

She tilted her head quizzically. His eyes followed the flowing curve of her neck to her shoulder, then to her long, slender arm, and finally to her hand, which she held lovingly over his chest.

THRUM!

"Oh," Shinji said. Warm light radiated from him. "There it is!"

The light and the low-pitched rumble spilled out between Asuka's graceful fingers.

Such heat...

The heart beat strongly.

THRUM!

Housed inside the badly cracked Center Trigonus was the window to higher dimensions that had opened inside Super Eva's chest.

When Super Eva's S^2 Engine had become damaged and slipped into the higher dimensions, Shinji and the soul of his mother, Yui, had opened a dimensional rift to restore the engine's connection. She'd given over Eva-01's body to her son and gone through to the other side, while Maya and the Nerv team had combined their efforts to control the torrent of energy that flooded out from the rift. They'd succeeded, and the heartbeat was born.

Shinji had almost forgotten how hot, ferocious, and wild his heart was.

He opened his black hand and tried to reach inside his chest to grab his heart. But just at the edge of the Center Trigonus, his hand froze.

《Don't touch me.》

"Who are you?"

《I'm Shinji. I'm the person you're trying to grab.》

The voice sounded just like Shinji's.

《Give me back my body and my prize. Without it... Without it, I—》

"Ikari-kun!" Trois shouted into Shinji's ear.

Shinji opened his eyes. He was inside his entry plug.

Super Eva was falling, about to crash into the sea of lava. Matching Super Eva's speed, a crest rose from the blazing, looming surface. *Something's there!*

Shinji intentionally turned his Vertex wings off-balance and put Super Eva into a spin. He thrust Kesara forward just as the lava burst upward, as if to block his path.

Kesara passed into the rising lava, into Sandalphon's mouth, and all the way through to the Angel's tail.

The Angel larva thrashed about, wrapping its long front fins around Super Eva's arm and trying to sear it off. But Shinji hardly noticed.

《I found my heart!》 he said, unable to contain his excitement.

"You what?" Trois replied.

Shinji's voice hadn't come from his mouth but from the entry plug's hydrospeaker. Trois realized what was happening. Shinji had entered the high state of synchronization that shifted his consciousness into Super Eva's body.

《Reforge the sword with Sandalphon's pattern!》

He wanted to use the thrashing Sandalphon's heat to reforge Kesara's blade and spare Trois from having to draw energy from the Q.R. Signum.

Trois touched Shinji's face. Just like last time, his body had become unusually stiff. When he spoke again from the hydrospeaker, he sounded like he'd just come home from a trip.

《There's...a lot going on, and it's bad. A Victor has my heart, and Asuka has turned into the other Victor—the one I thought we'd killed. I don't understand any of it!》

Trois tried to reconcile what Shinji was saying with everything they'd experienced.

"When we met Asuka in the tunnels," she said, "the *heart* had been calling to her. So, the Victor with your heart is the one calling itself Shinji?"

《I think my heart is calling itself Shinji. It wants a body and a weapon.》

"And that's why Super Eva has been moving on his own, especially when you're holding Kesara and Basara?"

《I think so. And so...》 Shinji sounded like he had an idea. 《This time, *we're* going to use my heart's power.》

Something pushed Super Eva hard from behind. The force surged against him as relentlessly as a waterfall and propelled the more-than-four-thousand-ton Eva forward, swords, Sandalphon, and all.

For a second, Trois couldn't breathe, and she felt like her body was going to be thrown backward.

She could've let go of Shinji and given herself over to the back of plug seat. But Trois wasn't the type to go against what she'd been told, so she kept pressing her forehead against Shinji's back, if a little tighter than before.

As she watched over Shinji's shoulder, Super Eva flew with incredible speed. Something distant one moment was right in front of her eyes the next.

While kidnapped by Seele/Kaji and forced to pilot Quatre's mutant Eva-0.0, Trois had learned how to draw power from a quantum resonance scale. Once she was inside Super Eva's plug with Shinji, where he struggled to do the same, she'd taken that responsibility upon herself.

Trois had been depressed because she felt unimportant as an individual, and Shinji's reliance upon her gave her happiness, even if it meant subjecting herself to the Q.R. Signum's corruption.

But now, a different kind of energy flowed into her from Shinji's faraway heart, warm and comforting, like a ray of sunlight. But it was also unrelenting, and it pushed the Q.R. Signum's cold reach away from her body.

Shinji realized that if the heart was exerting control over Super Eva, then it was still connected to him in some fashion. Just as the Angel Carriers had drawn power and become oversized, he was drawing power from his stolen heart.

Shinji stood still as a statue as she clung to his back. She let a shiver run down her body. The top of her black chiffon dress, stained with North African sand, rose and fell as she breathed deeply in the LCL. The color had returned to her cheeks. She stared into the distance.

She found herself at the junction of flowing energy and looked out across the network.

"It's true," she said. "Ikari-kun is on the other side, too."

Something about that struck her as funny, and she laughed.

Asuka is protecting Ikari-kun's heart. Well, then I'll be his heart over here.

The power flowed through her and filled Eva-01's body. Super Eva flew through the sky, burning an orange trail behind him.

《Reforging complete!》 Shinji announced.

The larval Sandalphon still thrashed upon the sword in its mouth. Suddenly, flames erupted from the Angel's body. It began to burn up and then exploded into tiny fragments, leaving Super Eva's right hand and the red-hot Kesara behind.

From far away, Heart-Shinji shouted, 《There! The weapon! Give that to me!》

Super Eva-Shinji shouted back. 《Yes, this is your sword and my sword. Now, let's bring them together! Give me your strength!》

"Ikari-kun," Trois reminded, "you have to temper the blade or the impact from the next strike will destroy the molecular arrangement."

《That won't matter if I kill it in one hit. This is going to get bumpy, so hold on.》

Super Eva fixed its sights on the flying Sandalphon carrier, which had lost the lower half of its body to Ramiel's particle beam. He charged forward, holding the still-hot sword behind him in his right hand, and tackled the carrier with his left shoulder.

Their shields clashed, but Super Eva kept pushing forward until the carrier slammed into the side wall at a shallow angle. It bounced off the membrane, and its body turned. Shinji waited until both of its Q.R. Signum scales were lined up just right, and then he swung the sword.

The blade, attuned to the same field pattern as the Angel the carrier had borne in its cocoon, pushed through the oversized giant's supposedly thick shield like it wasn't there at all.

By the time the Angel Carrier realized something was amiss, the sword had already split one Q.R. Signum in half and was on its way to the carrier's face. The white giant's head split open like a dropped watermelon, and the sword passed through to the second Q.R. Signum, shattering it.

Kesara had finished its job but didn't have time to slow down before it struck the membrane of the pyramidal tower.

CLAAAAANG!

The sword hadn't passed even one millimeter through the barrier, but the loud noise thundered across the surrounding battlefield.

PART 9

NEON GENESIS
KALEIDOSCOPE SKY
EVANGELION: ANIMA

NEON GENESIS
EVANGELION ANIMA

CHAPTER 45

INSIDE THE PYRAMID

*C*LAAAAANG!

The edge of Super Eva's sword struck the thin, transparent, soap-bubble wall from the inside.

The sound reverberated for kilometers in all directions.

On the battlefield, a reenactment of the myth of Babel was taking place.

The tower's influence had cut off all forms of communication—every language, certainly, but even diagrams, symbols, electronic signals, and power conductors had been thrown into disarray. With no way to find any meaningful mutual understanding, the Russian and European allied forces were beginning to panic.

But in that moment, when the sound of sword against barrier rang out, everyone reacted in unison. All at once, they looked up at the tower rising above the clouds of battle.

Some gazed up with fear, others with curiosity. With the smoke swirling inside it, the tower looked like a giant cloud-in-a-jar experiment but with colossal shadowed figures clashing within.

"I hold up your hand!"

《I swing your sword!》

From far, far away, in the chest of a Torwächter flying through the transdimensional passages, the heart's Shinji responded to Super Eva's Shinji on the arctic island of Novaya Zemlya. This time, the sword's downward swing synchronized with Shinji's perceptions.

When he'd destroyed the Angel Sandalphon, which had been creating a sea of lava within the tower, Kesara's tip had reached a velocity several times the speed of sound.

Tremendous power flowed into him from his faraway heart, and the Q.R. Signum scale began to belch black smoke, as if to express its displeasure. In reality, the scale's energy, now unclaimed by Super Eva, was overflowing.

The scale sent sharp pain into Super Eva's chest, but in that moment, Shinji's exhilaration overwhelmed all other feelings. At last, he'd found freedom from Armaros' black scale. Super Eva soared and so did Shinji's spirits.

The stolen heart claimed that it, too, was Shinji. But Maya had said that he and Super Eva were two distinct entities that existed together in a shared state of uncertainty. *Should I just think of myself as three now?*

Whatever the details, for the first time in too long, Shinji once again had all the Eva's energy at his fingertips.

From the air, Shinji looked down at Wolfpack bounding across the ground.

Super Eva was one being split into three, while Wolfpack was a great many souls in a single body. Though the pair had no way of knowing, they came from very different origins, despite their similarities.

《Now, who's next?》

As Shinji looked for another target, his voice came not from his mouth but through the entry plug's hydrospeaker.

He occupied a state of super-high synchronization. Under his orange coveralls, his body had gone completely stiff. He might as well have been part of the entry plug.

But he's still warm, Rei Trois thought as she held on to his shoulders. As she braced herself against the rapid changes in acceleration, she quickly scanned their surroundings through squinted eyes.

"Eight o'clock," she said. "The Ramiel carrier is getting ready to fire again."

A ring of light had formed around the oversized Ramiel carrier's waist—even with the cocoon—and it suddenly grew brighter.

"It's at full energy!" Quatre said.

Super Eva raised his sword and performed an uneven corkscrew maneuver, just as the Ramiel carrier fired its particle cannon from the right side of its ring of light.

Super Eva narrowly evaded the initial burst, but the light beam persisted for approximately 0.6 seconds, during which Ramiel swept the beam after the Eva's movements. For the briefest moment, the beam grazed the surface of Shinji's A.T. Field.

The air burst, as if from a mighty explosion, flinging Super Eva backward.

《Ack! What is that light ring? Three years ago, when the Angel was a giant polyhedron, it never attacked like that!》

Trois thought for a minute and then said, almost whispering, "Maybe the Angel needed to be that big..."

《What do you mean?》

"That ring seems to be acting like an accelerator for a particle beam cannon, and it would've fit inside the fully grown Angel's body. When Dr. Akagi modeled Ramiel's internal particle accelerator, she came up with a torus about that size."

《The Angels in the carriers' cocoons are stuck as larvae. Maybe their bodies can't grow to keep up with their weapons. In which case...what is Sachiel using as a substitute?》

Shinji was trying to figure out the answer when, without warning, Mari's voice spoke within the plug.

《Shinji, you attack from directly above, and I'll attack from below.》

《Mari?!》

Everything was always so sudden with that girl. The U.S. Eva leaped up from the blasted and smoldering ground and toward the flying Ramiel carrier.

Shinji followed suit, accelerating toward the carrier. The air burned in Super Eva's wake as he swung his sword.

He didn't come in from directly overhead but rather from the side. This didn't matter, however, as the beast had already drawn the Ramiel carrier's attention. Shinji's attack should still have taken the carrier by surprise. Yet without looking, the carrier brought its shield up and repelled Shinji's sword.

Super Eva was thrown backward, while Mari's Wolfpack tried to sink its teeth into the cocoon from below. The carrier managed to move its precious cargo out of the way, but Shinji saw the beast's front claws tear deep gashes across the white giant's thigh.

Shinji's attack didn't go as well as he'd hoped, but at least his sword had scanned the enemy's field data. He returned the weapon to its sheath and initialized the reforging process. This time, the burden wouldn't fall upon Trois. He could simply draw the power from his faraway heart.

Wait a minute... How did the American get through the carrier's shield?

《What's going on here?!》he asked.

"It's the ring around the carrier's waist," Trois said. "Ikari-kun, the carrier is anchoring its field in the shape of a torus. Here, look at the quantum flux inclinations."

She overlaid the measurement data on top of the external view display. Countless rings formed the wireframe outline of a tube that encircled the carrier's waist.

《Wait, so that means...》

Trois finished for him. "The Angel Carrier's field is acting as Ramiel's particle accelerator."

《And the field is fixed in that position?》

The carrier's field still served as protective shield, but it would almost certainly be weaker to attack from directly above and below—through the hole.

《Mari, how did you know?》

Shinji sensed Mari's puzzled reaction to his question.

《Those were the only places that didn't smell bad.》

《Oh. Okay.》 Shinji was disappointed, rather than impressed.

The girl and her Eva didn't think logically in the same way that he and Trois did. They felt like a refutation of human culture and technology.

And their enemies seemed to share an almost visceral hatred for the Eva that had taken the form of a four-legged beast. But why?

Whatever the case, Shinji had a new battle plan.

Super Eva dropped altitude and accelerated, skimming over the ground below the flying Ramiel carrier.

The carrier changed directions to try to block Super Eva from getting at its weak underside and fired another particle beam. But Super Eva deftly evaded the beam. The sword had finished reforging, and without stopping, he slashed the ground with the red-hot weapon to temper the blade.

Steam erupted from the earth.

Directly below the carrier now, Shinji burst up through the white cloud.

But something was coming back down at him—the tip of a spiraling, spiked drill.

Oh, crap! I forgot about that part!

When the original Ramiel had encamped itself in Tokyo-3, the Angel had used the drilling organ to penetrate all the way into the Geofront. On a subconscious level, Shinji had wiped the drill from his thoughts. After all, the organ was essentially an earth mover—a piece of construction equipment. What use would that be in an aerial fight?

His sword and the drill scraped past each other like passing trains, with shuddering tremors and fierce sparks.

Then a heavy weight fell upon Super Eva's shoulders, and in the next moment, something kicked him backward toward the sea of lava. As his view spun, Shinji saw a gigantic, tiger-like blur jumping over him.

Mari's Wolfpack had used Shinji as a midair springboard to leap onto the Ramiel carrier. The Eva beast scrambled up the carrier's wounded and bleeding leg and raked its claws across the cocoon in its belly.

《Hey, what do you think you're doing?!》 Shinji protested.

But he fell silent as he watched her nimble movements with awe—and then concern. She'd clearly gotten in too close.

Wolfpack crushed Ramiel's larva in its cocoon, and the Angel burst into mirrorlike crystal shards. The ring of accelerating particles around the carrier's waist began to wobble. But although the Angel was dead, its carrier was still alive. The oversized giant reached for Wolfpack with both arms.

The Eva beast dug its claws into the carrier's chest and flung itself higher, slipping underneath the carrier's arms and sinking its sharp fangs into the enlarged Q.R. Signum scale.

Shinji righted Super Eva and shifted power into his Vertex wings to go back on the offensive. The Angel Carrier was only moments away from grabbing the beast.

《Mari! Let go of that Q.R. Signum and escape!》

But her jaws remained clenched around the scale. *Is she not listening, or is she stuck?*

A large white hand took hold of the Eva beast. The Eva's slate-gray armor plates cracked and crumpled. The beast's neck snapped loudly.

《Mari!》 Shinji shouted.

The Angel Carrier flung the U.S. Eva away.

At the same time, the bright ring of accelerating particles came loose, flying from the carrier's body. *Is that because Ramiel was destroyed? And does that mean that the carrier's field is down?*

Trois saw the opening, too. "Ikari!"

《Damn you!》 Shinji cursed as he flew straight at the Angel Carrier. The white giant reached out one arm to grab him, but he batted it away with his sword. On the follow-through, the blade destroyed the Q.R. Signum in the carrier's shoulder. The carrier went still and began to disintegrate.

《Huh?》 Shinji said. 《But that was only one Q.R. Signum.》

But then Trois was shouting. "Twelve o'clock! Ikari-kun, move!"

Shinji leaped off of the falling Angel Carrier.

In the next moment, a sharp, razor-like ribbon pierced the bloodied white giant and split its torso clean in two. If Shinji hadn't gotten out of the way, his stomach would've been butchered, too.

《Zeruel!》

The Zeruel carrier had been standing still, with its back to the tower's northern barrier, but no longer. As if to dispel any doubt that the carrier had joined the action, flashes appeared from the smoke from where the ribbon had passed, and countless explosions burst across Super Eva's A.T. Field.

《Whoa!》Shinji said.

With smoke rising from his field, Super Eva dove downward. Shinji wasn't sure how much cover the terrain would give him within the large basin, but he'd take whatever help he could get. He flew low to the ground. Meanwhile, the Ramiel carrier's corpse splashed into the sea of lava amid a giant plume of fire.

Behind the veil of hot lava droplets, Shinji saw a light.

《But how?!》he gasped.

Ramiel's accelerated particles traced a wobbly ring around the U.S. Eva beast where it lay on the ground.

Wolfpack unsteadily got to its feet.

In between the wafting trails of gray smoke, Shinji caught glimpses of the beast forcing its head up. Its jaws held the Ramiel carrier's Q.R. Signum, still shining brightly. The accelerated particles circled the scale.

Mari had torn off the Q.R. Signum when the giant flung her away.

Even after the larval Angel's death, the Q.R. Signum continued the last task it had been assigned.

《What are you doing?》Shinji asked.

《You showed me I don't have enough strength like this.》

Wolfpack's powerful jaws crushed the quantum resonance plate—no, the beast was *devouring* it. All at once, the many shapes that had been circling the Eva beast converged, feeding on the Q.R. Signum like a pack of hunters sharing a kill. When a Q.R. Signum was broken, it typically shattered into a mist of crystal particles, but this time, the process was hastened by the hungry swarm.

《Wait,》 Shinji said. 《What happens when you do that? Trois?》

"I don't know," Trois replied.

But there was no time to think. Zeruel's ribbon came shooting out from the fog. Flying low, Shinji blocked the attack with both swords.

In a matter of moments, the pack of wolves had gorged themselves on the nearly double-size Q.R. Signum. Accompanied by a loud rumble, the scale reappeared, completely intact, over the Eva beast's chest. The air wavered, and the Eva's muscles swelled. Every part of the Eva grew larger.

《You're too reckless, Mari!》 Shinji said.

《All I want is a place where my pack can be at peace. But to get there, I need to...》

The orbit of the accelerating particles shifted around Wolfpack's neck, and when the bright ring crossed the empty super-directional N_2 explosive chambers, the field sent all four cylinders flying away.

CHAPTER 46

TRANSFERRED POWER

WOLFPACK'S TRANSFORMATION had drawn Shinji's attention away from Zeruel. Despite the distraction, he continued to block the sharp, incoming ribbons with his swords. But then, the thin, flat ribbon, as straight as a steel plate, did something different. It bent like paper.

Shinji barely had time to think, *Oh, crap!* before the ribbon wrapped itself around his right hand.

The ribbon yanked back toward the carrier and dragged the 120-meter-tall, 4000-ton-heavy Super Eva like a rag doll into the smoke.

Pulling back as hard as he could, Shinji brought his right arm to his chest and chipped away at the ribbon with the sword in his left hand.

After three whacks, the ribbon finally broke, but by that time, he'd already been carried directly in front of the Zeruel carrier. The oversized giant's white arms spread open and filled Shinji's view. It grabbed him by the head with one hand.

Yeah, but I'm inside your field!

Without a moment's hesitation, Shinji slashed the carrier's arm with his right-hand sword, Kesara.

But the carrier's armor held firm. The sword broke instead.

The SRM-61a Field Penetrator—a.k.a. Kesara—was unstoppable when the blade had been attuned to an enemy's field, but the repeated reforgings had weakened its structure and dramatically shortened its life span.

Shinji watched the fragmented sword tumble away.

He was standing beside the plug seat, bending over to hold the control sticks. Trois leaned forward against his back.

She lowered her head and whispered.

《Human. It is the duty of humanity to rule the wild animals of the earth. Those who do not adhere to that which has been ordained...who abandon the command...will return to the beast.》

Was it the voice again? Another message from Armaros?

《Trois?》 Shinji asked.

"I'm fine," she said after a moment.

The Angel Carrier's fingers covered Super Eva's eyes, but cameras elsewhere on his body reconstructed his vision. He struck at the carrier's wrist with his left-hand sword, Basara, but the carrier's shield was up, and the blade couldn't cut through. As the carrier's hand squeezed Super Eva's head, his armor let out a ghastly creak, and sharp pains shot through his skull.

His remaining Field Penetrator, SRM-61b—a.k.a. Basara— had scanned the Zeruel carrier's field data attack, but Shinji's head would surely pop by the time the sword could be reforged.

《Urk... Faraway me—my heart—if this keeps up, you're going to lose the body you want!》

Power coursed into Super Eva's body. When two ribbons shot out from Zeruel's cocoon, Shinji blocked them with the sword in his left hand and the prog knife he'd grabbed with his right. Sparks cascaded as the blades turned the ribbons off course. One ribbon flicked upward, out of control, and severed the carrier's right hand at the wrist.

The carrier dropped Super Eva and then lurched forward with its left hand to try to seize him again. The white giant's right shoulder pulled back, but it was suddenly struck by a beam of light.

《What?》 Shinji said.

The Q.R. Signum instantly shattered, its fragments melting into bloodlike droplets. The carrier had already been turning to grab Super Eva, but the explosion pushed its body into a complete spin, and the oversized giant dropped from the sky.

As Wolfpack leaped from island to island across the sea of lava, the ferocious four-legged Eva beast instinctively tapped into the ring of light around its neck and fired Ramiel's particle cannon.

The induced electric current left a lingering trail of blueish-white paw prints behind the beast as it ran. The same phenomenon hadn't occurred with the original Ramiel, or its Angel Carrier, because they fired the cannon from higher off the ground.

Shinji would have expected the particle cannon to be a one-and-done affair. Mari had inherited the particle accelerator created by the Q.R. Signum's field, but she didn't possess the Angel's original particle-generating organ. And yet, after she fired the cannon, the ring maintained a dim light, which gradually increased in intensity as it readied the next shot.

The trail of lightning tracks made the beast seem even more like something straight out of a myth. But in contrast to the beast's fearsome image, the little girl who piloted it spoke calmly.

《I wouldn't like it if you died before we got out of here.》

《I don't plan on it,》 Shinji said.

He might have come up with a better reply, but he'd felt something from Mari that had shaken him. He sensed that she was in intense pain.

A pilot and her Eva shared a deep connection. Certainly, such a radical change in an Eva would take a toll on the pilot. But Mari was acting calm—and Shinji saw that as cause for concern. He thought about animals he'd seen in wildlife documentaries—caught by predators, about to be eaten, their lives in terrible peril. They didn't cry out. They just stared into the distance.

CHAPTER 47

LEAVING BABEL

WITHOUT WORDS, WRITING, OR DIAGRAMS, no orders could be sent or received, and the chain of command was nonexistent. Outside the shimmering, rainbow-streaked walls of the tower, the terrified Russian and European forces fired blindly from their outer positions—and sometimes at each other.

Their enemies, after all, were entities beyond human comprehension and didn't conform to any kind of rationality. Once the soldiers began to question who the enemy actually was, there was no end to their doubts. Most of their unsanctioned attacks were against the tower itself and had zero effect—though, to be fair, if their commanders had still been able to give orders, the tower certainly would have been the primary target. But without any way to evaluate the results of their bombardment, the soldiers kept on shooting. The JSSDF maser howitzers, which had been dispatched with the observation team, fired from ineffectively long range, continuously searing the tower's walls.

But as this went on, many of the soldiers began to realize what was happening to them.

They weren't able to communicate, not because they'd *forgotten* language, but because their words were being received as unintelligible on the other end.

Not only could no one understand each other, their own machines were barely functioning. But even without any avenue for communication or coordination, each individual still believed in their own ability to make decisions and take action. And so, somewhere around half an hour after the tower rose, many soldiers had come to understand that all their fighting was accomplishing nothing.

Without a word, they began to walk.

They weren't allowed to speak. They weren't allowed to gesture. No one looked at anyone else. They just silently walked away. That's probably what the people in the myth had done.

CHAPTER 48

T HE ZERUEL CARRIER'S severed hand was still locked around
Super Eva's head. The hand had stiffened, and its weight threw
Super Eva off-balance and sent the giant falling yet again.

《Come on!》 Shinji growled as he pummeled the frozen hand
with the butt of his prog knife.

The hand shattered like plaster. Super Eva pried the last bits
away and looked over his shoulder where the molten ground was
advancing.

"Ikari-kun!" Trois said out of fear. But Shinji parted the sea of
magma with his flotation field and pulled up above the surface.

This time, Shinji flew very high. With the Zeruel carrier
focusing its attacks on Wolfpack, Shinji decided to look for an
opening from above.

He stored his left-hand sword, Basara, in his right shoulder
pylon and initiated the reforging process to attune the blade to
the Zeruel carrier's field.

Columns of fire exploded like geysers from the ground.

When Zeruel's cocoon flashed, the attacks landed almost immediately. The same had been true of Ramiel's particle cannon, but with Ramiel, the build-up of power had been observable. By not providing that same warning, Zeruel was far more troublesome, though Mari was adeptly dodging the energy bursts. The circling pack of air distortions alternated spreading out their formation and tightening it up again, enticing Zeruel to attack at moments when Mari was able to dodge. After each attack, she released the particles from the accelerator and fired them back at the carrier, then surrounded herself with her pack again—cycling from defense to offense and back.

The girl was undoubtedly cunning, but she seemed to be having a little trouble controlling her stolen hardware. Her attempts to fire in quick succession resulted in an unfocused beam, sometimes firing from multiple places on the ring at once. Even in this enclosed space of abundant energy, the cannon apparently needed a long recharge time before it would work at full power.

《Shinji!》 Mari's protest echoed inside Super Eva's plug. 《Don't stand there. I can't shoot!》

Now that she'd acquired a beam weapon, Shinji realized that positioning himself to attack the enemy from the opposite side was the wrong idea.

He wasn't sure if his field could withstand a blast from her particle beam at full power. But attacking from above still provided an advantage. The extra kinetic energy from a diving run would boost his attack. He'd just try it from the carrier's side rather than directly behind.

The Zeruel carrier flew upward. It still possessed one Q.R. Signum, and the Angel in its cocoon was alive and well.

In order to maintain his advantage, Shinji climbed higher as well—and then he realized he'd made a fatal error. The tower was a quadrilateral pyramid. The higher Shinji flew, the less room he had to maneuver.

Super Eva had unknowingly backed himself into a corner.

The Eva hastily dropped back down, but Zeruel's ribbon flashed below, cutting him off.

In its adult form, Zeruel's two ribbons hung like arms from its shoulders and seemed to have a maximum length. But in the larval stage, if there was a limit to the ribbons' length, Shinji hadn't seen it. Cutting the one ribbon had left it with an angled, razor-sharp tip but had done nothing to reduce its capability. And now Zeruel was weaving both into a latticework net that stretched from wall to wall, with the carrier at its center.

The Angel recognized that I was backing myself into a corner!

The netting was uneven and moved freely. Mari shot a hole through it, but the ribbons quickly filled the opening.

《How much longer on the sword?》 Shinji asked Trois impatiently.

"Seventy seconds," she replied.

It wasn't fast enough. He had to prepare himself to handle the net without his primary weapon.

Before Shinji had any time to think, Zeruel's light beam struck Super Eva. His A.T. Field managed to hold, but he still needed to stay alert. The ribbons' tips were hidden somewhere in the net's complex weave, and he couldn't tell from which direction they'd attack.

Something struck Super Eva's left arm, and Shinji grunted in pain. He looked down. A ribbon had sliced away his armor plating.

While he was distracted, the second ribbon split the empty scabbard of his broken sword directly through the quantum flux inclination sensors.

Now he'd have even more trouble sensing the shape and position of his opponent's field.

Keeping her hands on Shinji's shoulders, Trois sat upright.

"Four o'clock!" she shouted.

《Huh?》 Shinji rolled his body to the side and lashed out with his prog knife. The blade repelled the sharp tip of an incoming ribbon.

"Six o'clock!"

Trois was doing much better at deciphering the movements of the latticework net.

Super Eva turned where she indicated and blocked with his knife while he let his sword finish baking.

But then, as he dodged one ribbon, another came from a different direction, opening a shallow tear in his leg armor.

"Ikari-kun, this is a losing battle—nine o'clock! You should be attacking the carrier itself."

《But how should I do it?》

"Try to keep your maneuvers as small as possible. And stay out of reach of the carrier's arms. Dodge the field projections and the light beam and keep hitting and running. Then, when there's an opening in the net, drop through it."

《Okay!》 he replied eagerly, but not because he was in good spirits.

Shinji's error had gotten him cornered and stripped Super Eva of his greatest advantage—speed. He'd begun to panic a little, and though he'd understood Trois' directions, his mind was too distracted to really engage with her.

A large opening appeared in the net directly below him. Shinji didn't let the opportunity go.

《Now!》 he cried, as Super Eva accelerated.

《That way's a trap!》 Mari shouted.

Shinji reluctantly slowed his dive. But the Angel Carrier projected an invisible fist, ramming him in the back and pushing him down.

Mari fired her particle beam, as focused as she could manage to make it. Just as Shinji was about to pass through the opening, he saw the ribbon's tip sliding to meet him on the other side, but it was vaporized by Mari's beam.

He slowed to a stop. His haste had caused him to blunder into an obvious trap, but she'd seen the ambush coming from below.

《You're even more cunning than I thought,》 Shinji said.

With the netting once again closed below him, Super Eva crossed his arms and held his knife in a reverse grip as he flew toward the carrier.

Once Shinji began following Trois' strategy, he understood why she'd proposed it.

By consistently attacking from just out of the Angel Carrier's reach, he forced it to use its ribbons defensively.

Actually implementing the strategy, however, was easier said than done. In order to avoid the Zeruel carrier's light beams and shield projections, he had to keep circling away, without getting too close or too far, all the while attacking.

His target was the carrier's sole remaining Q.R. Signum. The range was too close for Super Eva's signature acceleration to be of any use, and his opponent had taken note of his aim and adjusted its movements accordingly.

《I'm sorry,》 Shinji apologized. 《I focused too much on the scale. The carrier is on to me.》

"Try going for its spine," Trois said. "You probably won't kill it that way, but you should be able to restrict its movement."

Her capacity for analysis seriously impressed him.

He couldn't understand why she criticized herself compared to the other Ayanamis.

Not only was Zeruel a formidable adversary, but the Angel and Shinji also shared a significant history.

When Super Eva was fitted with the Vertex wings, Zeruel had been among the invading Angel Carriers. Super Eva had overpowered the carrier and its larval Angel, but that wasn't the first time their paths had crossed. Three years before, Eva-01 had gone berserk in the fight against Zeruel, and the Eva had devoured the Angel's flesh, absorbing its S^2 Engine into its own body.

At the time, Shinji hadn't known what his Eva was doing. He'd expended the last of Unit One's internal power reserves and become trapped in the total darkness of his entry plug. He'd since watched the recorded footage of the event so many times he could have puked, but it still didn't feel real to him. Facing Zeruel again like this put him in a strange mood.

This thing gives me chills.

A section of the net rose up in front of Super Eva to cut him off, and Shinji veered around it with as little movement as possible. He realized that another attack might be hiding on the opposite side, and he was ready for it.

But he'd been outflanked.

Something struck him from above. The Angel Carrier had flipped upside down and done something the carriers almost never did—it kicked Super Eva from outside his range, knocking him down.

Shinji was more impressed than anything, though this might not have been the best time to admire his adversary. *Okay, I'll give you that one. You're really good at reading what I'm anticipating. Or is that just because Unit One took a part of you inside?*

Time seemed to crawl. As he was sent backward, a ribbon came rushing in, and he blocked it with his knife.

His left hand was reaching for the hilt of his not-yet-reforged sword. The second ribbon appeared and lopped his arm off above the elbow. Grasping at nothing now, his hand and arm were flung away.

In that moment, time returned to normal, and a loud rumble filled the silence.

Blood sprayed from his upper arm, and a scream tore from his lips.

Shinji shrieked in unbearable pain. His cry sent fear into the typically dispassionate Trois. In North Africa, he'd screamed in despair—as flames had engulfed his body—and then he'd rejected her. But despite lingering doubts from that memory, she clung to him even tighter now. She'd made the decision to protect him. If that meant she'd be burned, then this time, they'd burn together.

As he felt the faint thrum of her heartbeat, Shinji managed to step back from the brink of panic.

I haven't fulfilled my promise yet! he told himself.

He screamed again, but this time with purpose rather than despair. As the air left his lungs, he focused his strength and tried to think from a place of calm—at least, relatively speaking. But his next action came without conscious thought, and it took him by complete surprise.

The ribbon was still zooming past him. His right hand tossed the prog knife away, seized the ribbon, and pulled it to a stop in a shower of sparks.

If this is how it is...

《If this is how it is...》 he repeated aloud, as if spitting the pain from his body, 《then I'm taking you for myself. Only this time, I'm doing it of my own free will!》

He pressed the end of Zeruel's ribbon against the hilt of the sword still baking in his shoulder pylon.

《Take this as your arm!》 he said.

His heart responded from far away.

《I will!》

The sword drew in the ribbon. The Angel's thin, flat appendage throbbed and swelled grotesquely, until it had taken the shape of Super Eva's hand. His fingers gripped Basara's hilt tightly.

The next section of ribbon transformed into Super Eva's forearm, and the next became his elbow.

《My arm!》

《Yes! Your arm, and my arm.》

Unlike three years ago, Zeruel's larval form had no S^2 Engine to offer, but that didn't mean Shinji couldn't use its other organs. And so, Shinji brought down the wall between human and Angel, joining them together.

Trois could hardly believe what she was seeing. "Incredible. You're in berserk mode, yet you're still in control."

But then the ribbon pulled back. Trois had supposed that the transformed end of the ribbon would reattach itself to Super Eva's body, but instead, Zeruel yanked the arm toward itself.

The sword's sheath opened with a clang.

Of all the possible moments, the Field Penetrator chose this one to finish reforging, and the ribbon retracted with the sword in Super Eva's hand.

"Ikari-kun, the sword!" Trois gasped.

Zeruel had stolen Shinji's weapon along with his arm.

The ribbon folded back into the cocoon. Zeruel held the

red-hot sword directly in front of its face—right where the next light beam would come out.

Trois looked to Shinji as if to ask, *What are you going to do?*

《It's fine,》 he said. 《That's my arm. Watch.》

For an instant, Trois' mind reeled.

And then the feeling passed. She looked at the outside world on the display. The view had zoomed in on Zeruel's face—moments before it split open.

Wait...did Basara just stab the Angel's face?

Her eyes went from the sword, to Super Eva's left hand, to his forearm, to his elbow...which, had reconnected to Super Eva's upper arm, good as new.

Zeruel let out a loud, grating death cry. "Gyoaaaaaaaah!"

Super Eva added his right hand to Basara's grip and pushed the blade deep into Zeruel's face. He twisted the red-hot sword up and out, brutally shattered Zeruel's skull in the process.

Then he was wrenching the sword upward with both hands through the carrier's rib cage, to sever the oversized giant's arm at the shoulder.

The carrier couldn't comprehend what was happening. It tried to grab Shinji's hands, but the arm lost its fulcrum and fell through the air, the Q.R. Signum falling with it. Shinji swung his sword and shattered the scale in a spray of luminescent, bloodlike liquid. The liquid and the scale scattered into tiny crystals and vanished.

The air inside the tower vibrated, and the four walls began to ripple like the surface of a lake. As if on cue, the explosion of a massive cannon thundered across the battlefield.

Heurtebise had fired the eighty-centimeter Dora cannon at the tower's wall. The wall shattered, and the Tower of Babel melted like an ice chip on a skillet.

Hovering inside the tower, Super Eva moved to the side, and the Zeruel carrier fell. The tower's effects vanished, and the super-sized carrier began to compress in upon itself. Blood sprayed from every surface of its body, and by the end, the giant had crumpled into an unrecognizable lump of flesh, crashing into the smoldering earth.

《Please, call on me again.》

Shinji's voice sounded in the entry plug from far away.

Now that the tower's influence had gone, Shinji's heart felt even farther away than it had before. But that was okay. They were still connected. The flow of power had lessened, but Shinji didn't feel the same emptiness he'd felt when the heart had been stolen from him.

"About Asuka... Um... A word of advice. Don't make her mad."

Asuka—the Asuka/Eva synthesis—was likely still flying beside his heart. The warmth Shinji felt wasn't just from the Trigonus. Her warmth was there, too.

Out on the battlefield, some soldiers were still firing in a blind panic, but most continued their silent exodus. With the tower gone, their ability to communicate was resuming, but only gradually. Normalcy wouldn't return right away.

The radio frequencies offered only gibberish—languages weren't yet coherent again. Shinji tried to get through to Hikari, but she didn't even look his way. Heurtebise stood with its back to him, the Euro Eva pointing away from the battlefield.

Shinji and Trois were having trouble understanding what was happening around them, now that they'd emerged from the tower. But all things considered, the situation was favorable.

After barging into the middle of a chaotic battle, they'd defeated the Angel Carriers—but they'd also let the first Victor escape along with Asuka/Eva, who'd arrived as a second Victor. Politically, the fallout was going to be a challenge. But if Super Eva were to stick around long enough for the confusion to settle, the conflict might not just be political, but a violent, physical showdown.

Seeing no real option but to leave, Shinji flew through the thick smoke over to one of the Angel Carriers' staves that had formed the corners of the pyramid. He retrieved the weapon and flew back into the sky, where the heat of battle had summoned storm clouds heavy with rain...and the unmistakable scent of ozone.

"Home, then?" Shinji asked.

His body had relaxed again. He looked over his shoulder at Trois, who still clung tightly to him, and offered her a pained grin. "Could you maybe let go a little? You're kind of strangling me."

"My arms fell asleep," she said. "I can't move them."

He was fairly sure she looked sorry.

NEON GENESIS
EVANGELION ANIMA

CHAPTER 49

THEIR OWN WAYS HOME

MARI DECIDED to leave the battlefield.

The light of Wolfpack's new Q.R. Signum had calmed, but the Eva's body and armor had retained their enlargement even after the tower was gone, though the effect hadn't been as dramatic with her as with the Angel Carriers.

The UN giant-transport plane was circling the battlefield from a distance. Wolfpack's telemetry system temporarily reconnected and began sending its data. The Nerv U.S. staff stared in mute amazement at Mari's biotelemetry readings...and the video of the pilot.

Within the tower, she'd shared some kind of mental connection with Shinji and Trois, and had had no trouble communicating her thoughts. But now she couldn't speak at all—she merely barked like a dog. Her support robot was with her inside the entry plug, its four legs folded against it, and it transmitted an alert that Mari's body was rejecting several of its medicines.

In order to establish some form of communication with Mari, the Nerv staff tried converting the signal from her interface's image plotter into words on the comms display, but the results still weren't very clear.

Aside from the new powers provided by Wolfpack's Q.R. Signum, Mari's changes hadn't been unforeseen by the medical team, and guilt hung heavily among the crew in the control room. Indifferent to their feelings, the wild "pack" ignored the crew's commands and followed the terrain south.

The American Eva contained several remote shutoffs as a failsafe, but when the beast had gone berserk, its internal, organ-like systems had bypassed them all. Yet even if the U.S. military *could* somehow make Wolfpack stop, the Eva had become too big and heavy for them to pick up.

Wolfpack ran all the way to Novaya Zemlya's southern shore and then leaped into the Barents Sea.

When asked where she was going, her reply appeared on the screen: *To Asuka.*

A golden retriever nudged its way through the crowd and peered at Mari on the display. The girl apparently noticed, because she added: *Momo to Ayanami Rei Six and Azuchi.*

In other words, she wanted them to return the dog to Rei Six on Hakone Island. Mari didn't know that Six had exceeded escape velocity and was currently missing.

The U.S. Eva swam south with its head above the water. The cargo plane followed until the Eva crossed into a storm front where thick, electromagnetic clouds were gathering. The plane was forced to turn away, and the beast disappeared into the raging tides. With no satellites, Nerv U.S. had lost its Eva.

Super Eva flew over the Arctic Ocean, where the aurora borealis now shone even at midday. Trois didn't feel that using the tunnel network would be safe.

Shinji's faraway heart was sending power to the Eva, if only a modest quantity. The Q.R. Signum's effects had diminished, which might have hampered travel through the transdimensional corridors.

Though Armaros' darkness had retreated into the scale, the back half of Trois' hair remained black. But there was a brightness behind her blank expression, and her pale blue hair smoothly transitioned into the darker color as it floated in the LCL.

Before Super Eva accelerated into his suborbital flight back to Japan, Shinji and Trois opened the entry plug's hatch and stuck their heads out into the cold, desolate air. The feeling reminded Shinji of being on the desert side of the Apple's Core, the site of the Instrumentality Project's initial test. Shinji's long journey was ending. And an even longer one was about to begin.

The grotesque swollen moon began to rise in the east.

The Longinus Ring had lengthened in the time since the lance pierced the Earth and stole Shinji's heart. The gap between the lance's head and tail was shrinking. Before long, they would meet, and the ring would be complete. People were saying that when that happened, the Earth would end.

Kensuke didn't show up again. Nerv Japan Acting Deputy Commander Suzuhara Toji had been wounded on Novaya Zemlya, and his cybernetic arm was replaced with one that had been regrown from his own tissue years ago. Not yet able to walk, he was flying home to Hakone on a stretcher, with Lieutenant Colonel Kasuga and his vanguard unit.

While the moon had expanded, the Earth had drastically shrunk, and deformations frequently occurred in its crust. Geography had changed everywhere on the globe, but the transformation had been especially drastic at Hakone Caldera. The base of the Izu Peninsula had fallen several hundred meters, and the caldera became an island amid a newly formed straight between the former peninsula and mainland Japan.

Nerv Japan continued to search for little Rei Six, who'd become lost after her Eva accelerated beyond her intended suborbital flight path. Since the submarine communications cables had ruptured, and the satellites had flown away, humanity now relied on a stratospheric airplane network for nearly all communication. Nerv Japan had turned some of their antennas upward, while they also negotiated with various astronomical observatories to help search for Six's Eva-00 Type-F Allegorica.

In that process, they'd picked up a weak signal belonging to a few surviving scouting drones that the Euro military had flown through the Torwächters' gateway to see where they'd come out. The signal came from the moon.

But even more changes were happening in the abandoned area underneath Tokyo-3.

Lake Ashi's water level had been drastically lowered, and now, the lake's waters were flowing into the Geofront beneath Nerv Japan HQ.

The grounds of the former headquarters had been sealed away under a giant dome of hard tektite concrete. There, in Central Dogma, Lilith had gone dormant. Immediately following the failure of the Human Instrumentality Project, Lilith had shut itself away from the world in a giant sphere. Over 150 people had been trapped inside this timeless space, including Shinji's father, Gendo, Dr. Akagi Ritsuko, and a dozen or so JSSDF special forces soldiers who'd assaulted the old headquarters. For three years, everything had stopped within this black egg.

But years were nothing when time was frozen. At some point, everyone had taken it for granted that the egg would remain there forever.

Until, one day, it was gone.

PART 10

NEON GENESIS

IN THE BRIGHT NIGHT

EVANGELION: ANIMA

NEON GENESIS
EVANGELIONANIMA

CHAPTER 50

◄─── **LEAVING FOR A DREAM**

YOU SURE ARE a piece of work. Kaworu flashed a half-smile. *Do you remember what I told you when you got your wings?*

"I think it was something like... If a human tries to become more than human, their vessel won't survive." Shinji said.

Right. Even before your heart was stolen, you were starting to feel out of sync with your own body, weren't you?

"Was I?"

When he'd confronted Armaros in the Atlas Mountains, and failed to save Asuka, Super Eva had wailed in despair and erupted in flames. His flame body and his real body had fallen out of step with each other.

Your body was about to break down. But just before that could happen, a certain someone neatly divided you into two parts and allowed you to find a peculiar kind of stability.

"You mean what the Lance of Longinus did? You make it sound like having my heart stolen was a good thing."

Ultimately, yes. A miscalculation of the black giant. But he's merely a tool. I doubt he's capable of regret.

"Your advice... How do I say this? You cut right to the essence of things. It's hard for an ordinary person like me to figure out what you're talking abou—hey, what's so funny?"

Come on, how could you be ordinary? I chose you. Kaworu laughed. *When people try to get close to you, you turn them away. That's how you preserve who you are. That's your way. Beauty in self-reliance.*

"Are you making fun of me?"

At the same time, you also want someone who'll fawn over you endlessly. I could have done that, but if I had, the world would have closed at that moment.

After his creation, man's first failure came because he believed the words of the first person made from him—the beautiful imitation, Eve.

"What do you mean, beautiful imitation?"

Failures are repeated. Look at you now. You've handed your heart over to a red kitsunebi.

"Who, Asuka? Or are you talking about women, like, in general? I don't know if you should call Asuka a beautiful imitation. If she heard, it wouldn't go very well for you. I wouldn't be surprised if she yelled at you all night. Besides, if you look at our chromosomes, it's men who have an extra one mixed in. That makes us the imitations. At least, that's what Maya-san told me."

And you've given your body over to a white paper doll. Even as you dream, the embodiment of your power flies through the sky because she is deep within you.

"Oh, no..." Shinji mumbled. "I'm supposed to be—"

A little earlier, just as he flew past Hokkaido, Shinji had reestablished a comms signal with Nerv HQ. After that, he'd finally felt able to relax, and at some point, he'd fallen asleep.

While he was unconscious, he must have buried his face in Rei Trois' lap. When he opened his eyes, the first thing he saw were the ribbons on the boundary between her black lace underskirt shorts and the porcelain skin of her lower thighs.

"—flying," he finished.

"We're flying," she said.

Trois' left hand was on the control stick. Her right hand seemed to have been gently stroking the side of his head, but she'd stopped when he awoke. She lightly pressed her palm against his shoulder as if to say he could go back to sleep if he wanted. But he felt far too awkward positioned like this.

"When you're sleeping," she explained, "Super Eva reacts a lot more slowly. You're like a large ship. I can mostly keep you on course, but that's about it."

"Oh..."

He was surprised. Not only had Super Eva *not* fallen from the sky, as he might have expected, but Trois had been able to pilot him.

The Eva's control sticks—also called image controllers—didn't actually control anything. Instead, the entry plug transmitted the pilot's thoughts directly to the Eva as part of the feedback system. But thoughts weren't perfect.

In the realm of the mind, an indistinct boundary separated concepts like *yes* and *no* and *stop* and *go*. The levers existed to clarify such boundaries. The mind commanded, and the sticks sent the verification code. The controls also helped the pilot stay aware of their own thoughts.

And now, Trois had piloted Super Eva. Shinji had thought the Eva wasn't capable of moving while he slept—and before now, he never had. *Did that change because Trois has controlled the Q.R. Signum in my chest? What will change next?*

This time, Kaworu said as his voice faded, *the Eve is no imitation. That's why she's been prepared. But imitations quickly melt into the real thing...*

"What?" Shinji asked.

"I didn't say anything," answered a beautiful imitation. At least, according to Kaworu.

Inside the LCL, Rei Trois looked at him with her bright red eyes.

HOME AT LAST

T HE SKY WAS CLEAR, yet the moon was shrouded.

Its atmosphere had thickened enough to be observed by the naked eye. Now that the rocky satellite's orbit was drawing near, its pockmarked face should've appeared even more sharply detailed, but instead, the mountains and craters were blurred.

As the moon had expanded and cloaked itself in atmosphere, its surface area had begun to reflect more light. At night, the Earth remained as bright as just before sunset. The giant moon's radiance blotted out all the stars in the sky and left only black, while the horizon in all directions glowed faintly red from the moonlight reflecting off the ground.

Down below, the shrinking Earth's gravity had weakened, and the seas billowed into soaring, white-crested hills and plunging troughs.

The Hakone Caldera—now an island—stood atop the raging waters.

"The lights are on," Shinji remarked.

On his way home, Super Eva had flown over many large cities that had gone dark. But not Tokyo-3.

《Eva-01, this is the Nerv Japan command center. We'll handle your flight clearance, but be advised, a new airport has been constructed near the south rim—Mount Daikan Airport, letter code RJJN.》

"Hyuga!" Shinji said, thrilled to hear a familiar voice.

But Hyuga's response was strictly professional, and he spoke with clipped efficiency. 《Welcome back, Shinji-kun, Trois. Dock Super Eva in Cage Two. The restraint walls are still under repair, but we've set up two armament trees. You'll use their arms to hold the Eva in place. The cage crew will have further instructions. Command center out.》

So much for a tearful reunion.

Under the bright moonlight, Shinji easily found his way across the Nerv Japan facility.

The two armament trees towered from the Evangelion cage's open roof, casting long shadows over the surrounding concrete. An orange warning light topped each tree. But Shinji saw other lights, too. Two hundred meters below ground, visible through the hole in the center of the complex, work lights and heavy machinery had converged on the sarcophagus's dome.

It looks like they're lowering something down there.

He received the instruction to land, and he descended between the armament trees, which quickly and firmly locked down Super Eva...and its glowing Q.R. Signum. The trees' weapon holsters had been swapped out for mechanical arms—sixteen in total—that held the giant in place. The trees and the Eva submerged into the cage's LCL.

This was Shinji and Super Eva's home, but something felt off.

Trois seemed to pick up on his unease. "Ikari-kun?"

"I don't know. Maybe I'm just embarrassed at having been away so long." Into the comms channel, he said, "Controls neutral. Ready for plug ejection."

As they had approached Hakone, Shinji and Trois had reported on their adventures in digest, and the Eva pilot standby room had been converted into a medical inspection room in anticipation of their arrival. On opposite sides of a single curtain, the medical team stripped Shinji and Trois of their clothes and gave them each a standard examination. The process wasn't exactly pleasant, but it was hardly surprising, either.

If anything, Shinji wasn't sure if the precautions went far enough.

They didn't take us to separate rooms, which means they don't feel a need to interrogate us separately. Does that mean they believe our surreal story? Heck, I'm not sure I believe it myself.

Here they were, home after visiting an alien planet, and yet only a small team of scientists had come to meet them, their tests mostly perfunctory.

"So, the prodigal son and daughter finally return."

"Fuyutsuki-sensei," Shinji said.

The old soldier parted the antimicrobial curtain at the doorway and entered the room.

Smoothing down her white patient gown, Trois stepped through the cloth curtain behind Shinji and sat beside him on the examination table. Together, they looked up at Fuyutsuki.

"Sorry for all the fuss," he said. "I'm sure you have questions. We couldn't tell you what's happened over the radio, so I'll fill you in."

Shinji and Trois learned that Lilith and the Chronostatic Sphere had disappeared from the old Geofront and that Rei Six had gone missing.

Spearheaded by Chief Scientist Ibuki, the majority of the Nerv personnel had gone deep underground into the dome of the sarcophagus, which stood partially submerged in the flooding lake water. The staff were desperately searching for anything left behind after the Chronostatic Sphere had vanished.

The completely black, light-absorbing sphere—though, technically, it had been egg-shaped—had left behind an empty space neatly carved out from the Geofront. Gone was Lilith at its center, along with the old Nerv HQ and the more than 150 people who'd gotten caught within the timeless egg. There was no telling where they were now.

"Father...?" Shinji said.

As for Rei Six, the girl had gone missing in orbit. From the ground to the ionosphere, the Earth's electric field was an absolute mess, and any attempts to reach her were met with a waterfall-like roar of static. With nothing else to be done from Hakone, Nerv Japan had handed over the search to external space agencies.

But now that Rei Trois had returned, Shinji expected the last intact Eva-0.0 would soon be called back from orbit.

Quatre's Eva-0.0 had gone rogue and incorporated its powerful gamma-ray laser cannon into its body. The weapon's existence made it difficult to remember that the 0.0 series had been designed, unique among all Evangelions, with reconnaissance as their primary focus.

Even though Earth's diminishing gravity had scattered the satellite network into the depths of space, the last Eva-0.0 had still managed to stay in orbit. The Eva simply had a greater reserve of propellant to perform the necessary orbital corrections to maintain its altitude. But its fuel wasn't limitless. Regardless of Nerv Japan's immediate needs, Trois would eventually have to retrieve the Eva for refueling and maintenance.

As Trois reached the same conclusion, she softly pinched the bottom hem of Shinji's patient gown.

Engineering officers pushing equipment-filled carts bottlenecked at the security checkpoint into the command module's elevator lobby, while other staff added to the stressful mood as they tried to hurry past in both directions.

Assistant Acting Deputy Commander Fuyutsuki walked slowly toward the bank of elevators. Shinji and Trois followed. They pressed themselves against the wall, yielding to those in a greater hurry, and eventually made their way up to the command center.

"Send another inquiry to the Euro Rapid Response Headquarters in Brussels and to Nerv Germany about the situation on Novaya Zemlya," Misato was saying, "to see if they know where Asuka—Crimson A1, I mean—went. And try the UN Security Council."

"I don't think I'll get any response from the UN or the Europeans," Aoba replied. "The Tower of Babel effect hasn't completely worn off, and things are still a little chaotic over there."

"That's exactly why I asked. Establish a record that we kept trying to contact them. Make it look like we're still confused over here, too."

Misato noticed Shinji and Trois. She shook her head and snorted a laugh, as if to say, *See what I have to deal with?*

"It'll come in handy later, once we're all civilized again," she explained. "Welcome home, you two."

Between Misato's face and the row of empty energy drink bottles, the commander's exhaustion was evident. The two teenagers standing in front of her were at least half the reason she was exhausted. Because of them, Misato hadn't been able to take charge of the situation. Instead, she'd been forced to chase them and Asuka around, cleaning up the giants' messes.

The crisis had called her ability to command into question, at a time when her authority had already atrophied due to her thoughtless absence.

"Ikari Shinji," Misato said, switching to a more severe tone, "pilot of Eva Unit One."

Shinji stiffened his back.

"Did you lose control of the situation?" She was setting her own failures aside, but as the person in charge, she had to maintain discipline.

"Even if Unit One is physically your body, the Eva still belongs to Nerv Japan. As such, it must submit to the science and engineering departments for ongoing research and maintenance, and it must obey its commanders."

Her statement carried no real weight. Super Eva could operate indefinitely. As long as he didn't sustain any critical wounds or expend all his ammo, he had no need for support.

The same traits that made Super Eva a versatile, capable asset also posed a troublesome problem to the organization he represented, which had no means of reining him in should he fail to return home. With an Evangelion, a single pilot's actions could potentially designate Nerv Japan an enemy of the entire world. That kind of power needed limits. Even without going fugitive or defecting, the bonds of trust and duty could weaken.

For that very reason, Misato felt like she needed to keep Shinji from learning about Six's disappearance until after he'd landed in Hakone. Had he found out any earlier, he might have turned around and gone looking for her.

"Regardless of whether you were right or wrong, you made a unilateral decision to take the giant away. Do you realize the tremendous power—the evil power—you exercised?" Misato's voice carried across the command center.

Shinji lowered his head and raised his voice so that everyone could hear him, too. "I apologize for taking Trois and leaving you without Super Eva. I'm sorry!" He understood that she intended to handle the entire matter with a warning.

Nerv Japan had many pressing duties, foremost among them the search for Lilith's Chronostatic Sphere, Asuka/Eva, and Six's Eva-00 Type-F Allegorica. Misato didn't have the luxury of sentencing the only operational Eva and its pilot to long-term punishment. By reprimanding him in public, she hoped to make him feel guilty. But also, she was concerned that *not* doing so might isolate him from humanity.

Beneath her question lay another, unasked question—the ultimate question.

You are a human who has become an Eva. Are you prepared to continue living in human society?

As he looked at Misato's tired face, Shinji reminded himself that she was only angry with him because it was her duty.

He raised his head again and looked around the command center.

"We have the NATO designation!" an officer shouted. "Torwächter A1!"

A secondary display showed the new confirmation code for the Asuka/Eva synthesis. To Shinji's astonishment, she'd been designated a hostile threat. As the command center staff ran about with nervous energy, only Shinji—and Trois—seemed to be moving at a different pace.

THE JSSDF C-11 giant-sized transport plane landed at Mount Daikan Airport shortly after dawn.

The rear cargo ramp lowered, and the maser howitzers rolled out, along with Toji on a stretcher. His pale arm rested beside him. A medical team came to meet him, but of all the primary staff, only Shinji and Trois had joined them on the runway. The pair had come partly out of boredom but mostly because they didn't know where else to be.

"Hey!" Toji shouted to them over the noise of the jet engine. "You left together, and you came back together! I hear a bunch of other stuff happened along the way, but all's well that ends well, am I right?"

Hearing Toji's voice, Shinji finally felt at ease. *I'm back,* he thought. Of course, he'd been back for hours now, but this was the first time he'd felt at home.

Toji immediately noticed Trois' new hair color—the light blue in the front fading to a deeper blue in the middle and then black in the back.

"Ayahachi?" Toji said. "Trois? What's with the hair? Getting a start on your rebellious phase, eh? Have you gone punk rock on us?"

Toji called out to a JSSDF soldier who'd just stepped off the cargo ramp. "Could you wait a second?"

"No, you see, with Trois, it's more of a *back in black* phase," Shinji attempted to quip.

But Toji ignored this. "Sorry, Shinji, but could you carry that canister?"

Shinji took a waist-high metal canister from the camouflaged soldier. It was heavy.

"What is this?" Shinji asked. "All those gauges and lights make it look like some kind of bomb."

"It's no bomb, you idiot. That's my leg!"

"What?!" Shinji's grip slipped, and one end of the canister clanged against the tarmac.

For a second, the artificial circulatory system's indicator light turned red, but then it flashed green again.

"You idiot! Be careful with that!"

"S-sorry."

Trois knelt and lifted up the end of the canister.

Toji raised an eyebrow. "Oh?"

"What?" Shinji asked.

"So, you two are getting pretty close, huh?"

"It's not like that."

"Look," Toji said. "Whatever it is or isn't like is fine with me. Are you at least able to say whatever you want to say now?"

"Totally..." Trois said softly.

Shinji dropped the canister again. This time, the circulatory system had to reboot.

Misato was yelling. "What the hell am I supposed to do about a measurement error if I'm only learning about it now?!"

Entering the command center's middle deck, Shinji and Toji flinched reflexively, while Trois looked up to the top deck, where Misato's angry shouts streamed down.

Toji had insisted on getting out of the stretcher. What he really wanted was to walk on his own, but the post-op medicine's effects on his artificial leg weren't clear. For now, Trois was pushing him in a wheelchair. Shinji followed after them, carrying the metal canister. He'd been stopped by security three times, and now he held the heavy tube balanced over one shoulder.

Aoba noticed the trio standing near the elevator. He swiveled his chair to face them, covertly stuck up two fingers in a devil's horns gesture, and mouthed the words *pissed off*.

Toji nodded, glanced at the three-tiered display screen, and announced, "Suzuhara Toji, reporting in from the Euro-Russian operation. Requesting dissolution of my assignment and reinstitution of my duties as Acting Deputy Commander."

Tension crackled in the air, and all eyes turned toward the three teenagers. Shinji flinched. *C'mon man, what are you doing? Now everyone's looking at us.*

Misato was looking down at them, too. "Request granted," she said. "Welcome back. How are your injuries?"

"They won't interfere with my duties. As soon as the medicine wears off, I'll be able to walk. I think my new arm is going to need more rehab than the last one. It was only being exercised with electrical stimulation."

"Any signs of the Angel Bardiel?"

"The pattern measurements show zeroes all the way to the sixth decimal point—as far as the techs could get with noise filtering. But in the field hospital, the doctors were all over me. They kept me under constant surveillance. Everything was normal except that the post-surgery healing process went unusually fast." Then, without hesitation, he stated the inconvenient truth. "There's still a risk that the Angel will come out again if my whole body is put back together."

Toji had lost his left arm and leg in the fight against Bardiel three years ago. New limbs had been grown from his cell cultures, so he didn't *need* cybernetic limbs. But during the reattachment procedure, the Angel Bardiel had begun to remanifest inside Toji's body. The surgery was called off.

When he'd lost his cybernetic arm at Novaya Zemlya, the battlefield surgeons had replaced it with the pale, emaciated arm that had been grown for him years prior. Why had they attempted the surgery this time? Did the Nerv Germany staff at Novaya Zemlya have proof that the arm by itself would be all right? No, Toji knew there was no such proof. They just wanted to see what happened. If nothing else, it was a chance to observe the manifestation of an Angel. But the result was stable.

Someone had probably put them up to it. Most likely,

Kensuke had urged Nerv Germany to perform the surgery under the guise of returning the limbs to their owner. But if the leg in the case on Shinji's shoulder was ever reattached...

"That case Shinji-kun is carrying," Misato said. "That must be the leg. I'm going to launch an investigation and find out how those limbs ever left our facility. But Toji, it's too dangerous to keep you and that leg in the same location. I know you just got it back, but can you trust us to keep it for you again?"

Toji smiled broadly. "Of course."

Misato's eyebrows rose almost imperceptibly. *Oh?* she thought. *When did he become so resilient?*

Fuyutsuki had joined her on the top deck. As he looked down at Toji, the corners of his mouth turned upward, as if he was witnessing something peculiar.

Toji turned to Hyuga. "Get Dr. Noguchi from Tsukuba on the line."

He turned back to Misato and hooked his thumb over his shoulder at the measurement errors on the main display.

"You were talking about making corrections to the sensors around the Chronostatic Sphere? Let's get a sample reading from each sensor and put some real numbers behind this. We can work backward from the past data and find the answer."

How would we do that? Misato was about to say, but Hyuga spoke first.

"Acting Deputy Commander Suzuhara, I have Dr. Noguchi from the Tsukuba University of Technology on Line Three, with Level Two security."

"It would take us weeks to recalibrate our accelerator," Toji said, "so we just have to ask for help."

Ayanami pushed Toji's wheelchair to a nearby station, and he reached for the telephone receiver.

"Dr. Noguchi, good morning! Sorry to bug you so early in the day. I need you to fire one burst of measurement particles from your accelerator toward the ground under Hakone. Do you think you could do that for us?"

The professor said something, to which Toji replied, "Oh. Uh-huh. Yeah, we can do something about that. Yes. Okay, thank you so much. Three o'clock. Thanks again. Talk to you later." He softly set the phone back in the cradle. "All right. All crews currently inspecting the sensors should stop their work and prepare to take another reading. I want the sensors within the sarcophagus dome ready by 1430."

As soon as he finished, the technicians at their stations began transmitting his orders to the various departments.

"Shinji says that the quantum flux inclination sensors do a good job of predicting when something is going to come out from extradimensional space," Toji explained. "We've got five arrays positioned along the rim. Let's give them a test run and see if we pick anything up."

Misato, who'd been left out of this so far, thought for a moment and then said, "That's a good idea. We should do our best to reduce the background noise when the test particles arrive. We'll shut down all non-essential power transmission to the city for fifteen minutes before and after. That's a total of thirty minutes. Send word to the city government."

"What are you standing there for, Shinji?" Toji said. "You're heading out, too. You've got an hour to get to Tsukuba!"

Shinji had never seen a pigeon hit by a peashooter, but his expression probably resembled one.

"Huh? Wait, what? Why?"

"They don't have enough power to run the accelerator right now, so you're going to be a human power plant. Make sure Super Eva goes out with a phase-differential electric generator."

Shinji hadn't thought that Super Eva would be deployed so quickly again—not with the cloud of suspicion hanging over him. And from the look on Misato's face, the commander would never have allowed it, either. Toji looked back and forth between them, as if to ask, *Is that all right?*

On the top deck, Misato scowled and closed her eyes. But then she opened them again, nodded, and chuckled wryly. "On your way, then."

As Shinji was walking out, Aoba said, "The generator doesn't put out steady power. It comes in waves. Grab the highest-capacity constant voltage regulator you can find in Cage One."

"Understood."

Shinji took off running. He'd been feeling out of sync with the faster pace of everyone here, but now his perception of time sped up to match those around him.

His nervous energy had a direction. Events once again took to motion, like blood circulating through a body.

"I overstepped," Toji said. From his wheelchair on the middle deck, he bowed his head deeply to Misato. "I'm sorry."

She'd been planning to say something about it, but he'd beaten her to the punch. His thoughtfulness impressed her.

"I'll handle explaining the situation to the JSSDF, the airport, and the city," she said. "We need to make sure they're all fully on board, in case we need to keep the power out longer. Delays can happen."

She stood. It was time for the grown-ups to get to work.

Her expression still looked tired, but the weariness behind it was gone.

Even though she'd technically been taken hostage by the mutant Eva, she'd abandoned her duties as commander for a significant time. She'd needed to accept Shinji back after he'd done the same or else she might have faced major criticism from those around her.

As she left the room, the others followed after her with brisk footsteps.

The soapy cleaning solution rinsed down Super Eva's body. It would take more time to repair the countless scratches and dents from the Eva's long journey, but at least all the blood had been washed off.

Shinji had been watching Super Eva's bath from the other side of a small, blast-resistant window. He proceeded to the pilots' standby room. The partitions from his medical inspection had been taken down, and a wide, curtain-like cleaning laser slowly swept the room, searing the air and stimulating the antimicrobial effects of the photocatalytic walls.

Shinji opened the door of his plugsuit's bioseal locker. Behind him, Rei Trois—who'd been following him like a shadow—began to strip off her clothes.

"Whoa, whoa!" said a flustered Shinji.

Trois paused.

"I got this one," he said. "S-so if you could just rewind all that..."

"Rewind?"

To everyone who didn't listen to his father's digital audio tape player, that wasn't a word that held any meaning.

"This time," Shinji said, "I can go alone."

When Super Eva was adrift with no heart and the Q.R. Signum as his power source, Trois had managed the flow of Armaros' energy. But now, Shinji could receive energy from his faraway heart.

"But..."

Trois looked faintly displeased. Or...concerned?

《This is Suzuhara from the command center. Trois, are you there?》 Toji's voice blared from a speaker in the ceiling. 《We're going over plans for taking Eva-0.0 off ice. Come up here. We could use your input.》

Super Eva's external armor hadn't been fully inspected for structural fatigue. The Eva's internals had repaired themselves during the battle. But his new arm—the one regrown from the Zeruel's tissues—would need to be thoroughly inspected at some point. The cage crew had been given just enough time to replace the restraint armor around the Eva's abdomen, where the spear had passed through, and to switch out the sword-sheath shoulder pylons for the standard-spec pylons.

Super Eva's visor lifted. Something clanged into his back. Though the Eva no longer needed an external power source, he still possessed an umbilical cable plug in case of emergency. The noise must have been the work crew installing the phase contrast electricity generator into his socket. The module stuck out from his back like a bird's tail feathers.

"My systems are seeing the phase generator," Shinji said. "Power transmission test...check. The output is... Well, I won't know until I deploy the A.T. Field."

《Good to see you again, Shinji-kun,》 Maya said. 《Don't forget your weapons.》

"What? This isn't a combat mission. Are you sure I should go out armed?"

Fuyutsuki answered from the command center. 《Technically speaking, that would go against our treaty with Japan, but the time for minding that sort of thing is long gone. You never know when and where the enemy will appear. Or if the enemy might be human.》

"That's terrible..."

《You may not like it, but you must defeat *any* hostile and come back in one piece. Otherwise, we're all in trouble.》

Maya stood in the control booth directly in front of Super Eva's eyes. She looked small as she brought the microphone close to her mouth. 《You won't be able to take the Powered 8. When Super Eva repairs his body, the tissue growth breaks any unused electrical circuits. That means no weapons with high-power draw until we rebuild the connections.》

Super Eva took the prog knife and the KEG-46R Yamato Rebuild, a stand-alone cannon with high-explosive ammunition. The barrel had once belonged to a warship. In the Eva's hands, the weapon was more like a pistol.

The knife draws power from my palm, so I think it should be all right...probably. And what's that strange weapon on the wall?

"Maya-san," he asked, "is that a bow? A boomerang?"

《Well, you could throw it and hit something. But no, it's a guided weapon? Energy-based? It's called Azumaterasu.》

"Are you asking me or telling me?"

First Neyarl, then Kesara and Basara... Where was she coming up with these names?

《You saw the glass egg at the bottom of Lake Ashi, right? We found this down there with it. I've been trying to get it fixed up again. If I'm right, it's a weapon that works like Neyarl.》

"That would be amazing."

The Neyarl guided cannon had drawn undiscovered particles from the higher dimensions through Shinji's heart. Maya thought the particles were monopoles. When the cannon fired, the barrel couldn't withstand the energy, and it was blown apart. But the particles had struck one Torwächter and disintegrated it.

《In an Eva's hands, the weapon would be held like an over-sized bow. Crimson A1—Asuka—was abducted just before we were going to test it. These...things...came out of the ground—like tree roots, or whips—and wrapped around her.》

That sounded familiar to Shinji. *I think I saw something like that recently...*

"Those whips... Did they look like bundles of flat strips twisted tightly together? Like black film? Or tape, maybe?"

《How did you know that?》

He recalled when he'd been his heart, flying through the transdimensional corridors in a Torwächter.

As he'd passed through the dark tube, the walls had split apart like strips of film and gathered into a helix behind him, which was then sucked into the plate in his back.

"I'll tell you about it when I get back," he said.

Did the Victor abduct her? Er, Torwächter, I guess we're calling them now. Did my heart summon her from the Torwächter's chest?

A warning alarm sounded, indicating that Eva-01's flotation field was active. With Super Eva ready to depart, the thick, shielded ceiling opened, and warm, early-morning sunlight streamed into the cage.

CHAPTER 53

MOONLIT GATHERING

SUPER EVA flew over Kanto Bay, where Tokyo had been submerged following the Second Impact. On the north shore, at the High Energy Accelerator Research Center, he fulfilled his duty as a mobile power plant, and the proton accelerator ran right on schedule. Gold mirrors focused and directed the proton beam, which produced pions that traveled through 130 kilometers of bedrock to the sarcophagus dome in the old Geofront under Hakone—and into specially placed tanks of purified water, where the pions were converted into neutrinos and muons.

Now that the Nerv scientists had obtained a baseline particle sample, the observation system performed a series of minute adjustments and reinitialized. The computer performed corrections on the historical data, and the resulting logs indicated that the Chronostatic Sphere had disappeared half a day before the great collapse. That was when the sensors had first detected muons coming from the interaction of solar rays in the Earth's atmosphere. Previously, the sphere had blocked particles of any kind from passing through.

Seeing Super Eva's departure from Hakone, JSSDF Lieutenant Colonel Kasuga got an idea. He instructed the maser towers—designed to transmit power to Eva-02's rectenna—to turn their microwave antennas to the north, where the waters of the newly formed channel separated Hakone from mainland Japan. On the opposite shore, the Akashima carried a JSSDF maser howitzer equipped with a relay rectenna.

The N_2 reactor that powered Nerv Japan and Tokyo-3 had excess power capacity. Kasuga wanted to test to see if that excess power could be shared with less power-stable areas on the mainland in times of emergency. And so, when Super Eva came home in the early evening, he saw the faint purple glow of the focused microwave beams above the water.

Shinji walked down the hallway carrying a bag with cabbage and wheat flour for Toji's okonomiyaki.

Shinji had picked up the ingredients in Tsukuba. That was what had started this whole thing.

Vegetable fields had been hastily planted throughout the caldera, and unless the weather changed drastically, a sizeable harvest was expected. Only a short hop away, the old Izu Peninsula was historically known for its many orchards.

But there was a difference between obtaining something and having a steady supply of it. Once the flour reserves ran out, there was no telling when more would arrive from the outside. The same was true of meat—though Trois said they'd all be fine without it. But what about fish? Hakone was surrounded by water, but the changes to the Earth's crust had caused the fishing grounds to empty. Would the fish ever return?

That line of thinking only led to fear. If a typical disaster struck here or somewhere else, then the rest of the world could offer aid. But what about when the disaster was more widespread? What if it covered the entire planet?

Will this be the last time I have a chance to bring food to a party?

As he walked through Nerv HQ, he ran into Maya, who was carrying a bottle of vegetable oil. The oil looked like it could work for the okonomiyaki, but Shinji squinted at the bottle in doubt.

"I didn't make this in the lab, if that's what you're thinking," Maya said. "I'm not a mad scientist."

"But I smell flowers..."

"I was working underwater, so I took a shower after."

Shinji changed the topic before the conversation went somewhere inappropriate. "Working in the water tanks in old Dogma, you mean?"

"No, not the test tanks," Maya said. "They're filled with purified water. If anything got in, the water wouldn't be pure anymore, would it? I was outside the dome, in the Geofront—everyone's calling it the underground lake now. Drainage water. I hope I got the smell out. Did I?" She sniffed at the sleeve of her lab coat.

"It's not like it's sewage water. It can't be that gross," Shinji said. "Were you looking for the Chronostatic Sphere? The containment dome is still intact, right? So the sphere must have gone through the extradimensional tunnels, or something like them..."

When a large portion of the Earth's crust had disappeared under the base of the Izu Peninsula, and the land had suddenly sunk, the dome's earthquake sensors had tripped, activating an automatic lockdown of any passage, in or out.

Since the sarcophagus hadn't taken any major damage, the initial rebuilding efforts were focused elsewhere. Only later was a team sent to pry their way back inside. That's when they found a hollowed-out space exactly the same size and shape as the sphere had been.

Today's efforts had uncovered the time of the disappearance but nothing else.

The sphere had vanished without releasing all the people Lilith had trapped inside it three years ago, including Ikari Gendo and Akagi Ritsuko. The policy had been to act as if those trapped inside had died, if only so the survivors could go on with their lives. But now the sphere was gone. How would that feel to the people whose colleagues, friends, and family were gone with it?

"You idolized Ritsuko, as a scientist," Shinji said, aware that he was making light of any other feelings she might have had.

Maya let go of her sleeve and pointed at Shinji. "Idolized? That's a strong word. Watch yourself."

"Ah, sorry," Shinji said with an apologetic shrug.

But then Maya said something he hadn't expected. "No, the real shock is how little I feel now that the sphere's vanished and she's still gone." Clearly unsettled, she anxiously ran a hand through her hair. "I suppose that means I've made peace with my loss in the three years since Lilith froze time. But what about you, Shinji-kun?"

Shinji should've known this was coming.

"Well?" Maya said. "Director Ikari—your father—is gone, too."

Shinji didn't know what to say to that, even after all this time.

His father had abandoned and deceived him...but he'd also needed him.

If the sphere had lifted its spell, and Shinji had been able to see his father again, he hoped they could've gotten along.

He'd imagined running into his father one day. He'd even played out the scenario in his mind. Shinji wasn't averse to social contact the way he had been before. He was awkward, but so was his dad. Maybe this time, they could have been some kind of family.

But when he thought back to who he used to be—someone who only found purpose in other people needing him—he got chills. If he met his father again, would he revert to that person? Part of him wanted to find out, but another part wanted to delay the reunion forever.

When the Chronostatic Sphere disappeared, he'd been freed from a curse, in a sense. In that moment, Shinji realized he'd been feeling relieved.

"Well..." he said. "I feel the same as you."

She scrunched up her nose. "That's cheating."

Toji tried to flip an okonomiyaki patty on the hot plate, now that one side had finished cooking, but he couldn't quite match the movements between his right arm and his newly connected left. It was a miracle he could move the arm at all. He let out a panicked cry as the patty landed hard on the hot plate and split down the middle.

He shook his head forlornly. "There's nothing sadder than that to someone from Kansai. Ayahachi, do the rest, will ya?"

He foisted the twin spatulas onto Trois and pressed his fingers against the bridge of his nose.

Shinji was chopping up additional ingredients. "Suzuhara Toji, the greatest tragedy of Kansai."

Trois moved next to Shinji and began flipping the okonomiyaki.

"If Six were here," Shinji added, "she'd definitely want to do that."

"Next time," Trois said without looking away from the hot plate.

The group understood her optimism. The mental mirror link between the Ayanamis was still dysfunctional, but Trois had said, in an uncharacteristically roundabout manner, "She's still alive. I think she's sleeping. Once she wakes up, I'm sure she'll phone home or look for a way back herself."

"How about we take those okonomiyaki to everyone waiting for her call?" Shinji asked.

The okonomiyaki party had started as a small gathering, but as people invited others to join, it grew into something big.

The cafeterias were used by the night shifts, so they hadn't been an option. The party had started surreptitiously in the briefing room, but when the revelers set off a fire alarm—and received a dressing down from the fire watchers—they relocated to a cafeteria after all. Except by then, their party was over the room's capacity. The next step was to take it outdoors.

Beneath the aurora, and the long, thin line of the Longinus Ring, the revelers put up wing canopies, set down tarps, unfolded chairs and tables, and hung LED lanterns.

"Hey, Toji," Shinji said. "Someone brought a bunch of alcohol. Is that okay...Acting Deputy Commander?"

"What are you, stupid? Just pretend you never saw it. The adults can take responsibility for themselves."

Misato weaved her way through the people on the tarps. She'd taken her shoes off and was holding them. "Just be mindful of everyone who's still working inside," she said. "And no alcohol for people who are on the next shift." Then she added, "Mind if I join?"

"Er...sure," Shinji said. "Trois, would you split that patty in half and put it on a plate for her?"

The original plan for the party had long since been abandoned. People were grilling and cooking all kinds of different food, and through the mouth-watering smoke, someone had set up a tarp as a movie screen and was projecting pictures and video clips pulled from Super Eva's visual records, including from the battle at Novaya Zemlya.

Holding their drinks, the people watched the screen. The crowd stirred with each new clip, but their reactions to the footage of the Apple's Core—the site of the first test of the

Instrumentality Project—were far more subdued than Shinji had expected.

Toji leaned in. "Sorry to say it, but those pictures are so far beyond the realm of the ordinary that they come off as low-budget computer graphics."

Shinji shook his head. "I guess I wouldn't be surprised if that's what most people here think. Even seeing it in person didn't feel real."

But one cluster of partygoers was watching with rapt interest—the science staff.

Among them, Maya sat on a cushion on the ground. She was still working—her tablet in one hand, a drink in the other. She stood and, as an afterthought, picked up her cushion—apparently not wanting anyone else to use it—hugging it to her side as she walked through the seated crowd toward Misato.

"I think Armaros came to the old Geofront before the great sinking. Or at least, something as big as him."

"What?!" Misato nearly spat out her drink—oolong tea. She'd been resisting the array of alcoholic beverages.

The crowd went silent, the blood draining from everyone's faces.

The biggest of all the giants—the one blamed for the global catastrophe—had been right beneath their feet without anyone noticing?!

Is this a joke? Misato thought. "But there's nothing in the dome's sensor logs."

"He didn't go inside the sarcophagus. And you know how little we've been monitoring the Geofront since the lake flooded it. But that's where we found the evidence. *Outside* the dome, where all the water is."

Next to Misato, Fuyutsuki lowered his titanium mug from his lips. "Right. We're still watching everything inside the dome, but the flood wiped out our sensor network outside. So how did you find anything out there? Even if there *were* cameras on the outside of the dome, all they'd see is the water's surface. What makes you think we had a visitor?"

"I sent an underwater robot to inspect the foundations for damage. At the fifth level underground—now the bottom of the underground lake—we found this."

She thrust her tablet at Misato.

The commander sat up straight and took it, careful to keep the device perfectly level. Maya's drink was balanced on top of it.

Once Misato had the tablet, Maya retrieved her glass. Some condensation had gotten on the screen, but the image was difficult to decipher to begin with. It looked like underwater footage.

The camera showed sediment that had been carried into the underground cavern. Along the sediment's surface was a long indentation.

"What am I seeing?" Misato asked. The picture didn't seem like much of anything.

Still holding her glass, Maya used her pinky to swipe through the other images.

"The earthquake damaged the tracks, but we found several. And if you connect them together..."

The tracks formed two staggered, parallel rows.

"Footprints!" Misato said. "Are they from Armaros?"

"An unbroken line runs along one side of the tracks. I think his single back plate etched it into the sediment. Analysis of our visitor's stride also shows a likely match for his height."

Misato couldn't believe that something twice the size of an Eva had gone undetected so close to home.

"What about vibrations?" she asked. "They would've showed up on our seismographs."

But then she remembered that the mutant Eva-0.0 that had abducted her had also infiltrated underground without leaving any evidence.

"The prints are unusually long," Maya said, "like he was sliding. I don't know how, but he wasn't putting his weight under him. And then he went straight up to the dome."

"Straight up to the dome..."

"That was it. No tracks leading away."

Misato looked to Shinji. Everyone else followed suit.

Trois had been picking the meat out of her okonomiyaki and dropping it onto Shinji's plate. He'd accumulated a little pile and was nibbling away at it, but when all eyes fell on him, he got flustered and gulped the rest down at once.

"He...he went into the ground," Shinji said nervously. "Like with the...the dislocation."

Misato traced the footprints with her finger. The last two prints turned outward in the shape of an open "V."

"Just before he disappeared," she said, "he planted his feet and stared at the dome's wall."

The nearby partiers crouched down to get a better look at the screen, and the ones farther back got on tiptoe or stood on folding chairs. The crowd imagined the black giant standing in front of the dome wall with the water up to his chest and grew noisy again.

"He didn't need to see what was inside," Fuyutsuki said. "Didn't the first Angel Carrier break through the wall to get a look at the sphere?"

"So then, why did their boss come to visit this time?" Misato asked.

Trois mumbled something.

"Don't talk with your mouth full," Shinji said.

She swallowed. "Probably to come get it."

It? Does she mean Lilith, from inside the Chronostatic Sphere?

"Why do you think that?" Misato asked.

"Because the sphere disappeared." Trois seemed surprised by the question. "Wait, am I weird for thinking that?"

If the sphere had already gone, why would Armaros care about the empty space?

"I get it," Toji said. "After that, the ground came out from under us, and everything within twenty kilometers from here sank four hundred meters straight down. Lieutenant Colonel Kasuga told me once that this area's crust was probably stable *because* we had Lilith here. So after Lilith went away, the disaster came. It fits with what we know."

"Hold on," Hyuga cut in. "All that tells us is the order of the events. Let's not jump to any other conclusions."

Misato thought for a moment, tapping her finger against the tablet's screen.

"He's right. We don't have enough evidence to say what happened. And even if we did, the real question is, where did Lilith's sphere go?"

Trois looked to Shinji with frustration—a feeling she rarely showed. "Maybe I *am* weird..." she said, imploring him to speak up.

Shinji sensed that he'd come to the same conclusion as her. Probably everyone had. They just didn't want to say it because it sounded crazy. Shinji looked Trois in the eyes, working up the nerve to speak.

"Should we just come out and say it?" he asked.

Misato's eyebrows shot up. "Shinji-kun?"

"We're all acting like we don't know just because we don't have a physical explanation for it. The answer is simple, but we're pretending it's complex."

What am I saying? Shinji wondered. But it was too late to stop now.

"If we take this all as some kind of messed-up creation story, then we know what comes next. Everyone knows. Right? You're all picturing it. The stage for the next Earth..."

"Sengu," Fuyutsuki said softly. The relocation of a deity to its new home through a temporary shrine. "A pregnant spirit thundered in the heavens, and a voiceless herald moved her shrine. Her final destination—"

"The moon," Misato said. "The surface of the moon."

Making a scene wasn't in his character, but Shinji had come this far. He might as well follow through. He turned, pointing east.

"There," he said.

The bright, overbearing moon had just begun to rise over Gora.

Toji squinted. "So...Commander. We want to stop our stage—the Earth—from being cleared away, no matter what it takes. But if Lilith is up there already, we'll have to bring it back. And if Lilith is still on its way, we'll have to block it. Right?"

Misato downed the rest of her tea and thrust her empty cup at Toji. "How about the stronger stuff?"

"Sure thing. What're you having?"

The moonlight party took on an almost desperate rowdiness, especially from the adults, ignoring the objections of the security agents who came running over.

Some of the JSSDF undercover watchers must have been near the HQ, because word of the party reached the Akashima's team at the airport on the other side of the island. Armed with food and drinks, a band of burly, camouflaged soldiers soon joined, and the revelry continued with no end in sight.

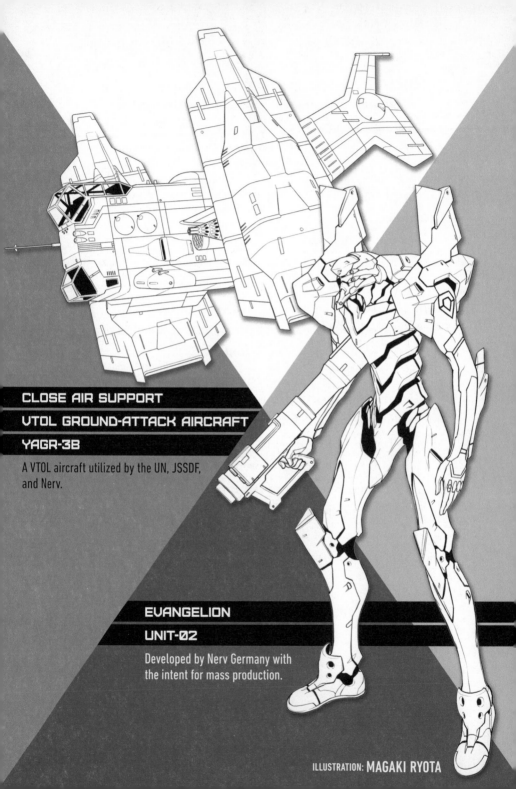

CLOSE AIR SUPPORT

VTOL GROUND-ATTACK AIRCRAFT

YAGR-3B

A VTOL aircraft utilized by the UN, JSSDF, and Nerv.

EVANGELION

UNIT-02

Developed by Nerv Germany with the intent for mass production.

ILLUSTRATION: **MAGAKI RYOTA**

POST SCRIPT

ALL RIGHT, and that was Part Three of *Neon Genesis Evangelion: ANIMA*, serialized in *Dengeki Hobby Magazine* from November 2010 to August 2011. It was the kind of third part that makes you say, "Hey, where is this going?"

The big earthquake hit during this period of *ANIMA*'s serialization, and creators of all kinds had to take a lot of different sentiments into account. Depending on the subject matter, scripts had to be rewritten. Theatrical runs were postponed. With *ANIMA*, I received the request to tone down the disaster elements. I'd built up an association in my mind between myths and natural disasters, and with *ANIMA* I had been so relentlessly destroying the Earth that the very title had come to mean cataclysm. I took a few measures to temporarily divert course—namely, setting the story somewhere that wasn't Earth and making the battle an embodiment of the character's internal conflict. Looking back now, I don't know if that added depth to the story or if it only acted as a detour, but I'll be thrilled if you come along with me to the final two volumes.

—IKUTO YAMASHITA,
EVANGELION MECHA DESIGNER

NEON GENESIS
CONCEPT GALLERY
EVANGELION: ANIMA

NEON GENESIS EVANGELION ANIMA 3

I told you to shoot, Toji.

DESIGNING TORWÄCHTER

I abandoned this drawing before I finished it.

This must've been from when they were on their way home from Novaya Zemlya...I think.